ONE FOOTPRINT IN THE SAND

One Footprint in the Sand

Stories of the Supernatural

Meg Buxton

WILLIAM KIMBER · LONDON

First published in 1979 by
WILLIAM KIMBER & CO. LIMITED
Godolphin House, 22a Queen Anne's Gate,
London, SW1H 9AE

© Meg Buxton, 1979
ISBN 0 7183 0266 4

Photoset by
Specialised Offset Services Limited, Liverpool
and printed in Great Britain by
REDWOOD BURN LIMITED
Trowbridge & Esher

Contents

Thing

I am the thing crouched under beds
And behind half-closed doors;
Everyone has a thing he dreads.
I am yours.

I am the branch – or is it a hand? –
That taps at the window pane:
I am one footprint in the sand.
I am insane.

I am the thing you dare not see
Just behind your shoulder,
When you are drawing close to me
The air grows colder.

When you're alone you are least alone,
I am here.
I am your own, your very own,
Nameless Fear.

I

The Flora Stone

Flora had been dead for nearly a hundred years when Mark was born. As the baby drew his first breath, and expelled it again on a long wailing cry, a slight tremor went through her and she raised her head to gaze eastwards in the direction from which she felt the message had come.

She recognized at once that he was to be the man for whom she had waited so long.

'He will become a great poet,' she thought. 'He will become great through me. He will love me and I will make him great.'

And so the little boy, as yet with no name, far away on the Lincolnshire coast, had already come under the aura of the lonely shade destined to walk the Cornish moors for all time.

Flora's short life had been lived in the village on the edge of the great stretch of moorland where she now stood, head thrown back, drinking in the intimation of the baby's birth from the east wind.

She had been a pretty girl, slight and graceful, quite unsuited to the farm life she was born to. Her mind had, fortunately, matched the fineness of flesh and bone and she turned what scant schooling she was granted to good use. She read every book she could lay hands on, few, alas, to be found in her own home, and copied the speech and manners of the ladies and gentlemen who passed through the village from time to time.

Her few clothes were carefully chosen to offset her clear skin and dark hair and her graceful movements and deliberately modulated voice set her apart from her brothers and sisters. Her parents adopted a resentfully deferential attitude towards

her and gradually it was accepted that she was different in a
way which entirely precluded her taking her turn at milking
the cows, collecting the eggs or scrubbing the kitchen floor.

She spent hours out on the moor, rejoicing in the beauty of
the wide spaces and in the grandeur of Haggard Tor, the great
hill which reared up out of the grey-green wastes of marsh
grass and tumbled boulders, an impregnable fortress of
towering rock watched over by buzzards, leaning against the
wind on nearly motionless wings like guardian angels.

She would sing with the larks, joining her small sweet voice
with theirs, and wander among the stone circles, mute
reminders of others for whom the moor had been home.

She accompanied her family to the fine granite church on
Sundays, picking her way along the muddy lane on high
pattens to protect her only pair of shoes, and she sat so still, so
upright, in the pew beside her lumpish brothers and fidgeting
sisters that inevitably she attracted attention.

Miss Amelia Crantock, the vicar's spinster sister, took note
of Flora's serious little face and graceful bearing and sent
word to the farm to ask if she could be spared for a few hours a
day to read to her and accompany her on walks.

Flora's parents were charmed and at once looked at their
daughter with some pride instead of surly bewilderment and
irritated deference.

The vicar and his sister were much liked and admired in the
district and the grand company they kept provided a welcome
entertainment for the hard-working villagers as they watched
the fine horses and carriages on their way to the stately
vicarage.

Flora adapted to her new surroundings at once. Each
morning she would walk the short distance from the farm,
except in foul weather when a carriage was sent for her, and
Miss Amelia became extremely fond of her: she taught her to
embroider, to arrange flowers and to speak a little French; she
encouraged her to use her pretty singing voice and to
accompany herself with a few simple tunes on the harp; best of
all she introduced her to the world of literature, of poetry.

Flora was an apt pupil. She had a deft hand and a good ear,
but it was the written word that she loved above all else. She

devoured books, carrying a pile of them home each evening to read far into the night by candle-light in her little attic bedroom.

Her days at the vicarage spent among books and flowers and beautiful furniture, and with people of refined tastes and manners, put Flora more and more at variance with her family. She was like a stranger in their midst, hating the stark practicality of the farm kitchen, the rough food and even rougher habits of those around her. She regarded the local boys who came courting her sisters with horror. Their uncouth voices, their huge red hands and coarse faces appalled her. She would rather die than wed one of these, she thought, and anguish wrung her heart when she compared them with the elegant young men, the vicar's nephews and cousins, whom she met at the vicarage.

These young men found her attractive, she knew, but she also knew that, although it would take only the slightest hint of invitation on her part for them to tumble her in a hay-field on her way home, never in a thousand years would they consider marrying her, a farmer's daughter with no dowry and no background, for all her fine new accomplishments and gentle manners.

In the summer these young men would sometimes accompany Miss Amelia and Flora as they went for their walks on the moor, and they would declaim poetry against the blue, wind-swept sky and towering crags of Haggard Tor. The heroic words would go winging away, sending the hardy cattle and long-fleeced sheep scattering at the unaccustomed sound. Flora's heart would wing away with them, full of emotion and ecstasy, but with the underlying sorrow of one who feels so much but has no way of expressing it.

Walking a little way behind Miss Amelia and the young men she would throw her arms wide as though to embrace both the beauty of the actuality and the beauty of the words. Oh, where, she wondered, was the man, the poet, who would love her and whom she would feed with her love and her inspiration? Would there ever be such a man in this world?

She thought not. For all Miss Amelia's affectionate teaching, and her facility in the minor arts she had learnt, there was no place for her among men of letters, no place for a lowly-born Cornish girl whose future inevitably lay in the mud of the farmyard.

The walks at the foot of Haggard Tor ceased when summer waned and Miss Amelia and Flora would take a turn round the large vicarage garden for their winter exercise. However, one early November a clear, still, sunlit day dawned, a borrowed day, and Miss Amelia took a fancy to visit the moor.

She and Flora strolled among the great out-crops of moorstone and stood in the ruins of the ancient circular huts, speculating on the harsh lives of those long-gone souls who had inhabited them: they mused on the scenes that had been enacted on this spot, surely often brutal and dramatic, totally unaware that the age-old rocks were about to witness yet another.

It was unseasonably warm and Miss Amelia had thrown off her shawl, the diamonds in the brooch at her throat and in her earrings flashing in the winter sunshine.

Suddenly from behind a great boulder a man rushed out. He had no doubt been watching them for some time and had waited until their strolling brought them close to his hiding place: now he leapt at Miss Amelia from behind, one arm round her neck, forcing her head back, his other hand tearing and wrenching at the flashing brooch.

The lady screamed and went down, the man on top of her, grabbing now at her earrings, the brooch and her reticule stuffed into his pocket.

Flora, agile for all her grace and elegance and with the latent strength of her forebears coming to her aid, fell upon the man, ripping and clawing at his face and neck with her nails, kicking him in the chest and stomach as he rolled over, releasing the terrified Miss Amelia in his efforts to defend himself. He beat off the slim girl-turned-hellcat and, picking her up bodily, he hurled her to the ground where her head struck an out-crop of granite with a sickening crack.

Flora felt nothing; she lay with her pretty head at an unnatural angle, blood spreading over the grey stone beneath it, her hands, with the man's skin under her nails, lying palms open to the blue sky and warm sun.

The man stood over her body for a moment, realizing with horror that he had killed; then, without a backward glance at Miss Amelia sobbing on the sheep-cropped grass behind him, he took to his heels and fled.

The village was appalled at Flora's death.

Miss Amelia had stumbled, screaming, to the outskirts of the village where people ran from their cottages to help her. When sense had been made of her hysterical crying, men with rake handles and pitchforks went to scour the moor, searching for the attacker, while others went to gather up the small corpse from where it lay, mourned over by curlew cries and caressed by the last red beams of the sun setting over the western sea.

The attacker was caught, tried for murder and duly hanged, and in due course Miss Amelia and her brother, the vicar, had a memorial made in gratitude to Flora. The rock on which she had died had its surface levelled and smoothed and on it were incised her name and the ghastly details of her death.

The story of the murderous attack spread across the district like wild-fire and the memorial on the moor became a place of pilgrimage. People came from near and far bringing flowers to place round the base of the rock, to sorrow at the waste of such a little life, to gaze around at the desolate moorland and shudder at the horror of it. Hundreds of feet beat a path to the place, which became known as the Flora Stone, and the village saw more strangers than it had ever done before.

Flora was enchanted. Her spirit, on leaving her broken body, had soared away into the sky to return, as sometimes happens after a violent death, to the scene of the crime.

She roamed the moor which she had loved, mingling with the sheep and cattle, the hares and foxes; she became part of the snow-laden winds of winter, the scented sun-lit breezes of summer; she became part of the aura of the moor, joining the spirits of those who had lived in the round stone houses. But they were unknown, faceless, she had an entity; she had a name.

Occasionally people would sense her, would catch a glimpse of her, but they were frightened and fled. Now and then someone, moved by the story, would write an article, a narrative poem about it, but they missed the real Flora; the sensitive girl eluded them.

Where was the man, she wondered, as she had in life, who would find her, would love her, who, through her, would become a great poet?

Over the years the path to her memorial became obliterated. Grass grew tall at its sides, partly obscuring it, and the letters cut into the rock were a little blurred with lichen. People had almost forgotten about her, but occasionally someone would chance upon the stone and she would feel their wonder and sadness as they walked round it, laying compassionate hands on its harsh surface.

'Touch *me*,' she would will them. 'Experience *me*. Love *me*,' but they would turn away, sighing, shaking their heads at the tragedy and the long-agoness of it.

Until Mark was born.

From the moment of his birth, when Flora had learnt of his being from the east wind, she drew him to her.

He was not a strong child; his chest was weak and the searing winds on the east coast damaged him.

It was decided that for his sake his family should move to the milder climate of Cornwall. Flora sighed a deep contented sigh. He was coming.

Mark had lived in Cornwall for ten years before he visited Flora. She didn't mind; time meant nothing to her and she could wait for him.

He had flourished in the western county whose worst winters were gentle compared with those that had racked his early years. He wandered the beaches, cliffs and moors drinking in their beauty, feeling that his mind was more attuned to the celebration of nature than to the intricacies of the law, which it had been decided he should study. Something somewhere in this glorious scenery was calling to him, willing him to understand and interpret it, something that as yet he couldn't define.

A few days after his twentieth birthday, Mark found himself gazing up at the pinnacles of rock leaning against the racing clouds which made the summit of Haggard Tor. The wind wuthered round the great boulders at its base and made the dry grass stems whisper and hiss. He walked slowly, his collar turned up against the gale, and allowed his gaze to rove across the moors, across to the other tors on whose slopes, as on these, herds of shaggy cattle, ponies and sheep worked hard finding enough grass to eat among the rocks; his eyes ranged across the grey huddled buildings of the farm and to the village, grown up close round its church; over the fields and away to the sea shining silver in a beam of winter sunshine.

This was an enchanted place, he felt. Not just for its wild and desolate beauty, not just for the mysterious remains of the round stone huts, but for something else. There was a numinousness about it which was reaching out to him.

His idle wandering had brought him to stand before a large stone whose smooth top had letters cut into it, overgrown with gold and silver lichen.

Flora watched over him as he knelt to read the inscription, watched as he threw back his head and took a deep breath, drawing the essence of the moor into himself. He spread his arms as if to embrace the wind and the love for him that was borne on it. His eyes were wide, the pupils dilated, as he spoke her name.

'Oh, Flora,' he whispered.

From then on Mark lived with Flora in his heart and in his mind. He spent hours on the moor in her company drinking in the wonder of it all through her.

He visited the farm where she was born and the vicarage where she had blossomed.

He searched newspaper archives for the reported details of her death, and parish registers for information about her family, the marriages of her brothers and sisters.

He tracked down men and women who were her great-nephews and nieces and who could remember their parents reminiscing about their sister, the sister they probably felt they knew better after her death than during her short life.

His family realized the futility of insisting that he study law and watched with increasing awe as his talent as a writer developed.

He roamed the moor with Flora, seeing through her eyes, thinking with her mind, writing, always writing: articles and short poems at first and then, as his confidence in himself and in her increased, book after book flowed from his pen, novels redolent with the magic of Cornwall, collections of poems, wild with the granite and the gale, gentle with the jewel-like butterflies and the moorland flowers.

He never wrote of Flora, never mentioned her name, but she was woven into every sentence, every stanza, every thought.

He was acclaimed. The Cornish poet, the great Cornish novelist, the authority on things Cornish.

But he burnt with too bright a flame. Never strong, the passion with which he wrote sapped what little strength he had. Out on the moor with Flora in all weathers his fragile lungs had suffered, and at the height of his fame it became clear that he was dying.

Anxious friends besought him to go abroad to warmer climes, but he could never leave Cornwall. They besought him to rest, to keep to his bed, and with this he complied, having no strength left with which to do otherwise. Until the evening which he knew to be his last.

The east wind blew bleakly, laden with sleet, as Mark, clad only in a light coat, struggled on to the moor for the last time.

His breathing was harsh and laboured and his frail body was racked with coughing as he made his way between the boulders in the grey January evening light, slowly but surely tracing the path he knew so well.

Barely able to lift his feet he came to the Flora Stone at last and wearily laid his body across it, his face resting on the incised letters that spelt the beloved name.

Sleet collected in the folds of his clothes as he lay, to be dislodged by the final deathly cough which shook him savagely, bringing his life's blood into his mouth to stream across the surface of the rock as Flora's had done so long ago.

Mark's spirit left his body, moving easily, part of the east wind which had first told Flora of his coming, part of the swirling sleet, and dissolved into the embrace of her outstretched arms.

II

Monkey Business

Wendy Huxtable was a very plain child. She was the daughter of pleasant and unremarkable parents and lived in a pleasant and unremarkable house. But she was neither pleasant nor, as it turned out, unremarkable.

She was nine years old, tall for her age, and thin. A small, pale face was framed in straight mouse-coloured hair; although she loathed the large glasses she wore, they actually improved her appearance by magnifying her myopic and too-close-together eyes, but there was no such help available to relax and soften the thin, hard line of her mouth.

Her plain little face mirrored a reserved and secretive nature and, apart from her parents, there were very few people who found anything to like in her.

She attended a small private day-school only a short distance from her home; it was purgatory to her. Preferring always to be by herself she made no effort to become friendly with the other children there who, finding their own overtures rebuffed, teased her about her large glasses, calling her 'Windows', and it was with enormous relief that she returned each afternoon to the tall Edwardian house in the quiet street where she lived, running up the short garden path and flinging herself through the front door.

But one day, the last day of term with the holidays stretching peacefully in front of her, when she stood, safe at last, in the hall, she was surprised to find it full of trunks and boxes, the air heavy with exotic scent and ringing with feminine laughter. She had forgotten that her Aunt Eileen from America was arriving today.

She had never met her aunt before, nor had she ever seen

anyone like her and she hated her on sight.

Aunt Eileen was beautiful. Her golden hair was piled on top of her head in shining coils and her face was exquisitely made up. Rings flashed on long red-tipped fingers, bracelets jangled on slim wrists and she moved with the nervous long-legged grace of a race-horse, on narrow feet in high-heeled sandals.

She had brought presents for all the family; a fur hat, Russian style, for Wendy's father, George; a froth of chiffon-and-lace nightgown for her mother, Caroline.

'And just wait until you see what I've got for *you*, you cute little thing!' she cried, having embraced the astonished Wendy and drawing her across the room. She pounced on a large, gift-wrapped box and tearing off the ribbons removed the lid.

'There!' she exclaimed. 'Isn't he lovely?'

Inside the box was a toy monkey made of golden nylon fur with a tragi-comic pink face. Half-lidded brown glass eyes gazed mockingly above the sardonically smiling mouth.

Wendy bent over the box and lifted out the toy. It was nearly as big as she was but surprisingly light and wonderfully soft. As she held it a huge, pink hand on the end of a long, limp arm flopped round her neck as though to embrace her.

She suddenly flung the toy from her.

'No,' she said coldly. "It's not lovely, it's hideous,' and she ran through the door at the end of the hall and into the kitchen.

Her parents were appalled.

'Oh, Eileen!' said her mother. 'I *am* so sorry. I expect she's just tired after school; I'm sure she didn't mean it.'

Even the exuberant Eileen was momentarily nonplussed, but recovered almost at once.

'Never mind,' she said brightly, and picking the toy up she placed in on a chair by the hall table. 'We'll leave it here and maybe she'll take to it later.'

The monkey sat in the hall completely ignored by Wendy for some days. It watched her from half-lidded eyes as she passed to and fro.

'*One day*,' it seemed to say. '*One day*.'

Mrs Huxtable gave her daughter a glass of milk each mid-morning, and on one particularly sunny day she suggested that she take it to drink in the garden.

'Such a lovely day,' she said, 'a pity to stay indoors.'

As Wendy walked through the hall towards the front door she tripped over the rug and fell, breaking the glass and cutting her hand. She sat on the floor regarding the blood trickling from the gash on her palm. Should she cry, she wondered? Should she make out that it hurt more than it did? Before she had made up her mind her eyes fell on the toy monkey; he watched her, smiling his knowing, mocking smile and it infuriated her.

She reached over and grabbed the offensive toy and, picking up a piece of the broken milk glass, slashed one of its huge pink paws so that the stuffing burst out. She rubbed her own bleeding hand hard onto that of the monkey.

'There!' she said venomously, 'that'll teach you to sit there and laugh at me!' But then, holding the damaged toy at arms length, she looked into its brown glass eyes for a long moment and suddenly hugged it tightly to her chest, rocking backwards and forwards.

'I'm sorry! I'm so sorry!' she whispered to it. 'I didn't mean it, really I didn't;' she smothered the slashed, smeared paw with kisses. 'Mummy will mend you, I know she will, and you'll be as good as new.'

'*Better than new*,' the monkey seemed to say. '*Part of you, now. Blood of your blood.*'

Wendy's mother did indeed mend the toy's hand very neatly, but the blood would not wash out of the pink nylon; a dark stain remained.

'Never mind,' said Aunt Eileen, relieved that her present had been accepted at last. 'It gives him character. What are you going to call him?'

Wendy thought for a moment.

'Arnold,' she said.

'Why Arnold?' her mother asked.

'Because,' Wendy said, with the irrefutable illogical logic of children, 'It's his name,' and from then on she refused to be parted from the toy and Arnold's reign of terror began.

Wendy and Arnold made a strange and unlovely pair, the thin, pale child and the large, lush toy. What had originally been a comic and amiable caricature of a monkey's face seemed to become more grotesquely human as time went by and the sight of the animal in her arms, its huge, blood-stained paw draped over her shoulder, was unendearing and invited irritated comment. There seemed, somehow, to be more between them than the love of a lonely child for a treasured toy.

Wendy was sitting on the stairs one day with Arnold in her arms when the daily woman went past her carrying a pile of clean laundry.

She didn't like the child.

'Great girl like you playing with toys,' she muttered, and one of Arnold's long arms flopped off Wendy's lap, wrapping itself round the woman's ankle and bringing her down hard onto her knees.

The woman screamed as she fell and sheets and towels spilled over the bannisters into the hall.

Caroline Huxtable ran from the kitchen.

'Mrs Williams! Whatever happened?' she cried, helping her to her feet.

'That ugly beast of a toy tripped me up,' the woman said angrily, rubbing her bruised knees and staring at Wendy as, hugging Arnold tightly, she ran upstairs to her room.

When mooning about on the front lawn one day Wendy saw the local riding school children trotting down the road on their way to the moors. She knew one of them, a little girl with red pigtails sticking out from under her hard hat. As she drew level the child reined in her pony and hailed Wendy.

'Hello, Windows!' she called, and then, pointing to Arnold lying spread-eagled on the grass beside her. 'What on earth is that hideous thing? Don't tell me you play with *toys*!'

Protectively Wendy ran to the monkey and picked it up, its long arms and legs flailing wildly. The red pigtailed child's pony threw up its head, side-stepped and then reared, unseating its little rider who landed with a thump on the pavement and immediately started to wail.

The lady instructor rode up and dismounted quickly. Picking the child up and catching the nervous pony she soothed them both.

'Quiet!' Quiet!' she said. 'No bones broken, you're all right dear, so stop that noise. Now, whatever happened?'

'It was that awful toy,' the red pigtailed child sobbed, pointing over the low hedge; but Wendy and Arnold had gone.

It seemed that, should anyone make a disparaging remark about Wendy and her toy, a minor accident immediately befell them. One of Caroline Huxtable's bridge-playing friends, on making a behind-the-hand remark to another on Wendy's plain appearance, was quite badly scalded when she spilt her tea in shock at finding Wendy, holding Arnold of course, just behind her. The twice-weekly gardener, after having remonstrated with the child for walking on a newly-raked seed bed, fell from his ladder while pruning the roses when she suddenly appeared at her bedroom window clutching the monstrous toy. Small boys who jeered at her in the street fell off their bicycles, old ladies in the supermarket who scolded her as she pushed past them dropped tins on their toes, but no lasting damage was done until the terrible day at the beach.

Caroline Huxtable had driven into the neighbouring town of Redbourne for her sister, Eileen, to have her great, shining coils of hair shampooed and set, and they had taken Wendy with them, carrying Arnold of course.

The hair, and a little shopping, duly done, they drove home, taking the longer coastal route so that Eileen could see some of the quaint Cornish fishing villages, and marvel at the great Atlantic rollers crashing onto wide sandy beaches below towering cliffs.

It was a day of fresh wind and intermittent sun, the racing clouds making purple shadows on the vast expanses of turquoise sea, and Caroline drove up a track and parked the car on a low cliff so that they could sit and watch for a little while. After a few minutes she suggested a walk on the beach.

'It really is so gorgeous when the sun's out,' she said. 'Too good to waste. Coming, Eileen? Wendy?'

Wendy got out, grudgingly, to join her mother, Arnold in her arms, but Eileen thought perhaps she wouldn't.

'The wind will blow my hair to pieces,' she said, 'And it seems silly since I've just had it done. I'll stay here and write to Joe, I bought some air-mail paper in Redbourne.' She looked at Wendy carrying the large toy.

'You can't run about with him, dear,' she said, 'Here, give him to me; he can sit and keep me company.'

Arnold was passed in through the window and Eileen put him on the driver's seat.

'There,' she said, 'Doesn't he look cute?'

'Yes, he does,' said Caroline. 'The car's in gear so you're quite safe. We won't be long,' and she and Wendy scrambled down the steep cliff path and onto the beach.

Eileen gazed at the view for a little while, it really was very lovely; and then she took writing paper from her bag and started the letter to her husband.

She had written two or three pages when she became cramped and uncomfortable. She threw the toy monkey on the floor where he lay, a mass of arms and legs coiled about the gear lever and brake, and putting her feet up on the driver's seat she resumed her writing.

– George and Caroline are very sweet – if a tiny bit dull – but the child, Wendy, is a nasty little creature, really quite sinister, not a bit like our darling Camilla. However, she seems to have taken to the toy I brought over for her and takes it everywhere with her –

Caroline and Wendy were at the far end of the beach when from behind them they heard people screaming. Turning, they were just in time to see their car plunging head-long down the cliff. The doors burst open and they saw Eileen flung out and hurled against the rock like a rag doll.

When they reached the scene someone had already called an ambulance. Eileen was alive but unconscious, both lovely legs and one arm broken and her beautiful face smashed beyond recognition, coils of blood soaked golden hair plastered across it. Sheets of blue air-mail writing paper fluttered about the beach, the contents of the shopping baskets were strewn around, but someone retrieved Arnold from where he hung suspended on a jagged rock and restored him to Wendy's arms.

Caroline was hysterical.

'I *know* I left the car in gear,' she wept, 'and why would the hand brake fail?'

Wendy hugged Arnold very tight, holding him to her chest so that no one could see the malice in his hooded brown glass eyes, burying her face in his fur so that no one could see the malice in hers.

Eileen's condition was critical. Apart from her broken limbs and shattered face she had severe internal injuries and her husband, Joe, and little daughter, Camilla, were flying over at once to stay with the Huxtables so that they could visit her in hospital daily.

Wendy, delighted to have got rid of her aunt, didn't like the thought of having another child in the house, and when Camilla arrived she turned out to be more than just another child.

She was, for a start, beautiful like her mother, all tossing golden curls and pink cheeks, smiling mouth and flashing blue eyes. To make matters worse she was a very nice little girl.

Although deeply distressed by her mother's accident, she managed to be perfectly charming to her aunt and uncle and tried very hard indeed to be nice to her cousin.

After days of anxiety when her life was in the balance, Eileen was pronounced out of danger at last, although still faced with weeks in hospital. Joe, her husband, had to return to America but it was decided that Camilla should stay on with the Huxtables to be near her mother.

She was a tomboy, dressed always in bright jeans and tee-shirts, her hair tied at each side of her head in beribboned bunches.

Ridiculous, Wendy thought, conscious of her own drab hair, ordinary clothes and lack of charm. She hated Camilla, of course, and held long, loathing, one-sided conversations about her with Arnold at night as he sat, too big to share her little bed, on the table beside it, and then she would fall asleep clasping the pink, blood-stained paw of the only thing she loved.

There seemed to be no point of contact between the two children and, tired of trying to play with her cousin, Camilla soon found other friends. At a house a few doors away from the Huxtables lived two boys, only a little older than Camilla, with whom she got on very well. They had a tree house out of which she often fell but never cried, much to their admiration; she fought with them when they jeered at baseball and called it rounders, they fought with her when she called cricket dull and stupid, and altogether they became the best of friends, Camilla coming home, ribbons undone and trailing, jeans grubby and torn, triumphant at some exploit in which she had done as well as, if not better than, the boys.

One evening after the girls had been put to bed she surprised Wendy by coming into her bedroom fully dressed in jeans and a thick jersey.

'Peter and Johnnie are having a secret feast in their summer-house tonight,' she whispered, 'and I'm going. They've got cake and biscuits and chips and things and I'm going to take some coke and some sweets. You want to come along?'

Wendy was horrified.

'No, I *don't*,' she said, 'and how are you going to get out without being seen?'

'Oh, easy,' Camilla said airily, 'I shall climb out of my window onto the porch and then down the creeper. I've done it twice already, just to practise. You are a draggy thing not to come. You're no fun at all!'

Wendy looked grim.

'What about when mummy comes and looks in last thing?' she said. 'She'll see you're not in bed and there'll be an awful fuss.'

'Oh gee! I hadn't thought of that!' Camilla looked stricken, but then her eyes lit on the monkey.

'Tell you what,' she said grabbing him from his perch on the bedside table, 'I'll borrow Arnold! He's nearly as big as me and he'll look just dandy under the covers! Your momma will never know!''

Wendy knelt up in bed in her striped pyjamas.

'No, no! You can't take him!' she cried desperately, 'You mustn't! I don't want you to!'

'Oh, go on,' Camilla said, 'you're just stupid. I'm not going to take him for keeps,' and, as Wendy started to cry, 'you're a big baby as well as stupid and draggy,' and she whisked out of the room with the toy, leaving Wendy desolate.

Later that night Camilla came home and clambered up the creeper and onto the porch. She had had a lovely time: it had been cold and earwiggy in the summer house and she hadn't really wanted to drink coke and eat damp biscuits in the middle of the night, but it had been really great all the same. Wendy was a *pain* not to have come, but still, she'd probably have ruined it all and the boys wouldn't have liked her one bit. She stealthily pushed open her bedroom window.

Arnold lay listening, his brown glass eyes gleaming with hatred under the covers, as Camilla pulled off her jeans and jersey and crept across to her bed. She slipped in beside him and his long arms wrapped themselves round her neck and squeezed, tighter and tighter, in a lethal embrace.

When Camilla was found dead in her bed Wendy did her best to look surprised and shocked, even to cry a little. She didn't tell anyone that when she had gone to fetch her beloved toy at first light, she had had the greatest difficulty in untwining his long arms from their stranglehold on her lifeless cousin's neck.

This time, however, she knew that Arnold had gone too far. Much as she had wanted Camilla out of the way she hadn't wanted her dead. Or had she? She caught her breath in horror at the thought. *Did* she want Camilla dead? *Had* she wanted her aunt's beautiful face ruined? She looked at the monkey's quizzical face as if for the first time. Who was he? What was he? Or who and what was *she*?

Clutching the soft nylon body close to her own she moved swiftly through the hushed, mourning house, running down the back stairs to the basement, hardly daring to think of what she was about to do, knew she had to do, until she was safely in the dimly lit, half underground room. Shutting the door and pushing the stiff rusty bolt across she sat down in an old broken basket chair with Arnold on her lap, one huge pink hand flopping over her shoulder. She buried her face in his soft golden fur and sobbed as though her heart would break.

The basement had once been the kitchen of the tall, Edwardian house, being underground at the front but at garden level at the back, and the huge dresser, wide sink and old-fashioned coke boiler still bore witness to its former usage: now it was used to store garden tools, the lawn mower, tins of paint and disused furniture.

Drying her streaming eyes as well as she could on a sodden handkerchief Wendy put on the large glasses she had taken off when her tears overwhelmed her and stood up, placing the toy monkey in the basket chair.

She took an old newspaper from the pile on the floor, crumpled it and placed it in the fire grate of the boiler, stacking some firewood, cut ready for winter fires in a box nearby, on top. Then she walked across to the can of petrol that stood beside the lawn mower.

The petrol can was heavy. Having unscrewed the cap she tilted it awkwardly to soak the paper in the grate of the boiler, slopping it on the floor and onto her skirt. Matches. There must be matches somewhere. She searched among the boxes of oddments and piles of old books and magazines on the dresser. Ah, here was a box. She shook it. Still a few inside.

Lighting a match she threw it onto the petrol-soaked paper and it exploded into flames with a roar, frightening her.

When the fire was burning steadily she turned back to the basket chair where Arnold sat and her tears started again.

'I'm sorry Arnold,' she sobbed, picking him up, 'but I've got to do it! I've got to!'

The monkey lay passive in her arms, his brown glass eyes gazing calmly into hers; but suddenly his expression changed, becoming one of horror as he realized what she was about to do, and he threw his arms round her neck in a loving, pleading embrace.

Wendy tore at the long soft, furry limbs as they wound and twined about her, not loving now, but becoming more frenzied every second. She struggled to get free and breaking his stranglehold at last she flung him from her, flung him into the flames.

The look of horror on the toy's face changed to one of pathetic entreaty, and then to agony as the flames licked at the golden fur; the acrylic material of his stuffing started to melt and contract, contorting his body with writhing anguish; the furry lids frizzled back from the brown glass eyes and the wide smiling mouth melted into a great, gaping, silently-screaming hole.

Wendy could bear it no longer; she had to save him, her beloved toy, had to pull him from the flames. She put out her hands but the fierce heat beat her back and at the same moment she saw the look of anguished entreaty on the half-consumed face of the toy change to one of purest evil. One writhing arm reached towards her, the scarred and blood-stained palm uppermost, held out not in supplication but to touch her petrol-soaked frock with its flaming fingers.

'*What I did I did for you,*' the creature seemed to say in answer to her screams, '*and where I go you go.*'

III

Department of Permanent Health and Social Security

The boredom, the utter crushing boredom of having nothing to do.

How much longer would this go on? No one to ask. Well, hundreds, thousands of people to ask, but somehow one didn't. Were they all wondering when this purgatory of inactivity was to come to an end, too?

Harrison looked wearily round the vast hall at the masses of people, waiting, waiting for something to happen.

Was it months or merely weeks since he had been brought here? The sameness, the lack of incident, made it difficult to measure time. Multitudes of people had arrived since he had been here and more were arriving all the time. They were roughly segregated according to duration of stay, and every so often one of the marshals would move a group, or an individual, further up the hall, or back in the opposite direction, retracing the way they had come where very distance made the hall narrow into darkness.

Harrison had been moved on in a forward direction: not that it made any difference. Each succeeding bay of the building was identical, totally without feature, nothing to focus the attention, nothing to like or dislike about the smooth white walls, the concealed shadowless lighting, the dark, soft floor-covering which deadened noise. Come to think of it, there was very little noise considering the enormous number of people.

From time to time one of the marshals would approach an individual and, referring to a thick file of papers, check a point here, ask a question there.

Harrison had been thus approached four times already, or possibly more often, he couldn't remember. The marshal, the one who, stressing that there was no formality here, had told them to call him Mike, walked smartly up to him and asked a string of questions, checking them off against information already on the file.

It was beyond Harrison's comprehension how they could find more questions to ask. From the moment one was born one's every movement was carefully noted by the authorities; practically every thought one had was monitored, or so it seemed. However, the checking and double-checking went on.

Harrison watched a man near him look up at the approach of a marshal, his face showing the mixture of anticipation and apprehension he had experienced himself when realizing he was to be singled out.

Did it mean some positive move? Anything would be better than this endless nothing, this limbo. Yet on the other hand, since one was never informed of the moves the powers-that-be had in mind, it could conceivably be worse.

When the marshal had finished speaking to the man his face registered relief, closely followed by the carefully controlled expressionlessness which masked all emotion here.

He looked up at Harrison and for a second their eyes met, but the comfort of communication seemed not to exist in this situation. Everyone was on his or her own, encapsulated in introspection.

Harrison went to lean against the wall and listlessly surveyed the thousands of people standing or sitting, only moving, deferentially, to make way for the marshals as they walked rapidly through the crowds.

This must surely be the biggest holding base of all, he thought. The other bases where he had been kept at various stages of his development and education had been vast, but nothing like this. In those other places everyone had at least been of one type, either of age, sex or intelligence and had been specially selected to carry out the assignment they were on their way to fill, but here there were people of both sexes and all ages.

Children were brought in at intervals and taken straight

through in orderly ranks by the junior marshals, who seemed little older than their charges but had the same assurance as their older counterparts.

Over to his right was a group of elderly, even old, men and women. What purpose they could fulfil in this gigantic project he couldn't imagine. Still, in every such enterprise someone had to do the back-up work; butter the buns and wash the socks. He nearly smiled at his own thoughts. There had been no buns to butter or socks to wash for a good few generations now, but such historic phrases somehow lived on in the language and filled a need.

His gaze moved over to a group of younger women, capable and efficient-looking girls with calm eyes. He looked at them with no sexual interest; such instincts had been trained out of him and all men at a very early age, to be drug-induced only when a breeding order had been made.

Listlessly his attention came back to the group to which he was loosely attached, men of his own age and younger. The presence of these and the young women he could understand. He, and presumably they, had been trained for this all through life. They had known that eventually they would be called upon to put into practice all that they had learned.

Processed as he had been since birth it was surprising that he still dared to question the rights and wrongs of the matter even in his own thoughts, but ever since he had been brought to this holding base Harrison had bitterly resented the speed with which his posting had been put through.

He had been constantly assured that there was never any need to worry about his wife and children in any eventuality; that they would be watched over and provided for. In fact on his various other assignments this had been the case and they had been brought on to join him in due course; in fact his youngest child had been programmed to be conceived and born when he and his wife were at an interstellar base.

Always, previously, he had been given permission to explain his leaving, to say goodbye, but not this time. Too secret, he supposed, and yet his wife had been so carefully screened before and since their marriage that he failed to see what harm could have been done by allowing him at least to take his leave of her.

With a sigh he raised his eyes and, looking at the man whose glance he had met earlier Harrison saw his face tense and following his eyes, noticed one of the marshals, known as Lew, approaching. Lew was different from the other marshals. He was dark while they were fair, and his compelling eyes held a depth of tragedy quite at variance with the aura of calm composure which the others radiated.

In low tones he questioned the man, made some amendments to the sheaf of papers he held and then together they walked back down the hall. Harrison watched them for as long as he could, until they disappeared among the throng, even the tall marshal's shining black hair indistinguishable in the distance.

Leaning his head back against the wall he gazed upwards, noting the small round eyes dotting the high vaulted ceiling behind which television cameras kept constant watch over the entire gathering. Harrison mused that it must make dull viewing. There was hardly any movement at all except when the marshals made their rapid way through the crowds, a path opening up before them and closing at once behind them, like a ripple in water.

Suddenly he noticed such a ripple and pulled himself upright and away from the wall as he realized two marshals were making their way towards him, their steady eyes fixed on his face.

In quiet voices Mike and Ray, a marshal Harrison had not come in contact with before, told him to come with them and turned to move further up the hall. It was the first move he had made without further reference to his file, which he noticed Ray was holding, a large official stamp having appeared on its cover starkly stating 'Processed'.

This move took him a greater distance up the hall than had the previous ones. There were slightly fewer people here, more isolated from each other, their trained expressionlessness still incapable of controlling the questions in their eyes.

The marshals stopped and Mike pointed further still up the

hall. To Harrison's astonishment he noticed a slight change in the construction of the vaulted building. There was a shallow flight of steps leading to a higher level up which another marshal was escorting a woman towards what looked like an enormous desk. It was so far away that he could make out no details, but Mike explained that in due course the marshal near the steps, whose name was Gabby, would come and fetch him and would give him further instructions. On giving him this information both he and Ray clasped hands with him, laying their other hands on his shoulders before they turned away.

Time passed, how much Harrison had no way of telling. The walls and vaulting of this bay of the hall were identical to all the others, but the difference at the far end, where the steps led to the higher level, galvanized everyone's attention.

Every so often Mike and Ray would bring more people to join Harrison's group and from the far end Gabby would come down to single out a man or woman to be taken up to the steps.

As before, children were marched through by the junior marshals, their little faces bewildered and wondering, straight up the steps and along the upper hall.

As Harrison watched them he wondered for the first time if this was where they had brought his first-born son, he who had been conceived in experimental conditions and who had been arbitrarily taken away when only a few years old. Hitherto he had supposed the child cancelled, but now he was not so sure.

As time went on Harrison felt his apprehension lifting a little. Perhaps it was only that he was becoming accustomed to the monotony of inactivity; perhaps it was because Lew was no longer to be seen in this part of the hall taking people back the way they had come; perhaps it was that surely soon he would discover the purpose of this operation.

For whatever reason a sort of serenity crept over him and when eventually the marshal, Gabby, came towards him, his glowing eyes fixed on his face, he went to meet him calmly and with assurance.

It seemed a long walk to the flight of steps, but having

reached them Harrison was delighted to see Mike and Ray, the marshals he had grown to like and trust, standing on the top step. They turned and accompanied him and Gabby to the great desk.

At the desk, files and documents piled neatly at each side of him, sat a man whose kindly, ordinary face seemed the very epitome of wisdom to Harrison. This man, whose candid eyes held compassion and understanding in their depths, for all the penetrating perception of their gaze, must surely know all there was to know about him, about everyone, he thought.

Ray handed the file he carried to Gabby. Harrison noticed that it now bore a further stamp on its cover, 'Approved'. The four of them stood some paces away from the desk, waiting for a sign from the man who sat behind it. Eventually he spoke.

'Yes, Gabriel?' he said.

Gabriel stepped forward and placed the file before him, at the same time gently propelling Harrison until he stood before the man.

'This is Harrison, Peter,' Gabriel said. 'He has been screened, researched, processed and judged fit to be promoted. All he needs now is your final word.'

Peter opened the file at the first page.

'Thank you Gabriel, Michael, Raphael,' he said, nodding at each of the three marshals as he dismissed them. 'I don't think I need to confer with Lucifer on this.'

He smiled at Harrison.

'Now, let us see,' he said.

It seemed to take another age for Peter to leaf through the file, seeking a pertinent question here, remarking on a point there, but finally he shut the book.

He stood up, fingering the vast gold key hanging from a chain round his neck, and gestured to Harrison to accompany him.

For the first time he noticed, some distance away and almost indistinguishable from the white walls in which they were set, towering gates towards which Peter walked, leading the way.

'You have worked hard and well, suffered much and achieved much,' Peter said. 'And we have found you worthy to fulfil this last and greatest assignment. I congratulate you.'

They had reached the great white gates by now and Peter held the gold key high in front of him.

Without a sound the gates started to slide smoothly aside as the electronic beam which controlled them was interrupted by the shining golden instrument.

Peter turned to Harrison.

'You will have wondered what we have been planning for you all this time,' he said.

A great peace, passing his understanding, enveloped Harrison as he crossed the threshold.

'Now,' Peter said, 'You shall know as you are known.'

IV

Cat Among the Bidding

'Quiet, ladies and gentlemen, please!' the auctioneer's voice cut across the buzz of conversation in the crowded drawing-room as he stood, large and jocular, on a stool by the window: his two white-coated assistants eased their way between the tightly pressed people to lift smaller pieces of furniture and ornaments high in the air so that those at the back near the door could see.

An auction in a large country house always draws a crowd, and this one had drawn a larger crowd than most.

Trescawen House had been the home of a recluse, Mrs Bowen, a semi-invalid who, on the death of her husband, had withdrawn completely behind the high stone wall which encircled the acres of garden and parkland in which the house stood.

For years she had seen no one except the married couple, housekeeper and gardener, who looked after her and the estate, and the doctor, on the rare occasions when she needed him.

She had almost ceased to exist for the people who lived in the district, only eliciting a brief moment of interest and speculation from tourists who chanced upon the tall wrought-iron gates as they explored the countryside, and later asked at the local pub or shop who lived within.

But when Mrs Bowen's death was announced, and later the auction, everyone wanted to see inside the gates, and now the long drive, and several hundred yards of the lane outside, was flanked with cars.

Inside the house fur-coated ladies, their bored husbands and blue-jeaned daughters in tow, jostled with elegant young dealers in fawn trousers, pure wool jerseys and hacking jackets. The dealers' discreet, small vans were parked outside the house with their names and 'Antiques' written tastefully on the sides in gold lettering, mingling with the estate cars and Land Rovers of others determined to buy, and with the foresight to arrive early.

The sale was nearly over, with only one more room full of treasures to sell after the drawing-room, and bidding was brisk: the young dealers conferred silently with their partners across the room, a slight widening of the eyes signifying a nod to bid higher, a narrowing of the eyes and mouth being recognized as a sign to go no further. Inveterate auction-goers among the ladies raised a hand and gave a confident 'Yes!' from time to time while their husbands winced visibly; others got it all wrong, causing the auctioneer to admonish them:

'Come along, madam! Are you bidding or just waving to friends?'

Young married couples, whose hopes of buying had evaporated as the dealers had got into their stride, stayed, their catalogues open at the relevant page, and assiduously marked in the astonishing prices beside each lot number.

'Now then, let's get on with it,' the auctioneer shouted, consulting his list. 'Lot number 408. A large painting in oils by the late owner of the house, who else? It measures 30 inches by 48, in carved gesso frame, and I'm sure I don't need to tell you that the subject of the picture is – cats!'

The crowded room rippled with laughter.

There was indeed little need to mention the subject matter of the painting. Every picture in the house, and there were several dozen, all in superb frames, was of cats. Grey cats, black cats, tabby cats, ginger cats, Siamese cats.

Cats appeared not only in the paintings but in the patterns of the carpets under foot, carved into the wooden fireplace surrounds and embroidered into cushion covers and the tapestry seats of chairs and sofas. Modelled in terra cotta and cast in bronze their reflections were caught in the highly polished surfaces of the mahogany furniture on which they stood.

Everything that could be embellished with a cat was so

embellished. Walking sticks and umbrellas with cats' head handles were tied in bundles and lot numbered; brass fire screens with cats' faces, the eyes pierced to let the firelight flicker through, stood before the empty grates, their eyes dull now.

Elegant china cabinets bore cats of every description on their shelves, from delicate procelain, ivory and jade beauties through more naive Staffordshire figures to cheap but attractive ones in pottery and pulled glass.

Book cases were crammed with volumes dealing exclusively with cats; books of cat paintings, cat photographs, cat poetry; books on their breeding and maintenance, their evolution and their place in history, religion and legend; books on every aspect of cats. In the hall were several piles of wicker cat baskets, dismally empty and bearing numbered tickets.

Mrs Bowen had been a cat-lover indeed.

On the edge of a chaise longue in the morning-room sat the late Mrs Bowen's housekeeper. She was a small, stout woman with grey hair, her pleasant face stricken now with grief. Her nervous fingers worked unconsciously at tearing the hem off a small damp handkerchief which she had rolled and twisted into a limp rag. Occasionally the handkerchief would be raised to her mouth, too late to stifle a slight sob, and she would clear her throat and move self-consciously on her seat, pulling her too-short skirt down over plump knees in an effort to cover up, not the knees, but her obvious unhappiness, from the few other people who sat about the room, waiting for the auctioneer to get to a lot number in which they were interested.

Beside her on the cat-embroidered upholstery sprawled a large, untidy woman in an expensive tweed coat. She threw the coat open and pushed her glasses up on top of her head, making her already wild hair wilder.

'I think it's all *terribly* sad,' she said, on a deep sigh, to no one in particular. 'I shouldn't think this house has seen as many people in thirty years, and now here they all are, tramping about and making jokes about the cat pictures; some of which,' she added in mild surprise, 'are jolly good.'

The housekeeper had been sitting with her back half turned to the large lady but now she moved to face her eagerly.

'Oh, madam!' she cried, 'I'm so glad someone understands!' Once again the tortured handkerchief was pressed to her lips.

The large lady pulled her glasses down onto her nose and examined the woman beside her.

'Well, I *do* think it's sad,' she repeated. 'This was someone's home. Everything in it had a meaning for the old lady, I don't care how mad she was. Now it's going to be scattered all over the place and I dare say all her paintings will be ripped out of their frames and burnt. I know it's inevitable but I still think it's tragic.'

The housekeeper leant forward. She was torn between warmth towards this stranger for her sympathy and anger at her for thinking Mrs Bowen mad.

'It's breaking my heart, madam,' she said, 'Ted, that's my husband, he said not to come, that it would upset me, and I didn't come, not until just now when I couldn't keep away any longer.' She sat a little further back on the seat, 'But my mistress was not mad,' she added firmly. 'She was the kindest, sweetest lady that ever lived. My Ted and me, we came here nearly thirty years ago, just before the master died, and we couldn't have wished for a better position: she was all the world to us. Us and the cats was all she wanted and she and them was all we wanted.' Once more her eyes filled with tears and the rag of a handkerchief was pressed to the quivering lips, but she suddenly remembered her place and sat up straight again.

'I'm sorry, madam. I promised Ted that if I came I wouldn't make a fuss.'

The large lady regarded her with interest and laid a heavily-ringed hand on her knee.

'You go ahead and make a fuss if you feel like it, my dear,' she said. 'It's about time someone showed a bit of feeling round here.'

Loud laughter, no doubt at one of the auctioneer's witticisms, came from the drawing-room across the hall. The housekeeper half-rose to her feet.

'Oh, that dreadful man, making jokes about madam and her cats!' she cried, '*How* she would have hated him!'

'He really is too ghastly, I agree,' the large lady said. 'That dreadful jocularity may be all right in his own saleroom, but he might behave with a little more dignity when he's out of it. But don't let it upset you too much,' she smiled kindly at the distraught woman, 'It will all be over soon.'

She looked round the small elegant room appreciatively.

'I gather you were Mrs Bowen's housekeeper? Well, I must say you kept it all beautifully for her. And the garden is heavenly. Your Ted looks after that I suppose?'

Diverted, the housekeeper relaxed again.

'Oh, yes madam, Ted does it all, the gardening and looking after the car and the shopping. He's out there now somewhere. Better keep busy, he said. He'll miss her as much as I will, the dear old lady.' Two tears rolled down the plump cheeks, to be scrubbed away with the devastated handkerchief.

'There, there,' the large lady soothed, patting the housekeeper's knee. 'What will you do now, the pair of you?'

'Mrs Bowen made sure we would be all right a long time ago;' the woman's eyes were tender behind the tears. 'She made the cottage over to us. You can just see part of it between the trees.' She pointed through the window behind the chaise longue and they both looked across the immaculate grass and drifts of daffodils beneath leafless oaks and beeches. 'She left us the car, too, and quite a bit of money. And the cats, of course. No one else was to have them.'

'Tell me about the cats,' the large lady said, glad that the woman beside her was less distressed. 'She obviously adored them. Were there many?'

For the first time the housekeeper smiled.

'Oh yes, she loved her cats,' she said, 'We've had as many as twenty-seven of them at times. Do you know,' she leant towards her companion, 'it was almost magical the way she trained them. They were as good as gold, they all knew their names and their places and did just what she told them, and they were as clean as clean. Lovely cats they were, all of them, and understood every word she said. Of course, when she became so poorly she knew she hadn't very long to live and saw to it that we didn't have so many. She didn't keep any of the kittens; made Ted get the vet in to them, poor mites, and only kept the older ones. There was six when she went: Ted and me's got them over at the cottage now. We dearly love them and they won't want for anything, she knew that.'

'Do the little tomb-stones in the garden mark cats' graves?' asked the large lady. Coming late she had had to leave her car in the lane and, walking up the drive, had noticed small slate headstones dotted about between the budding rhododendrons and azaleas, with primroses and daffodils planted before each one.

'Yes, they do,' the housekeeper said. 'There must be fifty or sixty of them because Mrs Bowen and the master were here long before we came and they always had cats. I don't think she ever forgot any of them. When one died she would send Ted over to Delabole to get a slate headstone made with its name and dates carved on it and then Ted would set it up over the little grave,' she sighed.

'Oh, yes, there must be quite sixty. She'd go out of an evening and walk about talking to them all, the dead ones and the live ones that went everywhere with her. Ted and me was sure they knew.' She glanced up at the large lady's face for any sign of derision but, finding none, relaxed again.

'I wonder if she can still communicate with them,' she said, her eyes far-away. The large lady's attention had wandered.

'Communicate with whom?' she asked.

'The cats. From wherever she's gone.'

'Oh I see. *Damn* that man Rundle!' the large lady said, irritated by more gusts of laughter following the auctioneer's latest sally. She got up and walked across to the fireplace, above which hung a large picture of a Siamese cat. It was emerging from a background of leaves and flowers and painted in such a way that the lifted forepaw seemed almost to move, the whiskers to quiver, the blue eyes meeting the eye of the beholder with lifelike directness; the leaves and flowers seemed ready to spring back to their original positions when the cat had moved on.

'Well,' she said, 'Your mistress certainly knew how to paint cats. I'm going to bid for this picture. It reminds me of a dear cat I had once. But I expect some wretched dealer is after the frame and will take the price way out of my reach.' She sat down again, pulling the silk scarf from round her neck and sticking her well shod feet out in front of her.

'It's jolly warm for March,' she said. 'Do you think we could open a window? It'll be dreadfully hot when that rabble come crowding in here.'

The housekeeper got to her feet and threw up the lower sash of the window.

'Oh dear,' she said, 'Here comes Edward!'

'Who's Edward?' the large lady asked without turning round.

'A cat,' the housekeeper said worriedly. 'Edward the Black Prince. Ted said he'd shut them all up but I expect Edward was too clever for him. Mrs Bowen said he was the cleverest cat she'd ever had. Said that he knew what she was thinking before she'd thought it.'

As she spoke a huge black Persian cat sprang onto the window sill and into the room, striding across towards the open door, his great yellow eyes baleful, his magnificent plumey tail lashing from side to side.

'He's a lovely creature,' the large lady said, as Edward turned his head to look at her appraisingly, 'And what a size! I've never seen such a big cat!'

'Oh, Edward!' the housekeeper said, 'Whatever are you doing? You know the mistress isn't here anymore.' She bent down to pick him up and cradled him in her arms, rubbing her chin against the side of his vast, angry black face.

'I'd better put you out and shut the window again.'

'No, don't do that, it'll be so beastly hot. Put him down here on the seat between us,' the large lady said, patting the chaise longue beside her.

'You'll be a good boy, won't you, Edward?'

Edward subsided onto the tapestry, ears pricked and eyes on the door, acknowledging the large lady's stroking hand absent-mindedly with slight undulations of his great body.

'He's not going to like all those people in his house,' the housekeeper said, looking at him anxiously, 'And, oh my goodness, here they come.'

· There were only the stacked cat-baskets and one or two articles of furniture in the hall to be dealt with before the morning-room, and people began crowding in to get into advantageous positions.

From beyond the door the auctioneer's jokes could now be heard.

'Lot number 439, four cat-baskets,' he said, 'I don't need to tell you sensible people that you could keep far nicer things in them than *cats*. Logs, for instance, or better still dogs! Now, what am I bid?'

Edward's tail began to lash backwards and forwards between the two women on the chaise longue, and they each kept a firm hand on him.

Very soon the morning-room was jammed with people. The young dealers marked their catalogues with the prices they had paid for things, scored out items they had lost to their competitors and made last minute appraisals of pieces of furniture. Quite a lot of the blue-jeaned daughters and young married couples had drifted out into the garden, the morning-room not being very large, but the fur-coated ladies pushed and shoved, easing their bulk sideways, dragging their husbands in their wake, speaking to each other behind their catalogues and eyeing the dealers.

The two women on the chaise longue tucked their feet in and moved closer together, sheltering Edward with their bodies in case someone sat on him, smiling at each other, seemingly old allies in the face of this the enemy.

'Come along now, move aside, please!' The auctioneer and his two assistants forced their way in, causing people to tread on each other's feet and making the cat ornaments sway dangerously on fragile, thin-legged side tables.

George Rundle was a tall, thick set man in his mid-forties. He was doing well in the removal and storage business and his expensive suit and the garnet ring which flashed on a little finger were outward, if vulgar, signs of the rapid expansion of his small firm.

'No room to swing a cat in here!' The joke was greeted, as usual, with laughter. Edward growled low in his throat.

'Lot number 447,' said the auctioneer.

The men in white coats held the picture of the Siamese cat high above their heads.

'That's the one I want!' the large lady whispered. 'I'd better stand up, if I can.'

The auctioneer continued. 'This is a picture in oils, 36 inches by 24, in a heavy gilt frame, and the title of this dubious work of art is Solitary Cat. No wonder he's solitary if he looks like that, the ugly beast! Now then, what am I bid?'

The bidding soon topped the limit which the large lady had set herself and she sat down again, defeated.

'That confounded dealer with a beard was determined to have it,' she said. 'Good heavens, what's the matter with the cat?'

Edward was growling and spitting and doing his best to escape from the housekeeper's restraining hands.

'He's taken an awful dislike to Mr Rundle, madam,' she gasped. 'I can hardly hold him.'

'I commend your excellent taste, Edward,' the large lady told the cat with feeling, 'but you really must be a good boy and calm down. Here, come inside my coat.' With strong hands she scooped up the struggling cat and wrapped him in the skirts of her tweed coat, holding him tightly against her body.

'He'll soon quieten down now,' she said, and indeed Edward lay, heavy and still, on her lap, with only the suspicion of a growl emerging from beneath the thick material.

The auction over, the crowds began to disperse.

The young dealers loaded their smart vans and others crammed roof racks and the backs of estate cars with their booty: groups of people drifted down the drive between the shrubs, a few touches of colour among the leaves brightening the grey March afternoon.

The large lady, accompanied by the housekeeper, carried the cat outside, still bundled into her coat. As she spilled him out onto the grass he streaked off between the azaleas in the direction of the little grave stones.

'I expect he's going to have a word with his ancestors,' the housekeeper said, relieved that the ordeal of the auction was over.

'What?' asked the large lady, polishing her glasses with her silk scarf.

'Oh, it's what Mrs Bowen always used to say when ever the cats went that way,' the woman looked indulgently after the rapidly disappearing cat.

They stood for a moment, comfortable in each other's company.

'Would you like a cup of tea before you go, madam?' the housekeeper said shyly. She didn't want the lady to think her over-familiar just because they had shared the chaise longue, that oasis of understanding in the unfeeling crush of the morning room, but she was loathe to end the chance encounter. 'I know my Ted will have put the kettle on, and he'd like to meet someone who felt kindly towards the mistress.'

The large lady looked round at the cars edging into line to begin the slow journey down the drive.

'Thank you, I think that would be very nice,' she said, putting her glasses and catalogue in her bag. 'It will be murder down there in the lane with people trying to turn and backing up. Much better to let them all get away instead of adding to the turmoil,' and the two women walked across the lawn towards where smoke could be seen above the trees, ascending from the cottage chimney.

George Rundle, the auctioneer, directed his two assistants in loading the larger pieces of furniture into the van backed up to the front door, his name in large letters on the side. Tomorrow they would be delivered to their new owners.

When he had assured himself that the grand piano, pathetic now with its legs removed and its body blanketed and strapped, had, along with the chesterfield, the sideboard and other large items, been roped securely to the slatted sides of

the van's interior, he helped lift the tail-gate into place and
fastened it.

'Right then, Bill,' he addressed the senior of the two men,
'I'm glad that's over. Queer old do I thought it was: all those
cats glaring at me from the pictures. I can't abide cats,' he
shuddered. 'Evil, creepy things, I think they are.'

Pulling himself together he got back to the job in hand.

'Now,' he said, 'I've got about half an hour's work to do
here. You take the van and put it in the garage. Drop Jack off
and bring the Mini out to collect me, will you?'

Bill nodded and climbed into the driving seat beside his
mate; Rundle slapped the side of the van and it started slowly
down the drive.

Having made sure the house was empty and all the
windows shut and fastened, the auctioneer let himself out of
the door and thankfully locked it behind him. He walked
smartly over to the gardener's cottage where he handed in the
keys, together with instructions about showing prospective
buyers round the house.

He had hoped that perhaps the housekeeper would offer him
a cup of tea, but she made no such suggestion as she sat at the
kitchen table, teapot in hand, having just poured a cup for a
large, well-to-do looking woman he had seen at the auction
and who now sprawled in an arm-chair by the fire.

As he stood in the doorway talking to the gardener he was
aware of the two women looking at him coldly and with
obvious dislike. Funny, he thought, as the gardener turned
aside for a moment to fetch something, that sort of thing
didn't usually bother him, but what with all those cats' eyes
glaring at him back in the big house, and now these women,
he felt the whole place had it in for him somehow, and it made
his spine creep. As if to endorse the thought a cat reared up on
the housekeeper's lap, a thin evil-looking ginger thing, and
then another appeared from under the table, and another
from behind a chair, all looking at him. He hastily said
goodnight to the gardener and was thankful to hear the door
shut behind him as he stepped onto the path.

Looking at his watch he found that this had taken him only

twenty minutes. Might as well walk down to meet Bill, he thought, strolling over the short grass towards the trees and shrubs that lined the drive.

Just out of sight in front of him, crouched low and urgent, Edward moved like a detached fragment of the coming darkness. He ran to each of the small, slate head-stones dotted among the shrubs, pausing at each one and mewing softly. From out of nowhere cats emerged like wraiths, silently and stealthily, more and more of them, until the big black Persian was leading a veritable army.

Rundle walked slowly on through the dusk. He was cross with himself for making mock of the pictures, and of the artist herself. Apart from anything else it was bad policy to run down the items he was selling as he got a percentage on all the prices they fetched, but the house full of cats' eyes staring at him had really got him down.

Although he didn't know the word his dislike, bordering on terror, of cats was ailourophobia, something he could not help and would have done well to admit and come to terms with, but it was his nature to mock and deride things he didn't understand. Nevertheless he was displeased with himself and strangely uneasy.

The large lady got up to go. It was nearly dark now, and she must hurry down the drive as her car was parked in the lane without lights.

'I'll come a little way with you, madam,' the housekeeper said, taking a coat and scarf from the hook behind the back door. 'Edward hasn't come back yet, and I must try to find him before it gets dark. Goodness knows what's got into him this afternoon.'

Together the women walked into the gloaming garden, their feet silent on the beautifully kept grass, talking in low voices, the housekeeper occasionally calling the cat.

'Edward? Puss-puss-puss!'

Suddenly the large woman stopped and pointed between the great black shapes of the bushes that lined the drive.

'Look!' she whispered. 'What's that? Is that him?'

Something was moving, but not just one cat; dozens and

dozens, an undulating stream, a writhing mass, a swirling cloud of cats, all moving swiftly and silently among the little gravestones.

The large woman clutched the housekeeper's arm.

'My God!' she gasped, 'They're hunting something!' and the women clung together for a second before running back to the cottage as scream after scream of anguished animal terror tore through the quiet garden.

The light was going as Bill turned the Mini in at the entrance gates and he put the headlights on as he started up the long drive. It was that peculiar time of day, between dusk and dark, when headlights seemed, if anything, to make matters worse, so he turned them off again.

His journey to and from the firm's garage had taken him rather longer than half an hour and he drove as fast as he dared until suddenly, rounding a curve, he had to slam on the brakes, slewing the Mini across the narrow drive and stalling the engine.

There in front of him was a seething, writhing mass of cats; cats of every colour, all crouched over something on the ground. Or so he thought but it must have been an illusion, a trick of the light.

Shaken, he had turned the headlights on again and now sat staring at the spot where he had seen, or thought he had seen, the struggling heap of cats.

In the middle of the drive, a great, dark stain spreading all round it like a shadow, there was only one cat, an enormous black Persian. Its eyes were slitted and glinted evilly in the headlights' glare: its head was tilted on one side as it gnawed on some appalling, bloody thing with strong back teeth.

Something else beside the cat's eyes glinted; something in the raw, torn, bleeding mass.

It was George Rundle's garnet ring.

V

The Chatelaine

The man stood in the shadows at the end of the hall watching the woman coming down the stairs towards him. She was wearing a long dress of grey or blue, the dim light shining on the shifting folds as she moved. Her hair was drawn back from her face and arranged in elaborate plaits and coils.

At first he thought that she had not seen him as her face showed no surprise or alarm at his appearance, unannounced, in the house. He took a step back into deeper shadow but, having reached the bottom of the stairs, the woman crossed the hall, her skirt brushing the polished boards until she stood in front of him.

Although the man had travelled untold miles and worked and striven for this moment of return he now realized that he had made no plan as to what to do when he arrived. Somehow the thought of meeting people, explaining to them, had not occurred to him, the seemingly impossible problem of getting there having obsessed him.

He raised both hands in front of him in a gesture of excuse.

'Please forgive me,' he said, 'The door was open and without realizing what I was doing I came in. This house was once my home.'

The woman smiled. 'You are a Chalice,' she said, more as a statement than a question. Her voice had a strange, almost foreign inflection. Was it French? He couldn't be sure, but found it attractive.

'Yes,' he said, 'I am a Chalice. My family lived here for five hundred years – my father thought perhaps even longer.'

The woman took a step nearer. 'Oh, yes,' she said, 'Chalices have lived here longer than that. The back of the house is very old. The walls are so thick,' she spread her hands, 'built to keep more than the weather out. They are all that remains of the very first house that ever stood here. It was built by a Chalice.'

The man was amazed at her calm acceptance of him. Was she perhaps expecting someone else for whom she had mistaken him? It seemed incredible that she should discuss the history of his family and the architecture of the house with him within minutes of finding him standing uninvited in the hall.

'I've been wanting to come back for a very long time,' he said, 'but there were obligations to fulfil, much to be done before I was free to return. It was quite unforgivable of me to walk in as I did and I sincerely apologise.'

The woman touched him lightly on the shoulder with one hand, her wide sleeve falling back from a slender white wrist encircled by a gold bracelet.

'You must not be sorry you have come,' she replied, 'I am glad. Always I welcome members of the family when they return. After all – I also am a Chalice.'

'*You* are a Chalice?' The man's embarrassment at this awkward situation vanished at the surprise he felt that this lovely, somehow un-English, woman should be a member of his family. He could not immediately bring to mind any young female relations, but then of course there were cousins whom he had never met. He wanted very much to ask who she was and how she came to be there, but since she had accepted his presence in the house and his identity without question, it would seem unmannerly to question hers.

'Who else,' she said, smiling at him, 'would you expect to find at Chalice Manor but a Chalice?'

His relief that the house had not changed hands made him suddenly relaxed and happy. This woman – this relative – lived in and loved this house as he and all the generations of Chalices had loved it down the centuries.

He looked round the shadowy hall, noticing that nothing seemed to have changed. The great dim looking-glass in its gilt frame still reflected the faint glow of polished mahogany and old silver, the muted colours of the Indian rugs on the floor, and the mellow velvet curtains.

The woman was moving about the hall, straightening a picture here, changing the position of a chair there in the sure way of a woman in her own home. He looked at her with gratitude.

'Thank you for keeping it as it was,' he said.

For the first time she showed some surprise. 'Why should I change anything?' she asked, 'How could I?'

Before he could ask her to explain she had crossed the hall to the stairs. 'Come,' she said, 'I was in the library when you arrived. I think there is a portrait of you there painted when you were a boy. Come with me and tell me if I'm not right.'

It seemed strange to be walking up what he could only think of as his own staircase at the invitation of someone else, and yet he found himself drawn to this serene and beautiful woman and content that she should lead him up the shallow steps of the curving flight. He was profoundly grateful to her for her surprising lack of feminine nervousness at the sight of him. He shuddered at the thought of what would have happened had she screamed. Servants would have come running, dogs would have barked, or were they, he wondered for the first time, alone in the house? It occurred to him that there had not been a sound in the house until she spoke. There had been no noise of servants laughing and chattering in the kitchen, no murmur of voices from the drawing room, no click and slither of dogs' claws on the polished floors. He smiled as he remembered his old nurse, kept on long after her job was done, scolding the maids in the kitchen, and the smile saddened as he thought of his own long-dead spaniel skidding on the rugs in the hall as it dashed to welcome him home in the old days. Odd that the house should be so quiet – but as well perhaps. He did not feel up to giving a more detailed explanation of his presence than had so far been required of him, and dogs could behave oddly with strangers.

By now the man had followed the slim, upright figure in the blue-grey dress across the upstairs hall which led to the library at the back of the house. As she approached the door she seemed to hurry a little, her hands stretched out in front of her as if eager to open it. Once inside she turned to the man, her face relaxed and happy.

'I love this room,' she said, 'Of course I love the whole house, but this – this is where I like best to be – this is home.'

She moved quickly about the room, her skirts rustling as they brushed against the furniture, pointing out various portraits hanging on the pannelled walls and giving a name to each, picking up an object here and there and handing them to him, saying, 'Do you remember this – and this?'

He followed her about the room, liking her, pleased that she should love the things he loved.

'Of course,' she said, pausing, 'This room is not right. It has been altered. But that is inevitable, I suppose. It is still, nevertheless, the place above all others where I feel at home. Do you understand that?'

The man looked at the deep window embrasures, felt the strength of the thick walls about him. He knew it all so well and yet had never looked at it quite this way before, the woman seemed to change it somehow. Vaguely surprised that he should not resent her possessiveness he nodded, 'Yes, I understand.'

Suddenly the woman stopped moving round the room and went to the open door and listened. Her attitude was that of a hostess listening for the arrival of expected guests. The man immediately felt himself a stranger and an intruder again.

'I'm so sorry,' he said as he hurried to her side. 'You're expecting someone and I've taken up too much of your time. It has been most kind of you to let me look at the old house again. I must go now.'

'I am expecting people, yes,' she said. 'But you must not go. They are only members of the family, yours and mine. Come, I think they have arrived.'

The daylight was nearly gone now, and as they crossed the upper hall a faint glow came from the stairway. The woman started to run, holding up her skirts in both hands so that her feet in their odd little pointed shoes could move unimpeded, the man close behind her.

When they reached the top of the stairs the man was

amazed at the scene below. The hall was full of people, with more coming through the front door, children running between them, servants carrying lamps and lighting the candles in the sconces on either side of the great looking-glass – and dogs. There must have been at least a dozen dogs, big and small, dancing delightedly among the people. One skidded on the rugs on the polished floor as it bounded towards the foot of the stairs.

The man turned to the woman at his side. 'There are a great many people,' he said, 'Is it an occasion? An anniversary?'

The woman took him by the hand and led him down the stairs towards a group of people coming upwards, their arms outstretched in greeting. In front of them the spaniel raced up the steps.

'Yes, it is an anniversary,' she said, 'The house was pulled down one hundred years ago to-day.'

VI

Fanny

St Merion's Road had once been what is known as a good address, but it had deteriorated. Now nearly all the large Victorian houses had been converted into flats, their garden walls taken down and their lawns concreted over to provide parking space for the residents' cars. But there was one house, halfway down the road on the left hand side, which, seeming to ignore the fate of its neighbours, had stubbornly resisted change.

Its large front gates remained in place, neatly painted a discreet green and firmly closed on mown lawns and a short gravel drive which led to the imposing fan-lit front door. Inside very little had been altered since it was built; electricity had replaced gaslight but apart from that the big, spacious rooms were maintained in their original condition, although very few of them were used.

The drawing-room furniture stood on the Aubusson carpet where it had stood for well over half a century, waiting for the afternoon visitors who no longer visited; the dining-room table, covered with a bobble-braided chenille cloth, could seat a dozen in comfort though now never called upon to seat one: only the small morning-room was in constant use.

In the basement kitchen the wide, shallow pottery sink, served by a brass cold-water tap, had never been replaced by stainless steel and chromium and the great black range still dominated one wall, though never lit now, its former function being carried out by a small, old gas cooker standing in one corner. The spacious larder had never achieved the status of utility room but was still a larder, the plates of sliced cold meat on its slate shelves a very faint echo of the huge hams which used to hang from the hooks in its ceiling, and the servants' rooms, pantry and boot-room all remained as they had been when lived in and used by a fairly large staff.

Upstairs the bathroom still held its deep, coffin shaped, mahogany panelled bath and temperamental copper geyser, and the bedrooms each contained a half-tester bed, high and comfortable and made up with linen sheets, although only one room was ever used.

Agnes Maitland had never felt the necessity to alter anything in the house in which she had been born seventy-four years ago; in fact it had never occurred to her to do so. A woman came in twice a week to clean the silver, to scrub the tiled floor in the hall and to see to Miss Maitland's bit of washing, after which she would flick a duster round all the rooms, giving each of them what she called a proper going over in their turn; a man came on Tuesdays to mow the lawn and keep the shrubs clipped and under control, and these were the only people who ever came to the house now, other than worthy ladies and intrepid children who came to collect for deserving causes.

Although Agnes's life was one of penance her surroundings were no part of it; they just happened to suit her. But would they suit Grace, she wondered?

Grace, her sister, had also been born in the house, two years after Agnes, but when their time in nursery and schoolroom was over their lives had been very different. Pretty, frivolous Grace had married twice, once well and once badly, her first husband, much older than herself, leaving her a small fortune to be squandered by her second, and much younger, one. Plain, serious Agnes had never married, knowing from childhood, with a conviction that grew steadily as she grew, that her life was to be devoted entirely to a demanding being of whom no one else was even aware, now.

She stood in the hall this evening, the fan light over the door admitting the green-tinged dusk which sifted through the tall trees in the garden. The grandfather clock ticked sonorously; nearly half past five, Grace would be here at any minute and indeed, as the clock struck melodiously, she heard a taxi draw up outside on the gravel.

The two women sat in the morning-room sharing an uncomfortable silence; small talk didn't come any more easily between sisters who had not seen each other for thirty years, and who had nothing in common except blood, than between any other two ill-assorted strangers.

Grace, her hair blue-rinsed and bouffant above her over made-up, elderly face, nursed a glass of whisky, a bottle of which had been produced from a hold-all within minutes of her arrival; Agnes, abundant, wiry, grey hair swept into a knot on the nape of her neck, her face innocent of any embellishment other than the lines and creases that seventy-four years had brought, fiddled nervously with the things on the tea tray. She had hoped that tea and biscuits would have made an appropriate offering on her sister's arrival, but apparently they had not. Anxiously she pictured the slices of ham and brisket of beef, the lettuce and few tomatoes she had bought for their supper. She could see that that was going to be inadequate, too; in fact it was all going to be very difficult.

It had not been Agnes's idea that Grace should come to live with her when her young husband, having spent all her money, had left her, but it seemed that none of her racy friends had any time for her now that she was practically penniless and she had had nowhere else to go. In vain Agnes had suggested any alternative she could think of in her letters, but Grace, humiliated by her husband's desertion, insisted on coming back to what she called home, to lick her wounds and to live the rest of her life on her memories of happier times.

'Besides,' she had written in her wild and barely-legible writing, 'I'm sure *you* could do with some company in your old age!'

Agnes had all the company, not that she wanted, but that she could manage. Her days were spent mostly dozing in an armchair in the morning-room, recovering from her sleepless nights and the thought of her sister's company was appalling.

Having rearranged every item on the tea tray Agnes cleared her throat nervously.

'I've put you in the green bedroom, the spare room, Grace,' she said.

'Oh? Why not in Mother's room?' Grace asked peevishly,

pouring herself another drink from the bottle at her elbow. 'But, come to think of it, I suppose you sleep in that yourself.'

'No,' Agnes replied, 'I still use my old room, the one I used to share with you when we were children. It never occurred to me to move out of it. I just thought you'd be more comfortable in the green room. It gets all the morning sun.' It was also more or less by itself, on the half landing at the front of the house, well away from the other bedrooms, she added to herself.

There was another silence during which she rearranged the tea things yet again, and Grace lit one cigarette from the stub of another and tapped with her long red nails on the arm of her chair.

'Do you remember Fanny?' Agnes suddenly heard herself saying.

'Of course not,' Grace replied, 'After all, I was only two when she was born. Why?'

'Oh, I just wondered, that's all,' her sister said. 'It's just that I – I think about her quite a lot.'

'Strange, isn't it? She would be, let me see, seventy now,' Grace said, 'had she lived.'

'Yes,' Agnes sighed, 'But as it is she always remains a baby.'

'What do you mean *remains*,' Grace said irritably, taking a deep drink from her glass, 'She doesn't *remain* at all. You let that silly business all those years ago upset you too much. For heaven's sake you were only a tiny mite yourself, far too young to understand. I'm surprised you even remember.'

But Agnes remembered all too well.

Her mother had been ill in bed for what seemed a very long time and she and Grace were taken to her room by their nurse, morning and evening, to kiss her good-day and good-night.

One morning they had found their big brothers in the room and Papa standing by the bed.

Mama was looking very pale, but smiling, and she held something in her arms.

'Come and see your new baby sister!' Papa had said, and Agnes had gone up to the bed.

Mama turned back the edge of an enveloping shawl to reveal the baby's face. It was very ugly, wizened and wrinkled with a wisp of black hair on its misshapen head and a bluish complexion.

Agnes thought someone must have made a mistake. Grace, behind her in Nurse's arms, was her baby sister and this new creature looked nothing like her.

'We are going to call her Fanny,' Papa had said, 'Come, dear, kiss Fanny.'

Agnes looked at the baby critically and then up at her father.

'She's very ugly, Papa,' she said candidly, '*Must* I kiss her?'

One of her brothers smothered a laugh, but Nurse grasped her shoulder and pinched it painfully.

'Do as your Papa says at once,' she commanded in a stern whisper, pushing her towards the bed, and Agnes had stood on tiptoe and done as she was told, not liking it and backing away at once, wiping her mouth on her sleeve as Nurse lowered the uncritical infant Grace to kiss the baby in her turn.

That evening she had been asleep in the night nursery, with Grace in her cot across the room, when Nurse had woken her. Papa stood by the door.

'Get up quickly, Agnes,' he had said, 'Fanny is going to be christened.'

Nurse wrapped a shawl round her and led her from the room. Agnes had no idea what christening was, but it seemed to be something very special to be taking place in the middle of the night.

'Isn't Gracie coming?' she enquired, glancing back at the cherubic child asleep in her cot, but it appeared that she was not.

In Mama's room her big brothers were there again looking very sad; Mama looked sad, too, and the baby looked even uglier than it had this morning, more blue than ever, and it made funny noises when it breathed. Mr Hawkins, the vicar, was there as well and Agnes found this very strange as she thought he lived in the church down the road and never came out.

In front of the vicar on Mama's dressing table was the big silver bowl which usually stood on the sideboard in the dining room with fruit in it, only now it was filled with water.

Mr Hawkins took the baby from Mama and said some things to it and then splashed water from the silver bowl on its face. Agnes was surprised that it didn't cry, but it just made funny choking noises in its throat instead and Mr Hawkins put it back in Mama's arms. At his direction the boys went up to the bed to kiss the baby.

'Come along, Agnes,' Papa said eventually and, as she didn't move, he held out his hand to her.

'Come dear, kiss Fanny.'

'But Papa!' she protested, 'I kissed her this morning!' and once again Nurse's fingers took her shoulder in a vice-like grip and propelled her across the room.

The next morning she was told that Fanny had died in the night, and once more the family assembled in Mama's room.

Mama lay back on her pillows sobbing uncontrollably and the baby lay in a cradle by the bed, dressed in a long, lace-trimmed and pin-tucked gown, a frilly bonnet framing its tiny wrinkled face: the face was no longer that strange blue shade but greyish yellow now.

'Come dear,' Papa had said in a low churchish sort of voice, 'kiss Fanny,' but this time Agnes had rebelled.

'No! Not again!' she screamed stamping her feet and beating her little fists on the side of the cradle, 'I won't! I won't!'

Mama had moaned, Papa had slapped her small furious face and Nurse bundled her out of the room and back into the night nursery where, after a sound spanking with a slipper, she was put to bed and locked in with nothing to eat and no one to talk to for the rest of the day.

Mama had died soon after that and in the general gloom of mourning that ensued Agnes had become convinced, in her four-year-old mind, that it was somehow all her fault. She should have kissed the poor baby, and now it was too late and she knew that, as long as she lived, she could never make up for that unkindness of hers. But she could try.

The sisters got through their first few days together as best they could, feeling their way towards some sort of understanding, Grace bored stiff and Agnes weary to the point of exhaustion.

Grace went out into town from time to time, to have her hair done and to replenish her stock of whisky and cigarettes, sometimes coming back with strange vegetables and other exotic food which Agnes did not know how to cook. She took advantage of her sister's occasional absence to flop down in her chair and close her eyes in blessed moments of sleep, but the absences were all too few.

When in the house Grace wandered about rediscovering her childhood.

'Really, Aggie!' she cried. 'It's like a museum! I don't believe you've thrown anything out in fifty years!'

'No, I don't suppose I have,' Agnes concurred. 'Everything's perfectly all right where it is. Why would I throw things out?'

They were in the day nursery, which had become their schoolroom when Nurse's place had been taken by a governess: the little desks were just where they had always been and the dolls' house, its paint dim and faded, and the rocking-horse, minus his tail, stood just where they had always stood.

Grace gave the horse a push and he moved on his curved rockers, painted eyes staring, painted nostrils flaring.

'It's all too nostalgic for words,' she said, 'Are all the other toys in the cupboard?'

They were, of course and Grace knelt on the floor to take them out one by one; boxes of bricks, a Jack-in-the-box, a monkey on a stick which hadn't ever worked properly, a Noah's Ark with only a few wooden animals missing, some stuffed dogs and bears and one or two faded and bedraggled dolls.

'There's one missing!' Grace exclaimed. 'My favourite doll, the big one with the wax head.' She sat back on her heels and remembered. 'Oh that dear doll! She had black hair and eyes that closed – and didn't she make a noise when you turned her over? I wonder what happened to her.'

It was a rhetorical question but it seemed to startle Agnes.

'Oh!' she said nervously, 'I gave her away.'

'You didn't!' Grace jeered at her. 'You never would have done that. You loved that doll too, in fact I remember you became positively possessive of her and hated me playing with her. Anyway you don't know any children to give her away to.'

Agnes retracted at once.

'No. Of course you're right. I didn't give her away, I *threw* her away. She was full of moth; her body was made of material if you remember and the stuffing was all coming out. Yes, that's right, I *threw* her away.'

Grace looked at her as she bent to pick up the toys and started to put them back in the cupboard. She was a strange old creature, this sister of hers, living alone in this mausoleum all these years, but as for throwing away a doll because it had moth in it, that she didn't believe. Some of the carpets had moth holes and the wool rep curtains in the dining-room were riddled, but Agnes hadn't thrown them away, so why did she get so fussed about a ridiculous old doll, she wondered.

Oh well, she shrugged her shoulders, it was another little mystery to go with the locked room and, although it really couldn't matter less, another thing to bait her sister with whenever she felt like venting her bored spite on her.

Actually the locked room did irritate her. It was their mother's bedroom and she would have preferred to sleep there rather than in the green room which she found noisy, the numerous families who lived next door coming and going in cars and talking and laughing at all hours. Their mother's room overlooked the garden and would be much quieter, besides which it was the biggest and nicest bedroom in the house, but Agnes remained adamant that the key to it was lost.

Once again Grace found the excuse unlikely. None of the other rooms was locked, each one being aired and cleaned once a month, and all had their keys in place, on the inside of the doors as they had always been. She nagged and teased Agnes about it, and the doll, whenever she remembered, but to no avail; the door remained locked.

In her more amicable moments Grace recognized her sister's right to be idiosyncratic about the house she had lived in and cherished all her life, but in her more belligerent moods, when the whisky was taking effect, she became annoyed and when suffering the noise of banging car doors in the middle of the night she became furious.

Agnes became more and more weary as the days went by. Her sister, bored and at a loose end, seemed to fill the house with noise. She had brought a transistor radio with her and this she began to have on more often, for company, she said, since Agnes was no conversationalist; she had been taught to play the piano when a girl and now, finding her old sheet music in the drawing room ottoman, strummed away on the badly out of tune upright, singing in her equally out of tune voice.

She hired a television set on which she watched what seemed to Agnes the most lurid and raucous programmes every evening and when at last the time came for them to go up to their rooms it was all the exhausted woman could do to resist the temptation of throwing herself down on her bed and sleeping instead of waiting until she saw the thin line of light under Grace's bedroom door extinguished before creeping across the landing and unlocking the door of her mother's room.

One evening she dozed off as she waited, sliding down onto the floor at her half-open door, coming awake with a start as the first eerie, piercing scream echoed through the quiet house, and the next morning she had Grace to reckon with.

'For God's sake, Agnes, what was that appalling noise last night?' she demanded, confronting her elder sister as she climbed the stairs from the basement carrying their heavy breakfast tray. 'The racket from next door is *bad* enough, but this seemed to be in the house, it was quite ghastly. Did you hear it?'

'No,' Agnes said, and then, realizing that it was ridiculous to pretend that she had not, 'Yes, of course I did. Cats fighting, I expect.'

'Cats? But this was in the house and we haven't got any cats. Anyway it sounded more like a baby screaming. It was weird,' she shuddered as she buttered a piece of toast. 'It quite upset me.'

'I must be more careful,' Agnes told herself, 'but dear God how am I to manage if I get no sleep in the daytime either?' Her head ached, her eyes smarted and she felt faint and dizzy with weariness as she poured her sister's coffee.

'Perhaps it was water in the pipes,' she said aloud. 'It does make odd noises sometimes.'

Grace looked at her over her second piece of toast.

'The old thing's cracking up,' she thought. 'She looks as mad as a hatter with those wild red eyes and her hair all over the place. Mustn't let myself go all to pieces like that,' she patted her elaborately waved and blue-rinsed hair complacently and sipped her coffee.

By dint of enormous effort Agnes saw to it that the eerie scream never wailed through the night to wake her sister again, but there was nothing she could do about the noise from next door.

One night, having tossed and turned to the revving car engines and shouts and laughter for a sleepless hour, Grace got up to fetch her whisky bottle. She had had a fair amount to drink that evening but obviously not enough. Maybe another stiff one would make her sleep despite the row, she thought.

She climbed out of the high old fashioned bed and put on a frilly negligee and feathered bedroom slippers, both bought in an attempt to rekindle a little of what she had once taken to be love in the eyes of her young husband, she remembered sourly.

As she stood on the half-landing outside her door a strange, faint sound made her turn towards the bedrooms further up the stairs. Was it singing? A low voice seemed to be singing a nursery rhyme, a lullabye. My God, she thought, I'm getting as dotty as Agnes, but she wasn't imagining it and it was not cats or the water pipes; somebody was singing and making soothing, crooning baby noises.

She crept up the stairs in the faint light from the landing window, carefully holding up the hem of her nightgown, and was astonished to see Agnes's bedroom door open and across the landing a ribbon of light from under their mother's door. She listened intently.

'There, there, my pretty one; there, there, my darling,' the low, sing-song voice intoned. 'Go to sleep, my precious, my little love.'

Stealthily Grace turned the handle of the door and silently pushed it open so that she could see into the room.

Agnes paced slowly back and forth across the room holding a bundle wrapped in a moth-ruined shawl, rocking it gently and gazing down between the woollen folds, her weary old face suffused with love. Her grey hair hung down round her face and over her shoulders in wild disarray and as she pushed a strand of it back she caught sight of her sister standing in the doorway.

She stopped rocking the bundle and immediately the eerie, piercing scream that Grace had heard once before shrilled out, cutting through the night like a rusty bladed knife.

Agnes turned and slowly walked towards her, pushing back the folds of the shawl to reveal the hideous face of the big, wax-headed doll. Its features were blurred and smeared with much kissing, only a wisp of black hair clung to its misshapen head; its arms seemed to move, weakly thrashing the air, the material pock marked with moth and bursting like putrescent skin. She held the thing out, the empty eye sockets glaring, for ever awake, screams emanating from the black hole of a mouth that no doll ever had, screams that froze the mind and lacerated the very air.

Agnes's eyes were hollow with lack of sleep and mad with the madness of overwhelming remorse, the madness of all-consuming love.

'Come, dear,' she said to Grace smiling a pathetic and ghastly smile. 'Kiss Fanny,'

VII

The Horse

It was May Day morning in Sawlyn and the little town was filled to overflowing with people who had come to witness an ancient ceremony.

The streets were hung with bunting and the shops and houses decorated with branches of sycamore, already wilting in the sun: people stood shoulder to shoulder as far as Ben Marcus could see in every direction.

He was very old and cruelly bent and twisted, the huge hump on his back throwing the rest of his body into hideous deformity. His thin, crooked legs seemed too frail to support the squat bulk of his body but the steel corset he wore strengthened his contorted back, the stout sticks he held in his strong, gnarled hands held him up well enough and his ancient, handsome face, dominated by clear, grey eyes, somehow made the onlooker forget the rest of him.

Ben stood, as he had always stood on May Day, at the bottom of the narrow street down which the hobby-horse would come, at a place where the houses formed a circle round an open space called the Penny-pool.

The air of suppressed excitement all around the old man brought inexplicable tears to his eyes and his heart beat a little faster, knowing what was about to happen, the same every year but never losing its magic.

Young men and women dressed all in white, bunches of spring flowers pinned to their shoulders, moved through the crowds. Their eyes were solemn and confident yet at the same time sparkling, aware that the ceremony in which they were about to take part made them unique in some way.

Ben Marcus knew them all, knew their fathers and had

known their grandfathers when they had carried the horse, but today when they greeted him with the respect due to his great age it was he who felt a reverence for them, god-like as they were in their youthful beauty, and he was proud to be singled out by them.

The crowd suddenly swayed and Ben took a firmer hold of his sticks to steady himself; all heads were turned to the building at the end of the street from which the horse would emerge. Was it coming? Yes!

The drum-beat that heralded it reverberated through the paving stones and above the cheering an accordion could be heard playing an old, strange song with a compelling rhythm and words which once meant so much, and still did to Ben, moving him deeply, although beyond his present understanding.

Here it was! The huge and hideous beast, a great cartwheel six feet across covered in white-painted canvas with a thrashing head and heavy swirling skirt concealing the man who bore it. In no way did it resemble a horse and yet – and yet it was primeval horse, terrifying, appalling but beloved. Ben bowed his head, acknowledging its coming.

The crowd pressed back to make way for the horse and its attendants and Ben staggered a little in the crush, steadying himself as best he could. His niece had told him not to come, he was too old and frail, she said, and should stay at home where the horse would visit him as it did other of its aged and infirm devotees; but no. As long as he could manage, no matter how slowly and painfully, to make his way to his accustomed spot he would do so. Maybe next year he would need the horse to come to him, but in his heart he was sure that this would be his last May Day.

The procession was in front of him across the open space now, led by one of the dancers who waved a wand decorated with flowers and ribbons and dancing an odd, ungainly dance to the archaic music, as did the others.

Suddenly the rhythm changed, the refrain became haunting and plaintive and the horse sank down to the ground, the man with the wand resting it upon its submissive head.

'What does it do that for?' one of the onlookers asked Ben,

sure that the bent and ancient man would know.

'It's drinking,' Ben said. 'River used to run down the street there,' he jerked his head awkwardly in the direction from which the horse had come, 'and it spread out into a basin, a pond like, just here where you'm standing; Pennypool, it was called. When I was a lad there was still some as could remember it, before they filled it in and put the river underground to make it easier for the traffic and that. The place is still called the Pennypool although there isn't a pool no more. I reckon the old horse still remembers though; drinks here every year, it do.'

'Why was it called the Pennypool?' the stranger asked. 'Did people throw pennies in it?'

'Perhaps,' Ben replied, 'But I think it's got another meaning, older than what pennies are. Always had a feeling about that, I have.'

As suddenly as it had gone down the horse was up again, refreshed, and the music rejoiced once more, and surrounded by the white-clad figures it pranced off, to visit every part of the town, returning late in the afternoon, to the Pennypool where Ben still stood awaiting it.

Once more it danced in front of him, the drum-beat so close that it rebounded on his barrel chest almost painfully and he became a part of it, physically a part of it all.

The horse swirled and cavorted, the great wheel of it tilting and turning, and he had an overwhelming urge to touch it, to feel that special feel of painted canvas, clutch a strand of its beribboned horsehair tail. Perilously he leaned forward, both sticks clutched in one hand, and his old fingers seemed to burn as he made contact: deep in his veins an ancient blood stirred, some antique element that had witnessed this over and over again down the centuries on this self-same spot.

He over-reached himself and started to fall, and the moment of falling stretched dream-like, into an eternity. His vision blurred and then cleared; he no longer felt the jostling crowds, not the crowds of now, but he was aware of other crowds as year after year spiralled back and back.

In that long second he caught glimpses of other years that he could remember and then of those that he could not,

although seeming to recognize a face here, a likeness there.
The years reeled back and then slowed and steadied.

The misshapen child lay in his mother's arms, his hump back
forcing his head to one side, his beautiful little face peering
over one hunched shoulder.

He was four, too old to be carried, but his deformity made it
impossible for him to walk. Some people thought the child
should not be taken out to offend the sight of God-fearing folk,
but should be kept hidden, thinking him devil-marked, but his
family was proud of him.

'It's a mark of grace,' they said.

His mother and the other women stood beside the
Ponypool, that circle of water in the heart of the little town
which was so named, some said, from the strings of pack-
ponies that drank from it, but which others thought had a
different and forgotten meaning, older than the pack-ponies.

The women scolded and shouted at the children who ran
about on the cobbles, telling them to hold their noise, and
anxiously discussed the rumour brought by a horseman who
could even now be heard clattering up the street, that a
French frigate had been seen in St Mewes Bay.

Most of the men of the town were away in France fighting
Napoleon, and those who were not were at sea in their fishing
boats or out in the fields: the women felt very vulnerable.

The crippled child's mother shifted him from one arm to the
other.

'Likely it's only a story,' she said, in an effort to calm the
nervous women, 'You know what they'm like up St. Mewes:
like a lot of clucking hens.'

But even as she spoke a boy, panting painfully and
streaming with sweat, ran towards the crowd of women with
dire news.

'The Frenchies are coming! he gasped out. 'There's a ship
drifting up the estuary on the tide!'

The women all started talking at once, some screaming,
some sobbing.

'Fetch the men from the fields!'

'No time, they're too far away.'

'The Frenchies'll burn our houses!'

'They say they're devils!'

'What shall we do? What shall we do?'

The messenger could still be heard, clattering up the street to raise the alarm in the next village.

'Horse!' said the crippled child, clearly and firmly, 'Horse!'

His mother looked at his solemn little face and realized what he had said.

'Quiet!' she shouted to the frightened women. 'Listen to me, will you!' and she climbed onto a mounting block nearby, the better to address them.

'The horse will save us!' she cried. 'It's done it before, they say, and it'll do it again! We must take it out to the headland!'

'But women have never carried the horse!' a girl said, breaking the sudden silence.

'Then this'll be the first time,' the crippled child's mother replied. 'Gertrude, Welthin,' she pointed to the two sturdiest young women in the throng, 'Go and get it out, and the rest of you take off your petticoats.'

'Whatever do'ee mean, Rose Marcus?' an elderly woman demanded, outraged. 'Us can't go without our petticoats! 'Tisn't decent!'

'Do it!' Rose commanded, suddenly magnificent and to be reckoned with in this moment of crisis. 'If they Frenchmen get here you'll have no decency left to bleat about, I'll tell'ee. It'll be more than your petticoats you'll lose!'

Gertrude and Welthin ran off to the ale house at the top of the lane where the hobby-horse was kept and the other women obediently hitched up their skirts to undo the tapes which held their red flannel petticoats tight at the waist, dropping them to the ground.

'Now,' Rose directed, 'Over your shoulders with them like capes! We'll make they Frenchies think we're a platoon of redcoats led by the Devil himself!'

Gertrude and Welthin came back dragging the white pipe-clayed canvas-covered cartwheel and the grotesque horse mask between them.

'Good girls,' Rose said, 'It'll take the two of you to carry it on your backs, it's some weight. Get underneath now, one arm round each other's shoulder, and see if you can do it.'

The other women, wearing their petticoats as Rose had told them and excited now that they understood, helped heave the great circle over the two stalwart girls and adjusted the heavy, hanging skirt round them. The creature came alive.

The women cheered, their spirits raised at once by the sight of the mystic, magic beast, and the child in Rose's arms recognized the beloved May Day horse and laughed with delight. Rose looked down at him as if only just remembering he was there, so used was she to the burden of him.

'Now, Benny,' she said gently, placing him on the ground, 'You're to be a good boy and stay here until we come back.'

It was an order he could not but obey, lying piteously where she put him, his twisted, useless legs bent under him, his short, crooked arms curved across his barrel chest, and he started to cry, but she paid him no heed as she marshalled the women into two ranks with the grotesque horse in front.

Dropping her own petticoat she swept it onto her shoulders with a grand gesture and prepared to lead the bizarre procession in the direction of the headland.

Benny stopped crying. His clear, grey eyes were wide with wonder at the sight of the hallowed horse, menacing and magnificent, prancing unsteadily down the lane led by his mother, her cheeks flaming, her hair wild, the other women, their red petticoats billowing from their shoulders, marching behind with their children running beside them.

But he realized that they were leaving him, lying helpless on the cobbles beside the Ponypool, and started to scream. He was used to being put on the ground where he could fall no further when his mother was busy; by the hearth in his cottage home and at the edge of the field at hay-making and harvest time, but she never went far from him.

'Mother! Don't leave me, Mother!' he cried, but she was rounding the corner of the fish-cellars, urging her little army onto the quay and up the cliffs to defy the Frenchmen, and could not hear him. His screams subsided into hiccupping sobs.

It was very quiet when the women had gone. Benny lay still,

the cobbles biting into his little body; he looked about him. From where he lay he could see almost all there was of the small town; a huddle of grey stone cottages grouped round the Ponypool with the ancient church behind them, fish cellars lining the tiny, land-locked harbour near the mouth of the broad estuary, and all backed by the heaving shoulders of the sheltering downs, scattered over with the moorstone from which the town was built. Not a soul was in sight to keep him company.

What if the Frenchmen came now when he was all alone, he wondered. He had heard his elders say that they were fiends, devils who ate little children, and his screams broke out once more.

A cat jumped down from a window sill and came to rub her body against the helpless child and he took comfort from her warm, soft fur and gentle purring as she pushed her head against his cheek. With difficulty he rolled over onto his stomach and, exhausted, fell asleep with the cat curled beside him.

The sun had dipped behind the downs when the child awoke, cold and stiff, to the sounds of cheering, laughing and singing. The cat fled as the crowd of jubilant women rounded the corner of the fish-cellars and came towards the Ponypool where he lay. The horse pranced and cavorted and the women waved their red petticoats like banners as they came, gloriously proud of their victory.

The crew of the French frigate had seen the red-clad figures marching, had seen the incredible beast that led them and, unfurling her canvas, had taken a broad reach of the estuary and made for the open sea. The plan had worked; the horse had saved them and they were nearly drunk with relief and joy. They sang snatches of the May Day song, the horse's song, adding new words, another verse, to commemorate their exploit.

Rose ran to the little boy, lying where she had left him, and caught him up, swinging him in her arms, showering kisses on his small, beautiful face and placing him on the mounting block out of the way of the excited women's feet. He lay on his stomach, laughing and shouting with delight at the return of his mother and the other women, and of the fabulous horse.

Gertrude and Welthin, tired as they were with carrying the horse's weight, whirled and stamped beside the water's edge with a final triumphant flourish before taking off the heavy wheel. The beast flounced and twirled before Benny's enraptured eyes, cavorted and pranced nearer and nearer, and suddenly he felt he must touch it, must touch its pipe-clayed canvas and horse-hair tail, and he reached out with one short, crooked arm.

As his fingers made contact with the hard rim of the circle a sunburst of sensation exploded in his infant brain, blood surged into his head and the song the women sang seemed to tingle in his veins. He reached further in an attempt to hold on to this feeling of oneness with the horse, reaching just too far and started falling, falling, time and space seeming to stretch endlessly before him.

He did not see his mother and the other women rush forward in an effort to save him, did not see his father and the other men running down the cobbled street, having learnt too late of the French frigate's approach: but he saw other women and other men as untold years reeled in front of his eyes, shifting and changing, whirling him back and back until the visions became suddenly clearer and steadied.

The young man sat on a pile of hay outside the thatched wooden hut, leaning against the plank wall. He shifted his position from time to time, automatically trying to find a comfort which the great hump on his back and his twisted, useless legs denied him; but he had more to think about now than the accustomed pain and discomfort his cruel deformities caused him.

While voices from inside the hut were raised in near panic he watched the flames of the burning village a few miles down the estuary which were luridly reflected in the water of the pool near whose brink he sat.

Maurauding Danes had come ghosting along the estuary in

their dragon-prowed longship, oars almost silently slicing through the water, devastating the little settlements dotted along the banks.

When the alarm had gone up most of the able-bodied men from the settlement by the pool, except those far away fetching the cattle from the moors, had gone to the help of their neighbours who were under attack. None had come back.

A small girl from the stricken village had run, gasping and sobbing, with the disastrous news that she, having hidden in a thicket of gorse, was the soul survivor; that the men had all been slain in the battle and the women and children killed in cold blood and then, all valuables having been seized, the thatched wooden huts put to the torch. Now the Danes, drunk with mead and blood-lust, were preparing to take to their longship again to repeat their massacre and pillage further up the river.

The voices inside the hut rose and fell, angry and frightened. Suddenly the young crippled man outside raised his head.

'The horse!' he cried, and again, 'The horse!'

There was a silence from within and then the Chieftain's son emerged, stooping to pass through the low doorway.

'What shall we do, Benyg Marghas?' he said.

'Fetch the horse skull from the great hall,' Benyg replied, his clear, grey eyes steely, 'And take the horse hide from the Chieftain's chair and bring it here.'

Several of the grey bearded elders had come outside now.

'You mean to use the sacred horse?' one said, having overheard. 'No! The horse never dances in the fall of the year!'

The Chieftain's son also demurred.

'I dare not touch my father's mantle,' he said.

Benyg laid a hand on the boy's arm.

'Your mighty father has been slain and you are our Chieftain now. The mantle is yours,' he said gently, and then, turning to the elder, his handsome face grim, he addressed him less gently.

'If you do not do as I say the horse will never dance again for there will never be another spring for any of us,' he said.

The old man's eyes fell before the fire of command blazing

in those of the crippled man. The new chieftain had already run to carry out his orders.

On the ridge-pole at the gable end of the hall which stood back from the cluster of huts hung a horse's skull of incredible size. It was never removed except on one day in the spring every year when the elders judged from their calendars of standing stones that the time was right. On that special day it was reverently taken down and, together with the great white horse-hide which draped the chieftain's chair, was carried with all due ceremony to the broad shoulder of down-land under whose shelter the settlement had sprung up.

Once there, among the no longer understood mounds and undulations which marked the turf, the people of the settlement would act out an ancient rite, dancing and chanting, while the Chieftain assumed the sacred character of the horse.

A stout pole, the horse's skull secured at one end, was placed across his shoulder and when the venerable white hide had been draped over all he would perform the ritual dance, making his way slowly down to the settlement near the sea, following the course of the little river which flowed down the valley until it broadened into a wide pool, the Ponapool, around which the huts were clustered. There the horse's head was dipped towards the water so that it seemed to drink, while the chanting, forsaking its triumphant rhythm for a brief spell, would take on a plaintive note, until, refreshed and jubilant, the horse and the song resumed their heroic mien.

When the new chieftain had gone to do the crippled man's bidding he turned to the rest of them, their numbers swelled now by the herdsmen having driven the cattle down from their summer pasture.

'Take clay from the pit,' he ordered, 'and daub your faces and those of the ponies and cattle; leave their eyes black but draw white lines along their backs and down their legs. Make haste for there is little time.'

Now even the elders had come under his spell of command, hurrying to do as he said, and soon the small, sturdy black cattle and ponies were unrecognizable as they milled about in their compound, as were the men and women, their faces ghastly white in the gathering dusk.

'Now!' Benyg Marghas commanded from his seat on the ground, 'Drive the beasts along the shoreline and up to the cliffs, and you,' he turned to the young chieftain over whose head the great white horse hide was being carefully lowered, 'Lead your army into battle as would have done your father!'

It was very quiet when they had gone and the young crippled man gazed across the flame-reflecting surface of the pool to where the river, narrowing again, spilled into the land-locked cove and out into the estuary. If the ruse failed and the Danes came he knew what his fate would be; his crooked body would be hacked and rent and he would be left, spread-eagled on the ground, to die slowly as they pillaged the huts and eventually burnt them; but he had faith in the sacred horse and there was nothing further he could do. His eyes came back to the waters of the pool, the Ponapool. Why was it so named, he wondered? Some said it was called after the first chieftain who had settled here with his family, but Benyg thought it had a deeper and more mystic meaning which as yet he had been unable to fathom.

Dogs crept out of the shadows where they had hidden to nestle at his side and easing his contorted body to accommodate them, grateful for their warmth, his chin fell forward onto his barrel chest and he slept.

It was quite dark when Benyg Marghas was awakened by cheering and shouting and the dogs slunk off. From out of the shadows loomed the ghostly horse followed by the white-daubed cattle and triumphant people. The plan had succeeded.

The Danes, drunk and befuddled, had been confronted by what they took to be a phantom herd of beasts, driven by phantom herdsmen and led by the skull-headed sepulchral horse. Terrified, the tall, blonde warriors had taken to their longship, had hoisted the great striped sail and with a following wind, the oarsmen rowing with a strength born of fear, had made for the open sea.

The beasts, still clay-daubed, were put into their compound

and the men and women, washing their faces in the Ponapool, rejoiced at their deliverance. They sang and danced, making up new words, a new verse, to the ancient song to commemorate their victory, pausing from time to time to take great draughts of potent, heady mead.

The young chieftain, having proved himself a leader and still wearing the sacred trappings of the horse, went through the ancient ritual dance once more, the fragile skull dipping and rearing, the great white hide swaying and swirling.

Two boys, drunk with success and mead, caught up the crippled man, the genius behind the plan, and bore him on their shoulders from where, despite the agonizing pain he suffered as they lurched about with him, his laughter of relief and triumph joined with theirs.

As the horse swirled before his eyes he felt he must touch it, feel the sparse white hair on the ancient skin, stroke the stiff strands of the tail, and he reached out with one crooked arm. As he made contact with the fragile, brittle hide emotion rent his twisted body and knowledge flared in his mind; power seemed to be transmitted from the horse through his burning fingers, to irradiate his entire being, and he reached even further to grasp the sensation, to hold it closer to him.

Reaching too far he unbalanced the young man, tottering drunkenly under his weight, and they stumbled, hurling him forward.

The seconds in which he fell expanded and magnified and he felt, not the pain of now but other pain, felt not the arms that sought to save him but some other saviour as he spun through time. Blurred visions of faces, some with the features of the young chieftain, some with those of the elders, cascaded before him until the images became clearer and steadied.

The ancient man, twisted and contorted so that he barely resembled his fellow men, lay beside the pool, the Epona Pool, and gazed at its wind-ruffled surface. The little band of people had left him at his own request and made their way to the downs. They had wanted to take him with them to the effigy of the great white horse which was carved into the turf, forever striding forward, its huge round eye fixed menacingly towards the open sea, defying whatever enemy might dare to approach, but he had refused.

They had carried him there every year throughout his long, long life on the day when the wise men with their complicated reckonings of moon and stars and portents judged that the time was right, and he of all people had had reason to worship, to reverence and adore the representation of the horse goddess, Epona, she who ruled the heavens, the white disc of the full moon being her lambent eye.

But the man was old, old beyond all reckoning and his twisted, useless limbs and hump back tortured him even when he was at rest and unbearably so when they moved him, so he had refused to be carried in his special litter, preferring to stay where he was at the reedy margin of the sacred pool round which the small dwellings of the tribe, mere holes in the ground roofed over with turf, were clustered.

It was quiet now that they had gone and his clear grey eyes left the surface of the pool to trace the course of the little river that filled it, looking to its source on the shoulder of the sheltering downland.

There beside the spring the vast figure of the horse, its outlines whitened with clay, shone in the sunshine: with the image of her to whom he owed his life imprinted on his mind he sank his head on his barrel chest and slept.

When, longer ago than anyone could imagine, the crippled baby had been born, a twisted travesty of humanity, the wise men had taken him from his mother and placed him up on the bleak downs to die.

In vain his mother had pleaded for his life.

'He has a lovely face,' she sobbed, but they took no heed.

'The crooked thing cannot be allowed to live,' they had decreed, taking the new little life in its cruelly distorted shell and discarding it.

But the baby did not die. Up on the downs among the small black ponies a huge white mare had appeared. She fostered the deformed scrap of humanity, protecting and warming him with her body and suckling him at her abundant udder.

In the course of time, when the baby was stronger, she

strode down the valley beside the stream bearing the child in her strong teeth, and confronted the astonished tribe. Some fled, terrified, others fell to their knees and worshipped. They had never seen such a fabulous creature before but knew her to be the horse of the heavens, Epona, come to visit them.

The huge mare gently placed the baby on the ground beside the pool into which the river flowed before it narrowed again and poured into the sea. She fixed the wise men with her vast, baleful eye.

'Here,' she seemed to say, 'is that which you discarded. That which you could least afford to discard,' and then she drank deeply from the pool before turning and galloping back to the downs where she stood for a long time, her brilliant whiteness shining against the green turf.

When finally the tribe had recovered from their awe and terror they climbed the hill, only to find the great horse dead, stretched peacefully on the grass.

They reverently brought the carcase down beside the pool, removed the milk-white hide and cleaned and preserved the colossal skull: on the spot where she died they carved her likeness into the turf, fetching clay from the other side of the country where they lived to whiten it and make it shine forth as had the living horse.

They treated the baby with deference when he was returned to them, calling him Benygys, which meant Blessed in their language, and his family, those children his parents had after him, and their children's children they called Marghas, the horses.

When he grew up he repaid them well, his agile mind compensating for his useless body. He worked out strategies to outwit their enemies, devised ways in which houses could be better built and crops could be made to provide greater increase. Every year on the day the wise men reckoned to be the anniversary of his rebirth they carried him up the hill, singing a strange song with a compelling rhythm and words which told the story of the wondrous horse whose image they worshipped. But this year he would not go.

It was dusk when he awoke from his sleep beside the pool and his clear grey eyes flew to the black bulk of the downs.

Epona's image shone, not with a reflected light but with a light of its own. As he watched the great figure seemed to move, the long, white forelegs extending to paw against the evening sky and she left the hillside, climbing the heavens as the full moon rose.

Bestriding the sky she descended beside the old crippled man at the edge of the pool, lowering her beautiful head to drink and then, turning her luminous eyes upon his tortured and hideous body, she extended her neck towards him.

He stretched his twisted, arthritic arms to touch her, felt the shimmering magic pelt beneath his fingers and was all but consumed by his love of her. Gone were the endless years of pain, extinguished in this moment of rapture, and he fell forward towards the water of the pool.

In the moment of falling through time, whirling onwards and onward, he caught glimpses of faces, of buildings, flashing and shifting before his eyes; not the faces of the wise men and others of the tribe as they rushed towards him, but other faces, hundreds of faces, some of which seemed to resemble theirs; he no longer saw the rudimentary huts but other strange buildings, getting larger and more numerous as the years reeled and spiralled forward, whirling him on and on until the visions became clearer and steadied.

Ben Marcus lay on the pavement in Sawlyn, his body grotesque in its helplessness but his handsome old face serene, his clear, grey eyes exalted, and with no longer any hint of the pain with which he had lived for so long.

The music and the singing stopped as the white clad men and women, tired now, ran to him. The man who carried the horse knelt at his side so that the beast's head dipped towards him.

'Who is he?' asked an onlooker, 'And how did he come to be all twisted like he is?'

'He's Ben Marcus,' said one of the white-clad men looking anxiously over the shoulders of those who crowded round the prostrate cripple. 'Born like it, he was. There's one like that gets born every so often in the Marcus family, right back to the beginning of time, they say. Might be something to be ashamed of in other families but to the Marcuses 'tis a sign of grace.'

Someone held a brandy flask to Ben's lips.

'Drink this, old man,' they coaxed, but Ben took no heed.

'He don't understand; he's nearly gone,' said a woman.

'But I do understand!' Ben's voice was surprisingly strong, 'I understand it all!' and he raised his short twisted arms and clasped the hobby-horse's neck.

He felt the shining milk white pelt of the great mare, and the rippling strands of her mane were twisted in his fingers as she lifted him, as easily as if he had been a tiny baby, and ascended, **Epona**, the horse of the heavens, bestriding the sky as the full moon rose from behind the sheltering downs to shine over Sawlyn on the evening of May Day.

VIII

Tears for Charlie

There was mud as far as Charlie Truscott could see. Trying to clean the bulldozer was a forlorn task, but he always tidied it up a bit before he left for the night.

He thought of it as 'his' bulldozer, talked to it and encouraged it when the job they were doing together was especially tough, and the great machine seemed to respond to his affection, working smoothly and efficiently for him like a sturdy animal: they were in complete harmony with each other. His workmates teased him good naturedly, but they had to admit that Charlie and his 'dozer made a grand team.

Rubbing as much mud off the yellow paint of the bodywork as he could with crumpled newspaper, Charlie patted the bulldozer affectionately.

'Good night, old boy,' he said, 'see you in the morning,' and tramped off through the mud to where his bicycle leant against the site hut.

The firm Charlie worked for was engaged in digging out a new road, which cut through a hillside, making a wide curve round a small town, thus relieving its narrow streets of heavy through-traffic.

The other men had already gone home in the firm's van, but Charlie preferred to bicycle the five miles to the village where he lived with his mother, talking to his bike as he went.

He was a thick-set man of about thirty, below average height – and below average intelligence, as his mother never tired of telling him. His short fair hair stood up in spikes all round a mild, open face, the blue eyes a little vacant, the kindly mouth a little slack. He could barely read and although he could write his name it was with difficulty.

However, what mental intelligence he lacked he made up

for with the skill of his hands. Big, square, hard worked hands they were, but as gentle and as sensitive as a woman's. Machinery of any kind responded at once to his loving, knowledgeable touch, and small injured animals relaxed in his huge palms and submitted to the large fingers gently coaxing them back to health. Within minutes the same hands could replace a vast working part of heavy earth-moving machinery and set a bird's broken wing, both operations being carried out with the same concentration and the same instinct for knowing when a thing was right.

All Charlie's love was directed towards the machines. He was happier at work than at home, for although he had very little it common with his workmakes except the job they did together, they at least respected his way with machinery and his hard work. His mother seemed to find him nothing but an embarrassment, except when the washing machine went wrong or a table lamp needed rewiring. She would not allow him to have a pet, not even a rabbit in the small back garden.

'I've enough mud and dirt to clean up having you about, let alone animals,' she had snapped.

'But the rabbit wouldn't be indoors,' he had pointed out.

'Fleas,' she had said, with such an air of finality that he had known better than to argue.

As Charlie bicycled home in the winter twilight, watching the rooks fly home in black, ragged flocks and hearing the sleepy twitterings of small birds in the hedges, Mrs Truscott paced back and forth in her small kitchen, impatiently looking at the clock.

On the table stood a new electric sewing machine gleaming in grey enamel and chromium, and holding a nearly-finished curtain in its clenched teeth, the purple material bunched up and enmeshed inextricably.

Mrs Truscott was a short, stout woman, her usually florid colour heightened now by her fury at the sewing machine's failure and by her impatience at her son's lateness. From time to time she rocked the balance wheel of the machine and pulled at the material crossly, but the brightly coloured stuff stayed firmly caught.

Draped across the other end of the table were three finished curtains. Only a yard more stitching and they would all have been ready for Charlie to hang up in the front room, in time to impress the ladies of the fête committee who were due in an hour. Mrs Truscott had only recently been elected on to the fête committee and she was determined that her front room, which she was trying to remember to call the lounge, should measure up to those of the other ladies.

Since her husband's death she had indulged herself by spending the carefully saved money he had left on doing up the small house to her own rather ostentatious tastes, unhampered by Mr Truscott's more modest ones.

The front room already sported a new purple carpet and a gold brocade three-piece suite, a cocktail cabinet and an enormous colour television set. She had seen the new curtain material yesterday and knew it would complete the opulent effect she was striving for. And now the wretched sewing machine had jammed on the last few feet of the final hem.

'Where is that boy?' she angrily asked the empty room, and at that moment she heard the back door bang.

'Where've you been?' There was no welcome in Mrs Truscott's voice. 'Take your boots off and come in here this minute!'

'Won't be long, Mum,' Charlie called back, 'I'm just going to clean the bike off a bit.'

'No, you are not!' his mother retorted sharply. 'You're coming straight in here to see to this sewing machine.'

Charlie stood in the kitchen now, in his socks, having left the mud-caked working boots in the back lobby.

Mrs Truscott looked at her son with contempt as he stood blinking in the harsh glare of the neon strip-lights, his hair on end, his heavy blue serge jacket and dungarees spattered with mud. What had she done to deserve a son like this, she wondered. Other women's sons were shop assistants, nicely dressed and with refined manners, or clerks or – or almost anything except labourers. She, so careful to be correct, to do things nicely, surely deserved something better than this.

She blamed her husband for her son's shortcomings. He had spoilt the boy; he hadn't beaten him when he couldn't do his lessons as a child: had let him leave school early; had encouraged him in his ridiculous passion for machinery. However, there were times when that passion could be useful, and this was one of them.

Having washed his hands at the sink, Charlie sat down in front of the sewing machine and, clucking at it quietly under his breath, he gently eased and coaxed it into releasing its hold on the vivid purple flowered material, and in seconds it was running sweetly again.

'You're too rough with it, Mum,' he explained, but Mrs Truscott wasn't listening as she rapidly finished off the hem.

'There!' she said, triumphantly. 'Charlie, get the step ladder and you can hang them up for me,' she directed.

'What about my tea?' Charlie asked.

'I haven't got time for that now. The fête ladies will be here in half-an-hour,' his mother said, gathering the curtains carefully over her arm. 'I don't want the house smelling of cooking. You can get yourself some bread and jam.'

'Can I watch telly?' Charlie's voice held little hope of his request being granted.

'No, you can't!' Mrs Truscott looked at him with distaste. 'Whatever would the ladies think? Now get that step-ladder and be quick about it!' She would seriously think of telling him to get out, to find somewhere else to live, she thought, if it weren't for the fact that he was making good money, all of which he handed over to her.

The cutting for the new road was going well, the gentle swell of the hill seeming to have split and opened up to let the raw earth ribbon through.

Charlie and his bulldozer worked at removing the soil which the massive mechanical digger lifted out from the level of the eventual road on to the top of the banks at each side.

Charlie admired the digger immensely. He thought it looked like a great, graceful animal with its long neck and delicate movements. He would watch enthralled as it swivelled on its track base and stretched out to gather up the earth and stones in its wide mouth, sometimes reminding him of a giraffe, sometimes, when it seemed to be digging almost

underneath itself, of a swan. When it was immobilized for the
night with the bucket resting on the ground it looked as if it
was meekly bowing its beautiful head.

But the man who drove the digger hadn't got a good word
for it. It was a devil of a machine, he said, always going wrong.
Almost every day a pin would sheer off here, a bearing run hot
there or the great hydraulically operated pistons of the jib
would jam. It was constantly needing attention. Charlie
privately thought it was because its driver, Fred, didn't treat it
right.

'Machines know who like 'em, Fred,' he said, one day when
the digger had been giving more trouble than usual.

'Crap,' Fred replied inelegantly. 'The thing's a bitch and
that's that. A real bad 'un.'

From up above on the bank Charlie would look down the
slope at the digger. When it was working well its movements
charmed him, he almost loved it, he and his bulldozer
accepting the loads of earth from its tipped-up mouth and
pushing them away almost reverently; but when it broke
down, stopped, sometimes, with its head at an awkward
angle, he would worry, sure that the way Fred cursed at it
made it unhappy and less likely to work well. Sighing, he
would pat the side of his own sweetly running machine.

'We know what it's about, old boy, don't we?' he would say
quietly to the bulldozer, and under his careful direction the
great beast would shoulder the loads of earth to their
appointed places with its angled blade, obediently and
willingly.

During the spring when the cutting only had a few hundred
yards of hill to eat through, Fred, the digger's driver, went
down with 'flu. Quite a few men in the firm were off sick and
those that were left working had to be moved from one job to
another in an effort to keep the work continuing smoothly.

Charlie couldn't believe his luck when his boss told him to
take over the digger; the great beautiful animal he had
admired for so long was to be his special charge. He would
show them that it wasn't a bad 'un, that it only needed
consideration and understanding.

He put down the grease-gun with which he had been attending to the bulldozer, wiped his hands down his dungarees and walked over to the digger without a backward glance. The bulldozer's small headlights stared after him wistfully, and it slumped slightly to one side as Harry, the man who was to take Charlie's place, climbed up into the cab.

During the next few weeks Charlie found that the beautiful digger had a less than beautiful nature. Fred had called it a bitch and Charlie agreed with him at least in so far as it was a female. It was petulant; it was truculent; it would swing its elegant head in response to Charlie's hands on the levers, but a little too far, not far enough; it would swivel gracefully on its track base and then the engine would cut half way through the movement.

Charlie adjusted the controls, tuned the engine, lubricated joints and above all talked to the machine, encouraged her, tried to make her respond to him, but she was flighty.

He would seem to make progress and she would work like a dream for a day or two and then another fault would occur and more adjustments, more delicate tuning would be necessary. He kept her clean and he replaced the great steel teeth when they became blunt, prized stones out from between the tracks and the ratchet wheels they rode on, but the digger remained intractable.

It was the first time in his life that Charlie hadn't been able to establish some sort of rapport with a machine.

Apart from his emotional involvement with them, his technical knowledge was sound and he could think of nothing to account for the constant malfunctioning of the digger. He spent more and more time with it after work, standing, hands sunk in the pockets of his working coat, gazing at it morosely, trying to understand.

His mother was furious with him as he came home late day after day, but he hardly heard the streams of abuse she poured out, his blue eyes, clouded and brooding, looking at her without seeing; looking, rather, at the hydraulic system which he knew like the back of his hand, knew to be right and yet could not fathom.

'You got a girl?' Mrs Truscott demanded one evening, her small eyes suddenly beady, 'You mooning about over some bit of a girl?'

Charlie brought his attention back to the small kitchen where they sat over their egg and chips and strong cups of tea, and looked at his mother.

'Yea,' he said slowly, 'You could say that, I suppose,' and then, as she opened her small tight mouth to express her astonishment and ridicule, 'I wish you'd just shut up and let me think.'

Never, in his thirty odd years, had Charlie spoken to her like that. By the time she had recovered from the shock sufficiently to ask him who he thought he was talking to like that, and after all she had done for him too, he had got up and left the house, taking himself off into the spring dusk to go over and over the digger's mechanism in his mind and ponder on her strange behaviour.

Working in the cutting with the unpredictable machine, Charlie would glance up at his old bulldozer from time to time as it worked high above him with Harry cheerfully and casually in charge of it.

He sometimes got the impression that it gazed down wistfully at him, its small headlights full of reproach. One day he was sure it did, its dirty, dejected appearance filling him with remorse for having deserted it, being so taken up with the digger that he no longer even wished it goodnight. But that was silly, he told himself, turning back to his work. Harry treated it all right. Perhaps he didn't talk to it as he had done but – well – it was only a machine wasn't it? Well – wasn't it? He suddenly felt the need to reassure it.

'I'll make it up to you when Fred comes back!' he yelled up at it, his voice drowned by the wind and the noise of the machines.

But the digger heard him. Suddenly, with her head swung round at an angle, teeth poised to take a great bite of earth, the hydraulic pistons seized and refused to answer to Charlie's hands on the levers in the cab.

For the first time Charlie lost his temper with her. Picking up a large spanner he jumped down from the cab.

'You jealous bitch!' he yelled at the machine, leaning down

towards the bucket head as though to look it in the face. 'What the hell's the matter with you now?'

He raised the heavy spanner and brought it down in a cracking blow at the nape of the machine's neck where the jib joined the head and where the two hoses carrying the hydraulic fluid lay on the metal surface.

One of the hoses split under the blow and fluid gushed out: the great metal head jerked sideways momentarily as though in anguish and then crashed to the ground, knocking Charlie down and embedding its huge steel teeth in his neck. He gave a great gurgling scream as blood flooded his chest, and then lay still.

Harry, on the crest of the cutting, leapt from the bulldozer, leaving its engine running, and started to climb, slipping and falling, down the steep slope towards where his stricken workmate lay, blood pumping out of his neck and soaking the raw earth round him.

As he half-ran and half-fell through the loose earth and rocks Harry heard a rumble and for a moment a great shadow engulfed him. It was the bulldozer, out of control and careering down the slope, its tracks, unoiled now for some weeks, screaming as it gathered momentum.

It hurtled past him, its headlights catching the pale spring sunshine and flashing with hatred, making straight for the digger, and charged into it. The cab, joined to the track base by a single spindle keeled over as the enraged bulldozer smashed into it and rode up and over the chasis.

As the digger's neck-like jib slammed into the earth the vicious teeth released their hold on Charlie's neck and the great bucket head reared up savagely to tear at the underbelly of the bulldozer, ripping out the sump.

The dying bulldozer came to a halt at last, straddling the crushed digger, its rear tipped up on the corpse of its rival, its front headlights clouded over with dust now, misted with grief, a few inches from the body of its murdered master as he lay on the blood-soaked earth, his head nearly severed from his body.

The machine's great throbbing heart struggled on and then, in a series of shuddering sobs, it stopped. Sump oil dripped from the ruptured tank; great black tears for Charlie.

IX

The Herb Garden

Mrs Petherick didn't believe in God, not as such. In fact, having no imagination, she didn't believe in anything she couldn't see.

She was as well aware as the next person that everyone needs something to believe in, and that it was convenient to give that something a name, be it Buddha, Tao, Mithras or whatever, but religion seemed to cause so much unhappiness, to be so doom – and gloom – ridden when surely it should be a joyful thing.

She certainly could not subscribe to the idea of an old man with a white beard, sometimes benign, sometimes brutal, sitting somewhere up in the sky on which her generation had been brought **up**.

No. As she pottered about in her large, rambling garden, she knew what *she* believed in; the unfailing yearly procession of miracles, the beauty that surrounded her, the peace and tranquillity that came from working close to the soil. She was deeply grateful, not only for so much so unstintingly given, but also for the eyes to see, the ears to hear and the fingers to touch the glories that were hers.

When her small, green-gloved hands were lifted to an arching spray of rambler rose, the impulse behind the movement was as much one of worship as an attempt to divest the opening buds of impudent greenfly; when on her knees before the pansies at the border's edge, her kneeling was as much an act of reverence as a comfortable position in which to pinch off dead heads to prolong their flowering.

Although she deplored the short poem by Dorothy Gurney, called 'God's Garden', thinking it mawkish, she agreed wholeheartedly with its last lines:

'One is nearer God's heart (whoever one might consider him to be, she added) in a garden Than anywhere else on earth.'

She supposed that if her sort of religion had to have a name she might be called a Nature Worshipper, but that conjured up a picture of earnest, thick-socked-and-booted people hiking about the countryside, wild-flower book in hand, which was not her style at all: or a sun-worshipper, perhaps? She chuckled to herself as she pulled up an intrusive wisp of couch-grass; that had a new connotation nowadays, one of nudist camps and naked sun-bathing, and the thought of her stout, exuberant little figure exposed to the public gaze amused her greatly.

There had been a sect once, she remembered, called Pantheists, Great Blue Domers. 'God in everything' had been their creed. Now that *might* have been something she could have subscribed to, but no doubt, if it still existed, it had become as hemmed about by dogma and rules and regulations as all the other organized religions, and as devoid of joy.

Despite her lack of religion Mrs Petherick had quite liked going to church on Sundays once. She was devoted to the small grey fifteenth century building, enjoyed a good rousing hymn tune and was glad of the excuse to get out of her gardening trousers and to put on a dress and wear a pretty hat once a week, but that was before the new vicar came.

The Reverend Jeremy Ballantyne had been the incumbent of Langarth for six weeks now, having replaced dear Canon Cowling when the old man had sadly breathed his last after half a lifetime of ministering to the little community.

Jeremy was an aesthete, a tall, painfully thin young man with a haggard face and great, haunted eyes. Not for him the old tweed jacket and grey flannels of Canon Cowling; he wore his cassock all the time, the tasselled girdle and the large silver cross he wore on a chain round his neck swinging wildly as he strode about in his sandals.

He owned a vast and ancient Rolls Royce in which he drove to the outlying parts of his parish. It stood high off the ground on spoked wheels, its brass radiator flanked by headlamps mounted on stalks like enormous anxious eyes, and was exceedingly difficult to manoeuvre, so he made shorter journeys on an equally antique lady's bicycle, clanking along the narrow lanes, his cassock flapping and more than once getting caught in the back wheel, despite the stringed skirt-guard, and precipitating him in the hedge.

The services in the little grey church had changed dramatically, becoming so high, Mrs Petherick thought, as to be practically out of sight, and she personally was totally lost. Besides this the incense brought on her asthma so she stopped going across the field behind her house and over the stile into the churchyard on Sunday mornings, putting in an extra hour among her precious flowers instead and letting the mellow pealing of the bells fill her with the peace which passeth all understanding, rather than wrestling with the earnest out-pourings of Jeremy Ballantyne as he leant perilously over the edge of the pulpit, his burning eyes greatly embarrassing the villagers in the front pews.

Since she had withdrawn from church it was with some surprise that Mrs Petherick, on answering the telephone one evening, heard Jeremy Ballantyne's urgent young voice addressing her.

'Ah! Dear lady!' he said, 'I wonder if I might ask a great favour of you?'

'Of course,' Mrs Petherick replied, intrigued as to what it might be. 'Ask away, by all means.'

'Well,' the young man continued, 'there's a parish meeting this evening and I wondered if you would be kind enough to allow me to leave my car in your courtyard. She's so large and has such a bad lock that I can't get her into the parking-space by the parish hall, in fact there is literally nowhere else I can leave her.'

'Of course you may leave her here,' Mrs Petherick said readily, 'I shall be charmed to accommodate such a handsome vehicle. But what is the matter with your bicycle?'

'Nothing is the matter with it,' the young man assured her, 'Unless you could call its uncertain temperament an affliction. No, it is I who am partially out of commission. The bicycle hurled me from it in a fit of pique this morning and I appear to have damaged a knee, which quite precludes my riding it tonight. However, many thanks indeed for saying I may leave the car in your courtyard. I look forward to seeing you.'

Mrs Petherick was standing in the courtyard when the great black Rolls Royce turned awkwardly in at the wide entrance, the earnest young cleric sitting bolt upright and wrenching the large steering wheel to manoeuvre the ancient vehicle between the granite gate posts.

The scent of the Albertine roses festooning the crumbling walls mingled with that of stocks and tobacco flowers which were opening as the day cooled towards evening. Fantailed pigeons fluttered down to alight on the roof of the small culverhouse which stood across the lawn.

Jeremy Ballantyne descended from the tall car with some difficulty.

'My goodness, you *have* damaged yourself, haven't you?' Mrs Petherick said solicitously as he limped towards her. 'You really must take more care.'

She was a kindly little woman, a great gatherer-up of stray cats and dogs, several of which basked in her affections and were to be found ambling round the garden or draped over the good old furniture in her comfortable house, and she looked at the young man before her very much as she might have looked at one of these.

'You're far too thin, Mr Ballantyne,' she observed severely, 'I'm sure you don't bother to cook properly for yourself. I know what it's like when you live alone, but it really won't do. You'll make yourself ill if you don't eat.'

The young clergyman laughed.

'You sound just like my dear mother,' he said. 'She was always on at me to eat more, but really I do very well on bread and cheese with the odd slice of cold ham. "Man doth not live by bread alone", you know.'

He looked round him at the flowers, the grey stone house, the tabby cat that pressed against his legs, all washed with golden evening sunlight.

'How perfectly lovely it is here!' he cried. 'So peaceful! So beautiful! And how nice it is to see a mediaeval pigeon house used for its original purpose,' he pointed to the small round building on the roof of which the white birds were alighting. 'This used to be monastic property, didn't it?'

'Indeed it did,' Mrs Petherick was pleased at his interest. 'It was a hospice for travellers who were benighted on their way to the monastery at Porthminack. The pigeon house – only we call them culver houses in Cornwall – was the only building of which enough was left standing to restore, but that,' she pointed to a wall against which hollyhocks grew tall and beautiful in shades of red and pink, 'used to be the dorter, apparently; where the monks used to sleep, you know,' she added, and the young man nodded, smiling.

'No one seems to know what the other ruins were, but at the far end of the garden behind the apple trees is a bit of wall with carving on it. I think it was probably the chapel. Of course the house itself was built of the material from the ruins after the Reformation.'

'I wanted to be a monk,' the young man said wistfully. 'An Anglican one of course; but my mother wouldn't hear of it, so the Ministry was the next best thing.'

'I'm quite sure your mother was right,' Mrs Petherick said firmly. 'I've never seen the sense in young people shutting themselves away from the world like that. Most unnatural. It must turn them in on themselves and make them very odd.'

Jeremy Ballantyne was not listening to her but to something else, his face intent, mouth open.

'I can hear chanting,' he whispered. 'Plain-song!'

Mrs Petherick listened too, and then laughed.

'It's the pigeons,' she said, 'they're all going in to roost and they always coo and bicker for quite a while before settling down to sleep.'

'No, not that!' Jeremy leant against his ancient car, his great eyes wide and wild. 'Vespers, they must be going in to Vespers,' he said, his hands feeling for the large silver cross on his chest and holding it in front of him.

Mrs Petherick looked at him sharply. He really did look extremely ill, and here he was practically having hallucinations in her yard.

'Nonsense,' she said. 'I tell you it's the pigeons, and I'll tell you something else. Before you go to that meeting you're coming indoors with me to have a glass of milk and a large piece of home-made cake, my boy.'

After that first evening Jeremy Ballantyne became one of Mrs Petherick's most frequent visitors. He would turn up at various times of day, in the Rolls at first, and later, when his damaged knee was better, clanking and flapping along on his tall bicycle.

She was delighted at first and would sweep cats and dogs off chairs and settle him down at the kitchen table to make him eat, which he did with the enormous appetite of the young when faced with food, all the more remarkable since they could equally well do with nothing at all; but soon Mrs Petherick was under no misapprehension as to why he came.

He liked her a great deal, she knew, and he enjoyed her good Cornish cooking, wolfing down pasties and saffron cake and great mugs of coffee, but it was after he had eaten and conversed with her that the real reason for his visits became apparent.

He would wander round the garden, scarcely seeing the glorious high-summer tapestry of roses, or the great beds of heavily-scented lillies, scarlet poppies and huge-leaved acanthus hemmed about by pansies and mignonette, but tracing the shape of the ancient buildings that once stood there, marked now only by fragments of crumbling wall, which Mrs Petherick used to great advantage to shelter and support a profusion of plants. Holding his silver cross in front of him he would pace along as though part of a procession.

Mrs Petherick would trot along beside him, taking three steps to one of his, pointing out to him this or that magnificent bloom, but, although he courteously gave her part of his attention, she had only to bend down for a second to snap a dead flower off here or uproot a daring dandelion there, for him to have drifted off without her, his eyes seeming to see that which she could not see.

'Ghosts,' she thought, 'he's taken to seeing ghosts now; *and* ghosts of wretched monks, I'll be bound!'

Mrs Petherick didn't believe in ghosts any more than she believed in God or approved of monks. Had she not lived here all alone for over fifteen years with never so much as a shiver running up her spine? He really was the oddest young man, this new vicar, and much as she had come to enjoy his visits, she resolved to put a stop to them for his own sake. Seeing ghostly monks couldn't be good for anyone, let alone anyone as highly strung as Jeremy.

Monks, indeed. She'd give them monks if she ever set eyes on them.

Jeremy Ballantyne was saddened when it finally dawned on him that Mrs Petherick was trying to tell him that his frequent visits were a nuisance. He knew she disapproved of his high church calling but he had been extremely careful never to talk about religion when he was ensconced in her comfortable house, cats covering his cassock with hairs and dogs sitting on his feet, or when happily following the brethren from brew-house to malt store, from woodshed to dorter, with her at his side.

He had been sure she liked him, and it had been a comfort to feel her concern for him and for his welfare, so much like that of his mother whose death a year previously had been such a sad loss to him.

But most of all the feeling of being at home, of belonging, that he had had when walking in the garden had been an utter joy. Behind the luxuriant and colourful blooms of which Mrs Petherick was so proud, he was aware of less flamboyant plants, feverfew, bishop's weed, comfrey, lungworth, tormentil and valerian, the descendants of which now sprung from every crevice of the fragmented walls, all in neat rows, all with their health-giving part to play in the life of the monastic community. Apart from being the site of a hospice, as Mrs Petherick had said, he was sure that the garden had also once contained an infirmary, planted about with carefully-tended herbs.

And it was not only of the herbs that he was aware. He had latterly made out the forms, shadowy at first, of cassocked brothers, looking very much like himself, singing at their

labours, glorifying their God, as they hoed and weeded, culled
and collected the plants. The place was alive with them and he
felt entirely at home in their company, looking forward
eagerly to the next time he could walk in their footsteps and
hear their endless chanting.

This, he decided, he could not do without and, though less
frequently, he continued to find excuses to visit Mrs Petherick;
delivering the parish magazine, begging flowers for the
church, collecting gifts for charity stalls.

Mrs Petherick was not deceived. She had grown fond of him
and treated him as she had done her own two sons before they
married and left home, fussing and scolding him about this
and that, sending him off with cake and biscuits in the large
basket on the handlebars of his bicycle as though seeing a
child off to school: but she could not be a party to the
nonsense that was going on in her garden. Being closer to
whatever gods there might be in a garden was one thing, but
seeing ghosts, or whatever it was he was doing, was ridiculous
and she became cold and forbidding to him, seeking to
alienate him all together, telling him, when he came, that from
now on she would be much too busy to put up with his visits.

So Jeremy became cunning. He took careful note of Mrs
Petherick's comings and goings. She was an orderly woman
and lived to a pattern, driving her little estate car into the
nearby town of Porthminack three mornings a week, going to
play bridge with friends in the village on two afternoons, to
dinner on alternate Saturday evenings, and always in bed by
11 o'clock at night.

He soon knew her timetable by heart and saw to it that he
was in the churchyard in time to watch her drive away on each
occasion, after which he would climb the stile, cross the field
and enter the hallowed garden by the small, arched gate
behind the house.

All summer long he roamed the garden, often accompanied
by one or two of the cats and dogs who, knowing him, were
glad of his company when their mistress was out and strolled
along the mown grass paths with him.

He could see the brethren quite clearly now, could even

recognize some of them individually and knew their names; Brother Martin was the infirmarian, Brother James the brewer, Brother Peter in charge of the garden, and it was to Brother Peter that he attached himself.

As he came and went about his appointed tasks Jeremy would join him, watching to see which herbs to pick, when and how, and helping to keep the neat rows free of weeds, but always careful not to step on, or harm in any way, the marigolds, antirrhinums and sweet williams which grew between them and which he could see but Brother Peter could not.

The young clergyman had a good ear and in no time he had learnt the chants with which the brethren accompanied all their labours. Although, since he was no longer being fed by Mrs Petherick, he was now appallingly thin, his face and arms were brown from the sun and, as he lifted up his voice in the ancient songs of praise, he had never felt so well, so happy, in his life.

His ministry suffered, all the time he should have spent on clerical and parish matters being taken up with his gardening, but his little flock had never taken to him, finding him too intense and quite frightening, and they were relieved when he no longer visited them in their homes and they only had to contend with his burning rhetoric once a week in church.

As the summer progressed Jeremy found the life he lived in the monastery garden more real than that which he lived in the other world. Mrs Petherick saw him only very infrequently when he sometimes passed her gate, and was shocked at his appearance. He was thin to the point of emaciation and his huge eyes were like holes in his weather-beaten face, burning with an unnatural light, she thought.

'Religious mania,' she told herself. 'That's what *he's* got.'

Why must the glorification of his God take him like this, she wondered. Why must it burn him up like a cinder? She worried about him. Should she invite him in again? At least then she would know that he had some good food inside him, but better not. He had this stupid idea about ghosts in the garden and that must be worse for him than not eating properly. No, she thought innocently unaware, she must not let him into the garden again.

Autumn came and the nights drew in, swathed about with mists and the drifting smoke of bonfires. Jeremy had never set foot in the garden when Mrs Petherick was at home, and he greatly regretted never having sung the night offices with the brethren, but now, with darkness descending earlier and more blackly as winter approached, he became more daring. He would wait in the churchyard every night until he saw the light go out in her bedroom and then, stealthily and silently, he would enter the garden through the arched gateway from the field and join the brethren, his hands tucked into the wide sleeves of his cassock, head bent, moving from dorter to chapel where, with them, he would listen to the strangely moving and sweetly monotonous chants. He grew more haggard as lack of sleep joined forces with lack of food to undermine his health.

Mrs Petherick had something else to worry about now as well as the condition of her young erstwhile friend. Autumn rains had softened the ground in her garden and during her annual clearing up and trimming back she had come across footprints in the soil of the flower beds, large footprints, made by a man.

On returning home from dinner at a friend's house one misty Saturday night she found, on going to bed, that she could not sleep. The heavy rain had made it impossible for her to get into the garden for several days and this always made her restless. Who, she wondered as she tossed and turned, had been walking about in her flower borders? Should she inform the police? Admittedly no damage had been done, not so much as a leaf crushed, but even so it was not pleasant to know that someone was tramping round out there uninvited.

As she pondered, the church clock struck midnight and almost at once a strange sound came from the garden, a strange melodious sound, that of a man – or men? – singing a sweet, solemn, liturgical chant. She leapt out of bed, threw on a dressing gown and ran downstairs.

Grabbing a spade from the porch she went into the garden,

and there by the light of a veiled moon she saw a figure gliding slowly across the misty lawn, and all the while the gentle singing rose and fell plaintively on the still air.

For a second she stood watching. Was there only one figure? No, several in a line and then, as the mist shifted a little and the moon cleared, only one again which vanished behind a ruined wall.

'Monks!' Mrs Petherick thought. 'That wretched young Jeremy Ballantyne, he's got *me* seeing things now!' and she ran, silent in her slippers, across the grass, carrying the spade like a club and following the melodious singing.

She rounded the corner where the hollyhocks had grown in the shelter of the wall, so tall and so beautiful earlier, now nothing but a cluster of stiff stems thick with seed-pods, and there among them was a hooded figure.

'Monks!' Mrs Petherick shouted out loud. 'I don't believe in ghosts and I don't approve of monks! Get *out* of my garden! Get *out*!' and she lay about her with the spade, hearing the brittle hollyhock stems smash and shatter under the blows, and snapping under her feet. But suddenly she stumbled over something and bending down her fingers closed on thick, coarse cloth wrapped round – a body?

She screamed. Of course! She hadn't been seeing things. It was the unknown prowler and she had probably killed him! Dropping the spade she ran indoors to telephone the police.

When the police arrived Mrs Petherick went with them into the garden once more, the beams from their powerful torches cutting swathes through the misty darkness.

In the wrack of broken hollyhock stems something lay, almost completely covered in a long black cloak.

'It *is* a monk!' Mrs Petherick breathed.

The policemen pulled the cloak back to reveal a thin frail body, the haggard face irradiated with a beatific smile and the skeletal hands clasping a bunch of rosemary.

'No,' said the elder of the two policemen, 'it's the young vicar, and he's dead.'

Mrs Petherick sank to her knees beside the pathetic remains of her former friend.

'Oh, the poor boy!' she sobbed. 'And I killed him!'

The younger policeman lifted her gently to her feet.

'No, you never, madam,' he said, 'He's been dead two-three days by the looks of him. Starved himself most likely. But God alone knows how he came to be in this here garden with his hands full of herbs.'

X

Disaster at Wheal Gratitude

The heat in the galleries leading off the main mine shaft was appalling: bad enough in normal circumstances but almost beyond bearing now.

Men scrambled along the narrow, twisting tunnels which were so low that they had to crawl on hands and knees. The terror in their hearts was mingled with anguish for the others they heard screaming their lives away as rock crashed and rumbled fathoms below them; their lungs were bursting from their efforts to reach the lifting engine before the buckling sides of the shaft put it out of action.

The man with the large nose and red hair clawed his way along the rocky bottom of the gallery, tearing the palms of his hands and his knees and elbows to ribbons, hard and calloused as they were; the tallow candle, which was stuck to his hard felt hat with a lump of clay, had long since gone out and he was in total darkness. He must reach the engine before it stopped, must get out, must see daylight again; claustrophobia, which he had had to fight all the time he was underground, gripped him now and he sobbed, panic mounting, as he crawled.

At last he could hear the clatter and wheeze of the engine at the end of the tunnel; a dim, grey vestige of light showed. Thank God! The shaft had not caved in higher up! The engine was still working!

The skips of tin ore were still being jerked to the surface on the chains which moved up along the articulated rods, activated by the great beam engine in the tall, stone house at the shaft head. Men jumped for the bucket-shaped skips as they passed the openings off the main shaft and balanced on the lumps of rock, clinging to the chains. Two, then three, buckets passed the man with the large nose and red hair as he crouched in his rat-hole, carrying sweat steaming men, filthy and terrified, their eyes huge and wild with horror.

He must get out! He would get out! With an animal roar he hurled himself at the man balanced on the next skip and through sheer weight flung him off. The dislodged man fell, his screams echoing down the shaft and mingling with those of others trapped on the lower levels; but the man with the large nose and red hair clung on with raw and bleeding hands, tears of relief making white lines down his filthy face, riding to safety.

There was another rumble as more tons of rock fell deep in the shaft: the rods bearing the skips shuddered but carried on through clouds of dust and grit and blasts of hot, sulphurous air. Through the noise all round him and the drumming of the blood in his head the man with the large nose and red hair heard the occupant of the skip beneath him yell:

'You bastard! You son of a bitch! That was my brother you flung off. By God I'll see you rot in hell for this!'

The engine stopped as the third rock fall jammed the rods fast against the wall of the shaft. The great beam which operated the lifting gear in the engine house above was wrenched off its mounting as it was about to complete its return stroke and it hung off balance, its massive head awry like that of a huge, stricken animal over the gaping shaft mouth.

The men still feet from the surface climbed hand over hand up the rods and were dragged by a dozen pairs of arms over the edge to throw themselves at last onto the ground in the blessed light of day. The man whose brother had been flung to his death was the last to get out alive.

The engine driver in the tall stone engine-house had shut off the steam from the cylinder and thrown the maimed machine out of gear; the great piston remained suspended between strokes; it still breathed rhythmically, but idling, achieving nothing.

By the time the last men had come, thankfully, to grass, as the surface was known, there was a crowd round the mouth of the shaft. The next shift, or core, was beginning to gather from the scattered hamlets and villages across the moor and the spallers and buddlers, the bal maidens and boys, the carpenters, wagoners and blacksmiths had thrown down their tools and raced to the shaft mouth. Among the child labourers, some of them only seven or eight years old, was a little boy with a twisted, crippled foot: he pushed and shoved his way through the crowd, almost being trodden into the ground in the great crush, his eyes searching the faces of the filthy, gasping men who lay on the muddy ground, or staggered to lean against the rickety wooden sheds. He did not find the face he sought.

Within minutes of escaping from the horrors below, men were roping themselves together to go down again, to climb down the jammed rods in an attempt to reach their trapped work-mates, but the man with the large nose and the red hair was not one of them. He barely stopped to catch a breath before running headlong from the scene, his sodden, filthy clothes plastered to his body. He ran past the sheds, round the winding gear of the horse-whims, through the spoil heaps, pushing between crowds of sobbing women and children out onto the heather stumbling and falling down the steep slope until he came in sight of a small huddle of cottages by the stream in the valley.

Women came running towards him, their eyes searched his face and then looked beyond him to where other men could be seen òn the skyline; then one – his Mary – her face contorted with relief, her arms stretched out, raced towards him to catch him as he fell to his knees.

That night, as the wrecked engine stood strangely silent, there came the sound of sobbing from some of the cottages in the hamlet by the stream, as there did from cottages in many other hamlets and villages in the neighbourhood.

The man with the large nose and red hair lay face down on the rough bed in his tiny cottage. Mary his wife had seen to it that the children were quiet on pain of a hefty smack, but the baby, a little boy, wailed shrilly from the pain of cutting teeth, knowing nothing of adult relief, terror, exhaustion and shame.

Mary took the baby outside wrapped in a fold of her shawl and walked a little way along the gorse-lined track, rocking him gently to soothe him and holding the small, hot face against her own.

Suddenly, in the last green glow of light from across the sea where the sun had set, she saw a movement among the gorse bushes. Straining her eyes and holding the now sleeping baby very close, she made out several figures moving like black shadows. Transfixed she watched them creep towards her cottage; her husband had told her what had happened at the mine, what he had done, and she knew instinctively what was to come now.

Too far away to give the alarm she saw the black shapes burst into the cottage, heard the children's first terrified screams cease abruptly. Clutching the baby she ran, sobbing and falling on the stony track. She looked back only once to see flames leap up and blaze across the thatched roof of her home before she plunged on into the night in the direction of the next village.

Henry Smith sat on a bench outside a small pub in the village of Treventon Vean. He stretched his long legs in front of him and took a deep draught from the pint beer mug in his hand.

The June day seemed to him sheer perfection; larks sang in the blue sky, pink valerian made a thick fringe on top of the dry stone wall to one side of him and cow parsley frothed at its foot. A large, tabby cat lay curled up asleep on the bench by his side and a black and white sheep dog lay across the threshold of the pub.

Over the road the fine, four-staged tower of the church with tall, ornate pinnacles at each corner, rose above the low roofs of nave and aisles. Rooks cawed and flapped among nests in the gale-ravaged elms at one end of the churchyard. Cornwall was a good place to be on a day like this.

An ancient man sat on the bench at the other side of the pub door; he wore a cloth cap and held a pint mug on his knee.

'You an Angove?' he suddenly asked in a wheezy, cracked voice.

Henry was aware, belatedly, that he had been spoken to.

'I'm so sorry,' he said, leaning forward, 'I didn't hear what you said.'

'Be you an Angove?' the old man shouted.

'All right! All right! I'm not deaf!' Henry protested, laughing, 'My thoughts were miles away, that's all.' He had no idea what the old man meant by his question.

'I'm English,' he said, 'And my name is Smith. I'm an accountant, down here on a visit to recuperate from an illness.' That should fill all the old man's requirements, he thought, whatever the question had meant.

'Certainly looks like an Angove,' the old man muttered to himself, peering into his mug, 'Got the nose of one, anyhow,' he took a long drink of his beer.

'Happen he'd know if he was one,' he went on, still speaking to himself. He bent his bleary gaze on Henry again. 'I don't know, though. Happen he wouldn't,' he mumbled, thinking his own thoughts.

After some minutes of silence during which the two men enjoyed the sunshine and finished their beer, the old one groped under the bench for his stick and stiffly got to his feet. Leaning heavily on the stick, which was a stout, knobby ash-plant, he slowly crossed from one bench to the other; his left foot was turned in awkwardly and he wore a surgical boot.

'Mind if I join you?' he asked Henry, ''Tisn't often I gets anyone to talk to this time of day.'

Henry rose to his feet and gathered up his own and the old man's glass.

'Delighted,' he said, 'Let me get you another pint.'

When the glasses were refilled the old man chatted away in his wheezy voice, decrying the change in the world in general, and Cornwall in particular, cursing the summer tourists and their cars – 'no offence, mind,' – the decline in local skills and the exodus of young people from the county.

'Take this yer village, now,' he said. 'When I was a boy there was three mines working within a mile of here. Not a family that didn't have someone working underground in them days.' He recalled record output of tin in the good years, the dejection and poverty when the market fell, and the emigration to America and Australia when the mines closed.

'Never went below ground meself,' he mused. 'Me foot, see? Couldn't never of managed they ladders and that man engine;' the heavy, ugly boot was held up for Henry's inspection. 'Put in my time as a spaller, breaking the rock before it went to the stamps, and after that I drove a spoil wagon.'

There was a short silence as they listened to the rooks in the elms and Henry stroked the tabby cat by his side.

'Got relations down here, have you?' the old man asked, eventually.

'No,' said Henry, 'Although my father did mention this village once, just before he died: seems my grandmother used to talk about it. Perhaps she came here on holiday once. I'd forgotten about it until I saw the place-name on a sign post. I read a book about Cornwall recently and it sort of got me. I had to come and see what it was all about, and I must say I haven't been disappointed.'

'Ah, yes,' the old man said, ' 'Tis a grand place, Cornwall. But you should have seen it like it was when I was a boy. Not that there wasn't terrible times, mind,' he looked round at Henry, taking in the strong-featured face, dominated by a long nose, and the greying sandy hair.

'Your father have red hair, did he?' he asked, inconsequentially.

'Yes, he did, as a matter of fact,' Henry said, surprised. 'Why do you ask?'

'Just wondered,' the old man said, burying his nose in his pint mug.

Presently he reverted to his reminiscences.

'Oh yes,' he said, 'There was terrible times. When I was a boy there was a disaster at Wheal Gratitude,' he waved an arthritic hand down the road to the right where it led to the rusty-coloured moor, gaunt, ruined mine chimneys and engine houses dotting the skyline. 'My dad was killed in that one.'

'I'm sorry,' said Henry, looking at him with interest. 'That must have been dreadful. How did you get on with him gone?' He had read of the crushing poverty of the old days and the appalling plight of families who lost their bread winner.

'My uncle looked after me,' the old man said. 'He saw to a lot of things for me, my uncle did.'

He resumed his account of the mine disaster.

'Fourteen men were killed that time,' he said. 'All buried over there under the elms,' he waved his stick towards the churchyard across the road. 'More'n fourteen, really, you could say.'

'What do you mean?' Henry asked.

'Well, there was another accident that night. Cottage burnt down; man and his four children died, although some say 'twasn't the fire as killed them. *They're* all buried over there as well.'

The old man picked up his empty mug, examined it and put it down again.

'Woman got away though,' he went on, 'She was out of doors at the time with the baby. Boy, it was, the baby. My uncle didn't know they were outside.'

Henry looked questioningly at him not understanding this last remark, but the old man's eyes were seeing far into the past and he didn't notice.

'She ran to the next village where she came from, we reckoned. Her father hid her away, most like. Changed her name of course and then they do say she got clean out of the county, her and the little boy. Often wondered about that, I have.' He was silent for a moment, then: 'You got any brothers and sisters?' he asked.

'No,' Henry said. 'I was an only child.'

The church clock struck half past eleven and three old men were seen coming down the road.

'Ah! Here come the lads!' the old man cackled. 'Hello boys!'

He leant towards Henry.

'Have to leave you now,' he said, 'Play dominoes, we do.' He rose to his feet, waving his stick at his cronies.

'Well, I shall go and look at the church,' Henry said, getting up from the bench, 'And then I think I'll take a walk out to some of the old mine workings: they look most romantic, covered in ivy as they are.'

'Romantic?' the old man glared at him. 'They wasn't

romantic,' he growled, 'They was hard work – and death to some. Hard work and death for precious little money. But you go and look at them anyway; go to the works where there's three engine houses close together: that's Wheal Gratitude. Go and see the graves I was telling about over in the church-yard first, though; specially the Angove ones. Angove means a smith in Cornish, same as your name. Funny that, isn't it?'

The old man slowly turned in at the pub door to join his friends, prodding the black and white dog with his stick to make him move out of the way, and Henry strolled across the road and up the few steps to the churchyard. Looking back at the pub for a second he saw that the old man had emerged again to fetch his cap which he had left on the bench.

'Over to your right under the elms,' he shouted, 'Angove is the name you're looking for, Angove and Polkerris.'

Henry waved to him and turned right as directed. In front of him among the slate and granite grave stones old and new, some with flowers in front of them, others leaning at crazy angles, those whom they commemorated long forgotten, was a large block of stone, almost like the base of a war memorial.

'To the Memory of Those Who Lost Their Lives in the Wheal Gratitude Disaster,' it read, and underneath were fourteen names, the date and a suitable biblical text. Among the fourteen names was Polkerris. Was that the name the old man had mentioned? Was it his father, Henry wondered?

To the left of the memorial was an ordinary, large, slate grave stone: it also had several names carved on it.

> To the Memory of
> Henry Angove Aged 28
> and his Children,
> Simon, aged 8,
> Adam, aged 5,
> Annie, aged 4,
> James, aged 2.
> Tragically Burnt to Death.

The date underneath was the same as that on the memorial next to it.

Henry stood and gazed at the two graves. How appalling, he thought; two dire tragedies on the same day in such a small village.

The Angove monument moved him, if anything, more than the other. Those poor children burnt to death, although the old man had hinted that they had died some other way. Odd. Oh, well. Old men *were* odd, and old Cornish men probably odder than most. He shrugged his shoulders and went to look at the church before striking out across the moor.

Leaving his car where it was in the yard behind the pub Henry walked down the road. Like a lot of Cornish villages, Treventon Vean straggled along, having left the nucleus of church and pub, until it petered out into moorland.

Away to the left the sea stretched blue and placid to the horizon behind the brown and green shoulder of the moor. No heather was in bloom yet, but the gorse, as ever, put out its golden, pea-shaped flowers, flooding the air with its warm scent.

The ruined engine houses and the tall, slim chimneys reared up against the sky with a gaunt beauty all their own: glassless windows gazed sightlessly over the now serene terrain which once had been torn and lacerated by man's efforts to tear the earth's riches from its bowels while the air throbbed with the rattle and clamour of machinery and reeked with smoke and fumes.

Henry wandered round, wishing he knew more about it all and could understand it better. Some things spoke for themselves; low broken walls, still standing a few feet high in places, marked tiny cottages, the gaps that had been their doors facing across a stony path to a stream which rattled down over a small precipice where even Henry's unknowledgeable eye could discern that a water wheel had once been mounted and from there to a jumble of twisted metal and rotting wood, a crushing machine of some sort.

He climbed the hill towards the three engine houses: Wheal Gratitude, the mine where the disaster had occurred.

Standing inside the largest of the roofless buildings he gazed upwards, wishing again he understood it better, marvelling at the strength of the walls and the meticulous way the great stones were placed together like perfect patchwork. Suddenly a rattle of loose stones behind him made him turn round. There stood the old man grinning at him.

'I see you done like I told you,' he wheezed delightedly.

'My goodness, you've walked a long way!' Henry said, amazed.

'Ah! I can walk a fair way when I've a mind. Trouble is I don't often have a mind these days,' the old man said.

He took Henry's arm and led him round the engine house.

'All white, it used to be, inside and out,' he said, 'And the woodwork was painted red. The engine driver used to sit here on a little wooden settle and the brass on the engine and the stairs and that used to shine like gold. Looked after everything like it was home, he used to, and it was a sight warmer than home, too. The beam used to balance on that wall,' he pointed to the particularly thick wall at the front of the building with a huge aperture at the top, 'half in and half out of that big opening, it used to be, with its head hanging over the shaft. Do you come outside with me and I'll show you.'

Together they left the engine house and walked through the tumbled stone and undergrowth.

'There's the shaft,' the old man pointed with his heavy, knobbed walking stick at a mound of gorse and bramble. 'Terrible dangerous it is, hundreds of feet deep and no cover on it. Still, nobody don't come up here much no more.'

Henry looked at the tangle of vegetation.

'You'd never think there was a mine shaft there at all,' he said, 'I can hardly believe it.'

'You'd believe it if you'd seen what I seen on this very spot,' the old man said, looking round. 'Course, 'twas different then, sheds and machines and horses and men all over the place.' He walked a few feet away, 'This here was where I stood while they came up that night. Watching for my Dad to come up, I was, but of course he never did.' He paused for a few seconds and then asked one of his inconsequential questions.

'You got any children, have you?'

Henry looked up from his examination of the ground round the shaft.

'No, I haven't,' he said. 'I'm a bachelor. Why do you ask?'

'No reason,' the old man replied, 'Just wondered. I haven't got none neither. Blessing really. Well, in your case it is. Look,' he went on before Henry could ask why it was a blessing, 'You come here with me and I'll show you where you can see the shaft from.'

He led the way back into the engine house, hobbling on the uneven floor where the machinery had been wrenched out, towards the massive front wall. Holding onto the masonry of the great arched doorway under the beam aperture he invited Henry to follow him.

There was a hollow square some few feet deep in front of the opening surrounded by a wall.

'That's the cistern,' the old man said, 'You walk along that wall and then look down and you'll see the shaft.'

Henry walked along the side of the square, tank-like structure and then halfway along its front wall.

'Good heavens, yes! Now I get more of an idea of the depth of it,' he cried.

He leaned over and gazed into the black depths in the centre of the encroaching gorse and bramble.

With surprising agility for one of his age and condition the old man joined Henry on the cistern wall. Raising his stick high over his head in both hands he brought it down with all his strength on the back of Henry's neck.

Henry cried out as he fell, grabbing fruitlessly at the prickly foliage round the shaft mouth: the cry seemed to echo back from the depths for a long time.

The old man edged his way back into the engine house. He took off his cap and gazed up at the sky through the roofless building.

'There you are, Dad,' he said. 'That's the last of they red-headed Angove buggers gone. The score's settled. You can rest in peace now and so can I.'

XI

The Weather-Dog

North Cornwall in January had seemed a mad idea to James Martin's friends when he told them he was going to spend a few days of the winter vacation there. Cornwall was a place to go in the summer, they said; it would be bleak and lonely in winter. James replied that they were probably right, but since he was a bleak and lonely person it would be quite fitting, wouldn't it? The friends laughed, slapped him on the back and wished him joy of his out of season holiday.

So here he was, sitting on a cliff-top with Cornwall and the Atlantic spread out on all sides of him, basking in a hazy sunshine.

To one side of the pale gold disc of the sun was an arc of rainbow, forming a partial halo round it. James had never seen this prismatic effect before and had remarked on it to a farm labourer he had met cleaning out a ditch at the side of the lane on his way to the cliffs. The man told him it was known in Cornwall as a weather-dog and foretold storms to come. Be that as it may, James thought, looking at it, today was idyllic and he seemed to have it entirely to himself. There was not another living soul in sight and he could indulge his three hobbies, bird-watching, photography and solitude, to his heart's content.

He looked down at the beach as it curved its golden sandy length far below him at the foot of the indigo cliffs which were streaked here and there with rust-red and ochre yellow from the mineral deposits bleeding out of the rock.

The lavender-grey sea, gentle today with no wind to drive it, rolled in sedately, wave upon wave depositing its white lace crown on the sand where it dissolved and sank out of sight.

It was about half-tide, coming in fast and curling round the miniature islands of rock which studded the beach in imitation of the larger islands sailing just this side of the horizon, following the line of the headland like the row of dots at the end of an unfinished sentence.

There was not a single footprint to mar the smooth sand and James wondered what was the matter with the people who lived here. They complained bitterly in the summer, he knew, that they couldn't get on the beach for trippers, and yet here it was, absolutely empty of people and no one except himself to exult in all this beauty, all this peace. No one except the birds, of course.

He picked up the powerful binoculars which lay in his lap and scanned the beach. At the water's edge was a small flock of turnstones, the little birds endlessly repeating the action from which they were named as though they had a reputation to live up to, turning over the slate pebbles, round and flat as counters, and eating whatever morsels they found beneath them.

Investigating the rocks at one end of the beach were oystercatchers, smart in black and white feathers, red legs flashing, and their liquid fluting calls cutting across the constant sound of the sea.

A few gulls had left the crowded cliff ledges and were standing on their flat yellow feet, heads hunched into bodies, gazing out to sea, quite motionless. They were joined from time to time by a pair of jackdaws that had been keeping James company on his cliff-top, walking round him and regarding him coldly with their strange blue eyes.

He let the binoculars fall, hanging round his neck on their strap, and started to pack his valuable camera into its large carrying case which stood on the grass beside him, full of lenses, filters and meters. He had taken a full pack of films this afternoon, wastefully he knew as the light, even using a haze-meter, was too diffuse and, although the scenery was utterly beautiful, the wide open spaces were too devoid of feature to make good photographs.

Zipping up his anorak and slinging the strap of the heavy camera case over his shoulder he stood up and started the walk to the pub where he was staying.

As he walked he remembered the last time he had been in Cornwall, with Daphne.

He had been engaged to Daphne, a fellow-student at Reading University where he was now a lecturer. She was pretty and sweet, loving and enthusiastic, and even now when he thought of her he felt a pang of regret; but it would never have worked out, in fact it hadn't worked out. The holiday in Cornwall, five years ago now, was the breaking point.

It had been August and Daphne had begged to go to Cornwall. James, remembering happy Easter holidays there as a child, had agreed, not very enthusiastically, but it was not his way to enthuse.

It had been a disaster. The beaches had been crowded with people, children and dogs, with all of whom Daphne had made friends. The sea was full of young men encased in black rubber, charging in on the rollers, riding their great Malibu surf-boards.

James had wanted to swim but the breaking surf and the surf-riders had made it impossible and further out he found the current too strong for comfort. He had wanted to watch birds but, apart from the greedy gulls waiting for scraps, there were none to be seen. The sand was churned up, dirty and littered with rubbish. Inland it had been no better. Cars blocked the narrow roads and sped, nose to tail, along the wider ones in an endless stream.

Daphne had loved it all. She loved the crowded hotel where they stayed, and the noisy discotheques to which she dragged him every night. She had wanted to see all the sights, and the final disaster had been Tintagel.

James could imagine the grandeur the ruins would have in solitude, in fact could dimly remember them from childhood, but thronged with noisy tourists and their running, screaming children, the ancient walls lost all their charm, all their meaning for him.

Daphne had seemed not to notice the other people at all. She had been enraptured with it.

'Think of all the knights in armour dancing with the ladies in their beautiful gowns! Think of the music and the singing!'

she cried, gazing round her, her blue eyes full of romantic visions.

James had turned on her, exasperated. He wiped the glamorous images out completely by explaining that the knights, probably rheumatic and bronchitic, would have found it difficult to move at all, let alone dance, in the vastly uncomfortable metal plates; that the ladies' gowns would have reeked of stale sweat, rotten food and worse, and the only music would have been that of the howling gales and the cursing and coughing of those who, for the sake of scant warmth, had to put up with the downbeating smoke from the central hearths.

To his surprise Daphne had burst into tears.

'You spoil everything,' she wailed, 'I've tried to enjoy myself, but you're a bad tempered, selfish beast and I've had as much as I can stand.'

The drive back to their hotel had been a silent one and the next morning she had packed her case and, giving him back his ring, left for the station.

Daphne had married another student a year later, Robert Mitchell, a Cornishman, now a lecturer at Camborne School of Mines. On impulse James had rung Robert and had been invited to visit them for an evening meal: he was going tomorrow. He could imagine Daphne, pretty and happy in her married state, and the home she would have made, bright and untidy and full of children and animals.

The light had quite gone by the time James got back to the pub, and the lit windows of the low building looked cheerful and inviting. After a bath and a change of clothes he went down to the bar for a few pints of beer and his supper, taking a newspaper with him.

The pub, with the church, a farm and three cottages, made up the original village of St Severan. A cluster of modern houses and shops half a mile up the road was developing fast, leaving the knot of ancient buildings, whose name it shared, in blissful seclusion.

It was a small pub with only two letting bedrooms and James was the sole guest. The bar, with its low beamed ceiling and slate floor, was exactly what a pub bar ought to be.

None of the plastic floral arrangements, reproduction copper warming pans and close-carpeting that the pubs on the main road seemed to think their coach parties would expect. Here what copper there was was genuine and the rough white walls between the small windows were hung closely with sepia photographs of local worthies, bell-ringing teams and wrecked ships, all long since dead or smashed to matchwood. The huge granite fireplace, piled with blazing logs, was flanked with high-backed settles, and benches and tables round the walls were the only other furniture.

James sat in a corner with his pint and his pasty, and covertly watched from behind his newspaper as the bar filled up. Burly men drifted in, several in navy-blue donkey jackets and seamen's peaked caps; others in suits, once 'best' but now, worn through at shoulder and elbow, used for working on the land.

As they came in the men would nod in James's direction, giving him a genial word or two. A man of few words himself, he appreciated their reserve, and they in their turn liked the 'foreigner' for keeping his distance while being in no way unfriendly. The Cornish prefer to take their time getting to know people.

Black and white cattle dogs, collie-type, slithered in after their masters with the odd, close-to-the-ground gait peculiar to them, and sat or lay at their feet, never taking their eyes off the men's faces, alert for every move. The deep voices of the men made a pleasant rumble, cut across by the laughter of the few women who came in; the fire glowed on weather-beaten faces and James sat, content to be with these honest people in this honest place. Anywhere less bleak and lonely he couldn't imagine.

That night a gale blew up, as the weather-dog by the sun had predicted. The wind tore at the low, slate-roofed pub all night and battered at the tiny windows, hurling rain at the glass like handfuls of pebbles.

In the morning the rain had stopped but the wind was still strong as James drove into the nearby town of Sawlyn to buy a paper and more film for his camera.

Sawlyn was a fishing town and small port and he parked his car on the quay. As he walked back to it, his purchases made, there was suddenly a loud explosion followed in a few seconds by another. Seagulls, which had been bobbing about in the harbour among moored boats, rose screaming into the air, pigeons clattered off the roof of the grain store and men came running down the narrow alleys.

'What is it?' James asked a woman who had come to her cottage door, wiping floury hands on her apron.

'Lifeboat,' the woman said, not looking at him, eyes on the running men. 'Some poor devil's in trouble, I 'spect.'

When James went back to the pub, to pick up his camera and eat a few sandwiches before returning to the cliffs, he was surprised to find the bar empty.

'Very quiet?' he said to the landlord, who was behind the bar polishing glasses.

'Boy gone off the rocks,' the man replied, 'Everyone's gone to help look for 'un.'

'The lifeboat's gone out,' James said, 'Would it be for him?'

'Yes. Helicoptor'll be over in a minute,' the landlord cocked his ear to the ceiling. 'There she goes now;' they listened as the machine clattered over-head, its rotor blades wuthering, flying sea-wards. 'Won't do no good, though.'

'Why?' James asked. 'Can't he swim?'

'Swim?' The landlord looked at him incredulously. 'With a sea like there is running now?'

James realized he had made an inane remark, remembering how he, six foot tall and a strong swimmer, had found it heavy going in a summer sea, but he was never one to apologize so said nothing.

The landlord looked at him sideways, contemptuously.

'Bloody foreigner coming here talking about swimming,' he thought. 'Nice enough chap, but bloody foreigner all the same.' However, he relented.

'Oh no,' he said, 'swimming in a sea like this don't do no good. The cold's enough to kill you in two – three minutes, and being smashed on the rocks –' He pursed his lips and drew in a long breath. 'Pity it is, though,' he sighed, 'He were a nice little chap. Tom Trenouth's boy.' He polished glasses in silence for a few moments, then went on: 'Reckon they won't find nothing till Thursday.'

'Thursday?' James said.

'They do say the sea keeps what she takes for two days and then gives 'un back,' the landlord replied, 'Happens like that most times. Currents and that.'

'Does it happen often?' James asked.

'Three – four times every summer. Once or twice in the winter; treacherous, the sea is. Know the rocks like the back of your hand you can, and she'll still get you. Freak waves, see? Bigger than the rest.'

They didn't speak for a few moments. James drank his beer slowly.

'Was the child by himself?' he asked.

The landlord nodded.

'Spent hours on the beach in his school holidays and weekends, him and his dog.'

James pushed his empty glass across the bar and fished in his pocket for money to buy another pint.

'How did they know it had happened?' he asked.

'Dog came back,' the landlord carefully pulled the pint of beer, 'Hysterical he was, barking and carrying on. Took them right to the spot where it happened. Child's footprints was all around. Clever old dog, he is.'

James thought about the black and white collies he had watched last night in the bar, anticipating their owner's every move.

'Dogs are clever,' he said, 'Uncanny, sometimes.'

The landlord moved to the other end of the bar and started unloading a crate of bottled beer. James spread his newspaper on the bar and read it while he finished his pint. Thanking the man, he picked up his camera case and binoculars and went out.

The next day James went down to the small beach on the other side of the headland which sheltered the village of St Severan. No cliffs here, but sand dunes backing the low rocks which reached black fists out into the water.

He found that the small bay was separated from a larger one only by a narrow neck of black basalt, veined and netted with white quartz, which led to a grass-topped mass of rock whose further end, long since denuded of turf, descended in a series of steps and ledges into the sea.

James climbed along the jagged neck of rock and up onto the grass. From here he could see the vast sweep of the larger beach as well as the smaller rocky one he had just left. The sight was magnificent.

The wind had died down slightly but was still strong and the sea was in turmoil, white water as far as the horizon. Breakers rushed in to crash against the rock thrusting out from the shore, and the ground shuddered under his feet from the impact of the mass of water, pounding in, dragging back, over and over again. The air was thick with spray and the noise was deafening.

James walked to the far end of the rock and sat down on a flat ledge some twelve feet above the water, exhilarated by the power and fury of the waves beneath him. He put his heavy camera case down beside him and gloried in it all, feeling almost a part of it.

As each wave flung itself at the clefts of the rock it streamed down, a mass of white foam, to become trapped, no time to return to the sea before another onslaught of water smashed in. The foam shook and shuddered in the wind, creamed and sculpted into whorled shapes as the water retreated from under it, only to be reshaped, recreated as the next wave thundered in, hurling its frothy crest of white spume to join the piled masses. It seemed incredible that transparent, volatile water could become something at once so fragile and at the same time so solid. Pieces of it became detached and blew like huge snow flakes over the rock to cling, quivering, to the short grass before being blown further inland. Fragments blew against James's face, hanging on his eyelashes or dissolving on his lips, salt and gritty with sand.

He was mesmerized by the steady roar of the sea and the constant change, constant repetition of water round him, the feel of the spindrift on his face, the clean salt smell, the shuddering rock beneath him, when suddenly he was startled out of his reverie by a stone hitting his boot. Another fell just short of him and bounced over his legs. He turned, furious, to see who was throwing stones at him.

On the beach behind and to the left of him was a small boy. He was dressed in wellington boots, jeans, a thick jersey and a bright red knitted cap, and was jumping up and down and waving his arms. His mouth was wide open as he yelled urgently at James, his face contorted with anxiety, and by his side a small rough-haired white mongrel dog barked frantically, its short front legs leaving the ground at each bark with the intensity of its efforts.

'What the hell?' thought James. 'Someone must be in trouble and he wants me to help.' He pulled the hood of his anorak off his head to try to hear what the boy was shouting, but the roar of the sea was too loud, he couldn't hear a sound from the child, although the dog's shrill bark carried well enough.

Leaving his camera case where it was, he started down the rock. It would have taken too long to run back along the neck of land as the child was becoming more and more distressed, his arms waving even more wildly, his mouth a square hole in his anguished face as he yelled.

James's boots slipped and slithered on the wet rock and he turned to go down backwards, the binoculars slung round his neck banging on ledges and getting caught on projections as he went. Finally he jumped, landing awkwardly in the shallow water and quick-sand at the foot of the rock. Righting himself he turned to find the child had gone. There was no one on the beach but the little dog, still barking frenziedly and making short runs at him.

'Where are you, you bloody child?' James roared, scanning the beach, but his only answer was to be knocked down by a colossal wall of water.

He went down with such force that his face was smashed into the sand, his mouth and nose were full of it and it rasped his cheek and cut his lips. The wave retreated and the tons of water tried to drag him back out with it, filling his boots and the hood and pockets of his anorak. He clawed with his hands, dug his leaden weighted feet into the sand and managed to pull himself free of the sucking water.

Staggering to his feet, wiping the streaming water from his eyes, spitting sand and small stones from his mouth, he let out a stream of curses as he realized that his binoculars were no longer round his neck; the strap must have slipped over his head as the mass of water surged over him. He glanced up at the rock where he had been sitting just in time to see the last foaming trails of the wave which had knocked him down stream from its sides. There was no sign of his camera case.

His boots full of water he stumbled awkwardly into the surf again, scanning the boiling, seething water, but in such turmoil it was impossible to see anything. He staggered back up the beach to the dry sand.

'Where are you, you bloody child?' James roared again. 'If I get my hands on you, Gold help me I'll kill you!' but there was no sign of the child, only the dog, not barking now but whining as it ran backwards and forwards, its little paws making a maze of prints in the firm sand round the base of the rock.

In the midst of his fury, emptying his boots, trying to wring water out of his sodden clothes, still cursing, James noticed the dog's paw prints. He looked down at his own, those made while wearing his water-filled boots and those made when his feet were bare having stripped off his socks. There were no others.

He knew roughly where the child had been but there was no sign of disturbance in the sand there except the dog's tiny paw marks. However, he was too angry at the loss of his valuable camera and binoculars to give the matter more than half his attention. He turned on the dog.

'Where's your damned little master, you wretched beast?' he yelled at it, but the dog was digging and rooting under the bladderwrack that hung down at the edge of the rock. It turned back to James holding in its mouth the red knitted cap the child had been wearing, now soaked and thick with sand and bits of weed.

'So he went up over the rock, did he?' James stormed, snatching the cap from the dog's mouth. He wrung the water from it and lashed at the dog with the heavy wet wool.

'If I catch him,' he roared at the frightened animal, who backed away from him, 'You can tell him I'll give him his hat back *and* a thrashing he'll never forget!' The dog retreated into the sand-dunes whimpering, its short tail tucked between its legs.

James let himself into the pub, frozen to the bone from his walk back from the beach in soaking wet clothes. He bathed and put on dry clothes, hanging the wet ones, including the red cap, over the radiator in his room. The cuts and grazes on his face were smarting badly and he dabbed them with antiseptic.

He saw no one as he went through the bar, it being not open yet. As he let himself out of the front door he vowed that tomorrow he would find out who the child on the beach was, who was responsible for the loss of several hundred pounds worth of photographic equipment. He would find the boy's father and tell him of his antics on the beach and tell him to knock some sense into him. He got into his car and drove, fast and angrily, to Camborne.

Daphne was a little plumper but otherwise just as he remembered her. For a moment he felt a twinge of regret, but after an evening in her company he knew he was well out of it.

Her home was, as he had known it would be, cosy and pretty and untidy. There were two small children upstairs in bed at whom he was made to look, two large dogs downstairs who looked at him, mournfully reproaching him for sitting on their sofa, and cats everywhere.

The meal was good but spoilt by Daphne's over-exuberance. She knocked over wine glasses and spilt soup in her excitement at seeing James again, but Robert was charmed by her and everything she did. They were obviously blissfully happy.

Daphne probably thought she was well out of their affair, too, James wryly told himself as he drove dangerously back to the pub. He knew he had behaved abominably.

Still in a furious temper over the loss of his camera and equipment, his face sore and burning, he had talked about nothing else. Usually a beer drinker, he had had too much whisky and too much wine and had got very drunk. He barely heard, after his third recital of the incident on the beach, Robert's quiet remark; 'That child probably saved your life.'

He certainly didn't see the far away look in Daphne's eyes or the little crease between her eyebrows as she considered the child's abrupt disappearance.

James woke late the next morning. The monotonous ringing of a church bell did nothing to improve his pounding head.

'Damned bell might as well be in the room,' he muttered ill temperedly.

He put on the clothes which had dried overnight on the radiator, stuffing the red woollen cap in the pocket of his anorak.

'I'll find the little swine this belongs to,' he growled.

The bell was still tolling when he got down to the bar.

'Sorry I'm late,' he said to the landlord. 'Bit of a party last night I'm afraid. Is there any black coffee going?'

The landlord eyed his bruised face and fetched him a cup.

'What's that damned bell ringing for?' James asked, screwing up his face.

'Funeral.'

'Oh?'

'Yes. They found the child.'

'The drowned boy?'

'Yes. Two days the sea keeps 'em when she takes 'em. But she don't do 'em no good,' the man sighed, 'Not a pretty sight, he wasn't.'

James didn't want to hear. His stomach was feeling none too good and the thought of the drowned child made it imperative for him to get out into the fresh air.

'Sad business,' he said from the doorway.

James went inland that day, cursing his lost camera as Cornwall unfolded herself to him in all her winter beauty, a patchwork of grey green fields and warm brown ploughland all topped by the massive crags of volcanic rock rearing against the sky, circled over by buzzards. As he climbed the rough slopes of Brown Willy, Cornwall's only mountain, his mind kept returning to the lost equipment. He must see about the insurance as soon as he got home and replace it, he thought.

It was late when he returned to the pub. The bar was fairly full, but quiet, the men's voices low.

In the corner where James usually sat was a large man whom he had noticed before, usually the centre of a hard-drinking, loud-laughing knot of men. But he wasn't laughing now.

Tears trickled unashamedly down his rough, brown face to be brushed away with the back of a large hand. From time to time one of the other men would go across to him and put a pint of beer in front of him. For a moment a kind, heavy hand would rest on his shoulder. The man would nod his thanks and drink the beer.

'Who's that?' James asked the landlord.

'Tom Trenouth', was the answer, ''T'was his boy was drowned. Fair creased Tom, this have, poor bugger. Thought the world of his boy, Tom did.'

James went over to the man and sat down beside him.

'I am sorry about your boy,' he said gently.

'He were a lovely boy, our Tony,' the man said, taking a large handkerchief and mopping his face. James noticed he held a piece of binder twine in his other hand. Probably a black and white sheep dog under the seat, he thought.

The man blew his nose resoundingly. 'Didn't ought to be here really,' he said, 'But the missus is in some state, poor girl, and the dog crying and carrying on do make her worse, so I brought 'un out;' he tugged at the binder twine.

From under the seat crawled the small, rough-haired white dog. It looked up at James with large brown eyes, its short stump of a tail moved ever so slightly, tentatively wagging.

'Is this your boy's dog?' he asked incredulously.

'He were Tony's dog, all right,' the man said, looking down at the animal. The dog didn't take its eyes off James who sat, gazing back at it, with his hands on his knees. He turned one hand over and the dog's soft muzzle dropped into his palm as it shuffled nearer. With his other hand he pulled the red woollen cap out of his pocket and handed it wordlessly to the man.

'That's our Tony's cap,' the man said, 'Christmas present

from his Granny.' He buried his face in the red wool and his broad shoulders heaved.

James put his hand on the man's arm, pressing hard, until he recovered himself and took a pull at a fresh pint of beer which had been placed before him.

'You find this on the beach?' he asked shakily.

James nodded and they sat in silence. The dog stood up on its hind legs and put its little front paws on James' knee. It quivered and its small red tongue flipped out in the direction of his face.

'You want to take the dog?' the man asked, 'He ain't doing the missus no good. Someone'll have to have him. I'll have to put 'im down else.'

James cupped both hands round the dog's small furry face and looked into its brown eyes. He remembered the little boy on the beach, wearing the red woollen cap which the man now held. He remembered the open mouth yelling a soundless warning. He remembered the force of the summer sea five years ago, and the suck of the undertow as he lay face downwards in the surf yesterday, and tried to imagine what it would be like to be a small child fighting for its life in that maelstrom. He remembered Robert's quiet remark and Daphne's thoughtful look. Most of all he remembered the small urgent dog on the sand, barking, barking.

In all his life he had never felt so humble. He knew that in all his life he would never feel so grateful.

James felt the dog relax under the gentle stroking of his hands deep in the fur of its neck. It collapsed into a ball at his feet, asleep.

'Yes,' he said, 'I want to take the dog.'

XII

Felina

Christopher Lyndhurst sat in the car and watched the twilight deepen outside. The dog lay on the seat beside him, asleep now and mercifully relaxed, its beautiful lacerated head on his lap.

Gently Christopher stroked the feathered ears, taking care not to touch the deep scratches across the delicate muzzle, the vicious slash across the eyebrow which the vet had stitched. The fur under his hand was damp where the blood had been sponged away and smelt faintly of antiseptic.

There was no sound in the car except the deep gentle breathing. The twilight had become darkness now, and gradually the stroking hand slowed until it rested on the domed head protectively.

Christopher sat still, not wanting to disturb the animal, not wanting to go home, afraid of who or what he might find.

Christopher's first marriage was over almost before it had started. His wife had been killed in a car accident three weeks after the wedding. She was driving the car he had given her, a sleek and beautiful sports car. It was too fast and too powerful, but she had wanted it so much. He held himself responsible for her death and had thereafter retreated from close friendships of any kind, feeling them too great a responsibility.

His friends, in the country town where he lived and worked as an architect, accepted him for the pleasant, intelligent and somewhat withdrawn character that he was, thinking of him more as a bachelor than a widower, and his housekeeper ran his home for him capably and understandingly. He neither gave nor expected more than the affection of friendship and respect.

Then he found the dog.

He had been driving a friend to a golf course some distance away when they passed a sign at the end of a drive-way: 'Saluki Puppies For Sale'.

'What in heaven's name is a Saluki?' the friend had asked.

'Something like an Afghan hound, I think,' said Christopher, 'or is it one of those little fluffy things from Tibet?'

Neither was sure and, since they had time in hand, they turned the car and went back to where they had seen the sign.

Although Christopher had always liked dogs, and got on well with the retrievers and spaniels his friends kept, he had never particularly wanted to own one. The Salukis changed all that. He was immediately captivated by the sheer elegance of the adult dogs, their slim lissom shape, their feathered ears and tails, the grace with which they carried their beautifully shaped heads and moved on their narrow feet, and amused and enchanted by the leggy, awkward puppies.

The friend never got his game of golf. The rest of the afternoon was spent buying collar, lead, basket, rugs and puppy food, and in the evening Christopher drove home with an eager, quivering puppy beside him, feeling more alive, more involved, more actively happy than he had in years.

Christopher and the dog settled down together into the sort of close relationship that sometimes springs up between a basically lonely person and a sensitive animal. The dog's undemonstrative devotion seemed to fill a gap in his life of which he had been unaware and its needs were of paramount importance to him. His housekeeper, Mrs Carter, treated them both with indulgence, scolding them in much the same tone of voice for bringing mud into the kitchen, for eating too much or too little, for getting dog hair and cigarette-ash respectively all over the carpet. She confided to her friends that, whereas Mr Lyndhurst had never been a difficult man to look after, he laughed more and seemed friendlier and more relaxed since he got the dog: 'And a nicer sweeter-tempered animal than that dog you never came across,' she added.

During one summer about four years after getting the dog, Christopher attended a cocktail party at a neighbouring house. He arrived just after the 'new people' for whom the party was being given and his hostess flashed a welcoming smile at him and gestured towards the drinks table.

'Christopher dear, forgive me. I *must* introduce the Harringtons to everyone – be an angel and help yourself to a drink – and mingle. I think you know everyone except the Harringtons – oh, and a weird girl the Kents have brought,' and with another smile she turned to do her duty by the newcomers.

Christopher did as he was told and poured himself a drink, but allowed himself some minutes to survey the scene before launching himself into one of the nearby groups. What nice people these were, he thought, as he watched. The women, pretty and middle-aged, most of them, their faces animated, their voices eager, touching their newly-set hair with little self-conscious gestures, giving little screams as they backed into people or had their elbows jogged, making the usual small fusses about the difficulty of holding a drink, a handbag, a cigarette and trying to accept pieces of cheese and pineapple on a stick at the same time, the men rocking back on their heels, apologising for a spilt drink, talking to each other over the heads of their wives, eyes narrowed against cigarette smoke.

Christopher smiled, liking them, liking the way they played the cocktail party game according to the rules, this party almost identical to those that had been before and those that would follow, pretty pointless, quite harmless and rather nice.

But this party was not to be like any other.

Turning back to the table to pour himself another drink before joining a group of his golfing friends across the room he realized that he himself was being watched by the strangest and most beautiful woman he had ever seen.

She was standing in a group to Christopher's right, a group where the men's laughter suddenly seemed to boom a little too heartily, the women's chatter to be brittle and over-bright, a group to which she was contributing absolutely nothing, not a word, not a look, not the slightest interest.

The girl turned away and Richard could admire her at his leisure, although he felt she was aware of his scrutiny.

She was slim, almost to the point of leanness and yet her movements had a fluidity that made the slightest gesture beautiful. Her small creamy-skinned oval face was framed by dark hair and dominated by enormous eyes of the most pellucid blue Christopher had ever seen. She was wearing a simple dress of cream shantung silk and dark stockings and gloves. She had an air of calm about her which made the other women seem over-coloured and fussy, the men clumsy and awkward.

As he watched she turned her wide, blue unblinking gaze on him again, and very deliberately detached herself from the group and walked over to him.

'I'm Felina,' she said. Her deep voice was almost a purr.

Christopher's friends were at first amused, then alarmed and finally saddened by the way Felina spun her web of enchantment round him.

They were married a bare month after their first meeting and he seemed almost hypnotized by her.

She introduced an air of exotic luxury into the hitherto comfortable but unremarkable Georgian house where Christopher lived. Her sense of colour was superb and her knack of arranging flowers, ornaments and pictures against backgrounds which doubled their impact was extraordinary. Mrs Carter still ran the house calmly and efficiently, but kept almost entirely to the kitchen which remained much as it had always been. The rest of the house, she hinted darkly to her friends, didn't look as though it were meant to be lived in, but more like a picture from a glossy magazine.

'Beautiful of course,' she said. 'But it isn't home any more.'

There had been one tremendous hurdle that Christopher and Felina's marriage had to cope with. Felina hated dogs.

When Christopher first took her to his house the lovely, gentle dog, which had been his sole companion for so long, strolled across the drawing room to where she sat, waving its plumed tail gently in welcome, ready to lay its head on her lap.

It was the first time Christopher had seen the almost unnatural calm on Felina's face shattered. She drew her lips back from small, even, white teeth, gasping in horror as the dog approached her, and beat at its face with short striking movements of both hands. The bewildered animal backed away and went to stand by its master. It had never received anything but kindness and love in its life and was at a loss to understand the attack.

Christopher was dreadfully hurt, both for the dog and himself, but such was Felina's hold over him that even this could not disenchant him.

He stroked the dog's head and reassuring it, led it off to the kitchen, from whence Mrs Carter could afterwards be heard soothing it, her voice raised a little unnecessarily to enquire of herself, 'Someone not like *dogs*? In *this* house?'

The dog found itself spending more and more time in the kitchen and Mrs Carter was given more and more to enquiring, 'What he ever sees in that woman I don't know. Just you tell me what happiness she brings him?'

Other people were asking the same question among themselves. Gradually Christopher's friends had stopped coming to the house and gradually he had stopped asking them.

Sometimes Felina could be charming, using all her beauty and all her wit and grace to make a dinner party something to remember. But at other times she barely seemed to notice her guests, almost as though she found them beneath her contempt, and often would take herself off to her room upstairs with no word of explanation or excuse.

She spent hours in her room, made beautiful and luxurious by her genius for colour and texture, brushing her hair, doing her nails and generally attending to her immaculate grooming, or simply doing nothing at all, lying on the draped and cushioned bed, seeming to make her very languour an exquisite art.

Christopher was only occasionally allowed into her room. On these occasions she would create an ecstasy for him by her ardent and beautiful love making. She would wrap her supple sleek body round him, her deep voice purring endearments, seeming to exist for him alone, loving him almost savagely.

At other times if he tried to kiss her cheek or put his arm round her she would abruptly withdraw herself from him, seeming almost to spit with dislike as she told him to keep away from her. She would love and be loved when she wished and he soon realized he would do well to remember it.

Nevertheless, Christopher was so bewitched by her that he was willing to put up with anything, do all she asked, just so that he might be allowed to watch her, to be with her and to join in her unbridled passion when she felt so moved.

There was only one thing on which he stood firm. The dog.

Time and time again she had asked – demanded – that he get rid of it. Time and time again she had withheld herself from him for weeks when he refused.

And yet, hurt and bewildered as he was, he *did* refuse. He could not turn away the devotion of so long, could see no reason why he should as his love for the animal in no way diminished his love for his wife.

Felina and the dog rarely met, Mrs Carter saw to that, and Christopher still managed to spend a great deal of time with it when Felina was cocooned in her silken world upstairs, yet he knew she resented its very presence in the house.

On the few occasions when the dog took advantage of the kitchen door left ajar and Felina happened to be downstairs, she would go stiff with horror at the very sight of it, holding her hands in front of her as if to ward off an attack. The dog, sensing her utter dislike, would retreat to the comfort of Mrs Carter and the kitchen, the fur along its lean and lovely back rising.

Mrs Carter found things more and more difficult as time went by. She was too fond of Christopher to complain, but more than once he found her crying into the fur of the dog's neck, and gathered that Felina made a habit of summoning the housekeeper to find fault with some trifle to do with running the house.

With part of his mind he was aware that his comfortable happy life had been changed beyond recognition but with another part of his mind he knew that Felina, with her beauty, her strange charm for him, was something he could never do without.

One cold, early autumn evening, Christopher had been seeing to the repair of a fence at the far end of his extensive garden. The dog, having realized that no walk was forthcoming, and tired of sitting beside its master in the cold wind, had gone back to the house where Mrs Carter, hearing it scratch at the back door, had let it in.

She was busy lighting the fires in various rooms so that, if and when Felina should choose to come downstairs, she should have no cause to complain of the house being cold.

'Go to your basket, my love,' the woman told the dog. 'I've got one more bucket of coal to fetch from outside then I'll get your supper.'

The dog yawned and stretched and did as it was told, seeming not to have noticed the open door to the hall and Mrs Carter went out to the coal shed.

Christopher was walking up the path to the house, when he heard Mrs Carter's screams and started to run. He met the distraught woman rushing into the kitchen from the hall from which other screams, higher, more piteous, were coming. Pushing past the woman, he nearly fell over the bucket of spilt coal and righting himself, saw the dog. It was shrieking with pain, trying with its long front paws to wipe the streaming blood from its eyes and to reach him at the same time. Blinded, its usually sure supple feet slipped on the polished floor.

Christopher raced to the dog and gathered it into his arms. He held it very tightly, pressing its head against his cheek, its blood soaking his collar, and the shrieking gave way to long, shuddering whimpers.

Still clasping the dog he strode to the drawing room door and stopped dead.

'Felina!' he gasped.

The unmistakable blue eyes blazed pure hatred. As the Siamese cat started to advance menacingly towards him he could see blood on her mouth and claws.

XIII

Were There Ever Roses?

The village of St Melloran lay in a heavily-wooded valley, a picture-postcard group of cottages which seemed to slither down between the trees towards a small grey church, a school and a shop.

Celia Tolcarn stopped her car and got out to ask the way to the farm which was selling the slates. She was a tall woman in her mid-thirties with incredible red hair: it had none of the gold or ginger tones which most red hair had but was almost mahogany, rich and dark, and she wore it very short with a thick fringe from under which brown eyes now surveyed the pretty village with interest.

Although it was only some ten miles from where she lived Celia had very seldom been here before and she was enchanted by the compactness, the seclusion of the little settlement, so unlike the straggling villages she was more used to.

Her father had had a positive dislike of St Melloran, she remembered, saying the deep valley was claustrophobic and that it never saw the sun. He had preferred the open downland where they lived within sight and sound of the sea, and where, two years ago, he had died.

Celia's mother had died soon after her birth, of an accident about which her father would never speak. He had brought her up himself, with the aid of a devoted housekeeper, and taught her to share his love of the land he farmed and the things that lived and grew on it, to use her senses to the full and to enjoy each day as it came.

When he died Celia had found the big old house, where she and generations of Tolcarns had been born, had become an empty shell, a mausoleum, and had sold it and all the land that belonged to it, keeping only a small field on a gentle south-facing slope which ran down to the estuary. In this field she had had a house built for herself, exactly to her own design and using, wherever possible, old materials.

She described her house as being a modern hand in an old-fashioned glove; central-heating, double-glazing and a labour-saving kitchen, all were incorporated in the design, but the proportions of the house were traditional and the stone walls, granite lintels and rag-slate roof looked comfortable and appropriate in their surroundings.

Indoors the carefully selected pieces of old furniture from the big house and the cherished portraits of her father's family, whose faces she searched for a likeness to herself, looked at home in the large low rooms; the muted colours she had chosen for carpets and furnishings blending with the views of hills and sky and water to be seen through every window.

Now she was tackling the garden. There was to be a broad terrace in front of the house and she wanted old slate flag-stones with which to surface it. In the local newspaper she had seen a small advertisement of slates for sale at a farm near St Melloran and had decided to drive there at once to see them.

The village street was deserted except for two old ladies who had just come out of the shop. Celia walked over to them and asked the way to Pencoid Farm and, eager to help, they immediately began to argue with each other over which way she should go.

'Up over the hill, dear, and then turn right –'

'No, no! She'd be better to go along by the church, up through Biddick's wood and then turn left –'

'Whatever would she want to go that way for? Up over the hill would be quicker –'

Thanking them Celia got back into the car and started off again, smiling to herself and within a mile was quite sure she had taken a wrong turning somewhere. The lane was very narrow and, having climbed up steeply, was now going down hill; there were no houses where she could ask and no room to turn so she must go on.

As she drove she reflected on the misconceptions people had about Cornwall. They thought it had very few trees and yet here, only a few miles off the main road, was this great area of woodland with the lovely village she had just left embowered at its heart.

She was proud of being Cornish. There were Tolcarn tombstones in the churchyard near her old home going back to the sixteenth century, and the not very good, but deeply loved, portraits which had accompanied her to the new house, were of Cornish men and women who had, in all probability, never left their native county. Come to think of it she had done so very seldom herself, never tiring of its beauty and variation.

It was fun driving along the hitherto unknown road. The February afternoon was mild and grey, no wind, no sun but dry and with a very clear light.

There had been a lot of rain recently and water streamed down each side of the lane which led through scrubby woodland between high hedges brilliant with the copper-coloured foliage which clung to the stunted beeches and oaks all winter, with here the acid yellow of a few last-remaining ash leaves and there the crimson of a bramble-spray.

Turning a corner she saw a triangular road sign. 'Ford', it said. Celia was delighted. So many fords had been bridged over that one almost forgot what fun it had been to drive slowly through the shallow water, and it was nice to find one which had been left alone.

A stream in the valley bottom swirled through a gap in the hedge, spreading out in the shallow basin of the road to several times its original width, until, having to pull itself together again, it passed under a narrow footbridge and through another gap in the opposite hedge.

There were three muscovy ducks squatting in the lane at the far side of the ford and four more swimming fussily about in the stream, skimming the surface of the water with their red-knobbed beaks and quacking gently to themselves. Celia stopped to watch them, thinking them very like the old ladies in the village, comfortable and comforting as they bickered quietly in conversational tones. Behind them on a raised bank, and shrouded by trees, was a small cottage.

The cottage must once have been picturesque, but it was not now. It looked sodden and dank, its once white-washed walls stained with patches of mould and streaked with green where the blocked gutters leaked: what paint there had been on the small window frames and narrow door was colourless and peeling. Standing in its forlorn plot of dead grass and weeds, once no doubt a garden, it looked derelict, but Celia noticed a thin thread of smoke above one of its squat chimneys. Good! Someone was there and she could ask the way again.

Driving very slowly through the water, as much for the ducks' sake as for the car's brakes, she stopped, parked opposite the cottage and walked up the steep steps let into the bank.

On closer inspection the little house seemed even more dejected. Rags of curtains hung inside the dirty windows and the path was green and slimey from the constant dismal drip of the guttering. At the far end of the weed-choked patch of ground were the collapsed remains of bee-hives, keeping company with heaps of rusty tins and sticks of broken furniture.

She barely expected her tentative knock on the door to be answered, but after a long pause she heard movements from inside.

A key rattled in the lock and the door creaked open to reveal a tall old man. His collarless shirt was filthy and over it he wore a fusty knitted cardigan which hung, ragged and holey, almost to the knees of his ancient trousers. The man's hair was white and sparse and bleary grey eyes looked out of a haggard, wax-pale face.

Before Celia could apologize for disturbing him and ask her way to the farm the man uttered a cry. His long-nailed, dirty hands flew to his mouth and his eyes seemed to start from their sockets.

'Oh dear God!' he whispered. 'It's never you come back, Ruby girl, is it?'

Celia was completely taken aback.

'I beg your pardon?' she said inadequately, and was about to explain her visit when the old man started to cry, tears pouring from the already swimming eyes.

'Oh God, oh God,' he sobbed, 'Haven't I suffered enough? I can't stand any more. No more, Ruby, no more. T'is too late now to come begging my pardon for what you done to me.'

He put up both hands as though to ward her off and at the same time to shield himself from the sight of her. He pushed the creaking door shut, and Celia found herself facing the patchy, peeling paint. Once more the key rattled in the lock.

She retreated to the car as fast as she could, feeling shaken by the encounter. Sitting still for a few seconds to recover she looked up at the cheerless cottage and a wave of pity for the old man swept over her.

Why was he all alone, as she was sure he was? Who had he mistaken her for? Should she go back and try to explain? Try to help? No. It would only make matters worse. And besides, she thought, pulling herself together, she must find this farm with the slates.

A little further up the hill, out of the wood now and in more open country, she saw a man cleaning out a ditch and was directed to the farm she wanted. Within half an hour she had arranged with the owner of the slates for them to be delivered to her house, had written a cheque and was on her way home.

That night in her comfortable bed in the spacious bedroom she had designed for herself she slept badly, troubled by dreams of the sombre cottage and the sad old man. Every detail seemed oddly disturbing; the ducks, the swirling water, all were redolent of gloom and doom and led up to a crescendo of nightmare as the creaking door opened.

It was with thankful relief that she struggled awake from the clutches of the dream to find herself in her own beautiful room, the heavy silk curtains open at the wide window to reveal the field at the bottom of the half-made garden and the waters of the broad estuary placidly flowing to the sea.

She sat up, still distraught, and gazed round at familiar objects, her flower paintings on the eau-de-nil walls, the deep-piled white carpet, her hair brushes and scent bottles on the rose-wood dressing table. She ran her fingers through her short red hair and shook her head to rid herself of the terribly disturbing images that had plagued her sleep.

There was a lot of work to be done in the garden-to-be and Celia took advantage of the mild dry spell of weather to plant roses, shrubs and specimen trees and to plan exactly how it would one day look.

She was going to plant all the old-fashioned flowers that she had known from childhood in the large rambling garden at the old house and which her father had taught her how to cultivate, but weaving among her memories of the gentle, kindly man and her visions of how the garden would be, other pictures crept unbidden into her mind of the dank little garden patch in front of the dejected cottage by the ford. Had it once been pretty and well tended? Had flowers and vegetables once flourished in it? Did bees from the derelict hives once gather honey from sweet-william, bergamot and candy tuft? Were there ever roses?

Had the old man once been young and strong, proud to care for his little house and bit of land? Who was Ruby and what had she done to him?

She cursed herself for thinking so much about it, for minding so much. After all, one fleeting encounter with a sad, mad old man should not be so important to her.

But the memory of that encounter kept drifting into her mind and almost every night the dream came back so that she dreaded going to sleep. She would tire herself out in the garden during the day and then read in bed for as long as she could keep her eyes open, but to no avail.

She had friends to dinner and accepted every invitation to go out, but still the images swam into her mind, ducks, swirling water, the drip of the gutters, and the horror in the man's grey eyes, over and over again.

The slates should have arrived within a few days of Celia's visit to the farm but they did not. She began to be irritated by the farmer's delay in delivering them; after all she had paid for them and the work in the garden would be that much easier when they were in place.

The farmer was not on the telephone and her questioning postcards went unanswered so Celia decided she must drive over to see what might be holding things up.

She drove straight to the farm and was greeted apologetically by the farmer. The lorry he was going to borrow had broken down, but it had been repaired now.

'I'll get they slates over to you first thing tomorrow, and that's a promise!' he said.

Mollified, Celia got back in the car, and on impulse decided to try and find the desolate cottage again. It would be rather like biting on an aching tooth to see if it still hurt, she thought wryly, but on the other hand perhaps seeing it again in reality might exorcise the melancholy memories that haunted her.

She took a detour round the pretty village so that she could approach the cottage from the same direction as before, and as she drove down the steep lane towards the ford her hands gripped the steering wheel a little tighter and her heart began to pound.

The muscovy ducks were sitting in a row on the footbridge preening their feathers with their beaks and shaking their tails. The small chuckling noises they made should have been endearing but Celia found them menacing, like malicious laughter. There was less water in the stream now but the noise of the car's tyres driving slowly through it sounded sibilant and sinister.

The cottage seemed almost to be waiting for her. It was just as she remembered it, dreamt of it. It was steeped in loneliness and neglect, the dirty bleared windows seeming to film over as she looked at them, like the eyes of a dying animal, all hope gone.

She had stopped the car on the opposite side of the lane and was gazing at the cottage through the open window, one arm lying along the sill, when suddenly she heard a footstep behind her and her wrist was gripped by a dirty hand. Horny finger nails dug into her skin and shock and pain made her cry out as she looked up into the old man's deathly pale face, so close to hers that she could smell the musty, unwashed stench of him.

'Why d'you come here, Ruby girl?' he whispered. 'Haven't you treated me cruel enough already? Do you come back to gloat over what you've brought me to? Dear God, why can't you leave me alone!'

His eyes looked wild, the pupils tiny in the pale irises, and two patches of red mottled his yellowish cheeks as he let go of her wrist and reached into the car with both hands, reaching with clawing fingers for her throat.

Celia switched on the ignition and let the clutch in with a jerk, the movement of the car nearly knocking the old man off his feet. As she accelerated erratically up the hill she glanced over her shoulder in time to see him regain his balance and raise both hands to the sky as if in anguished entreaty. She was crying hysterically and the car scraped the banks at the side of the lane as she drove, desperate to get out of the wooded valley.

Celia became ill. She was weary and listless; too tired and jaded to work in the garden, too restless to find comfort in her beautiful house, too frightened of what her dreams might hold to sleep. Eventually she called a doctor.

He was a young man, new to the district. He listened sympathetically to the careful recital of her symptoms and prescribed a tranquillizer, suggesting she had been working too hard in the garden. He took some sleeping pills from his bag and said she should take one at bedtime.

The consultation over, Celia asked if he had time for coffee as she was about to make some.

'I should like that very much,' the man said, 'I have no surgery tonight and no more calls to make.'

He wandered round the room admiring an ornament here, a picture there, while she switched on the percolator and set the tray.

When they were sitting over their coffee Celia asked him how far his practice extended.

'Does it take in St Melloran?' she asked.

'Yes, indeed it does,' he replied, 'I have a surgery there once a week; I was there this morning in fact.'

Casually she mentioned having seen the strange old man at the cottage by the ford, and the young doctor leant forward.

'You must mean Jack Tregaskis,' he said. 'How odd that you should mention him! He was not my patient and indeed I'd never heard of him until today,' he went on. 'He drowned himself last night in the stream, quite deliberately lying face down in about four inches of water. He appears to have had quite a brainstorm because he killed a lot of ducks which lived in the stream before killing himself: their bodies were all over the lane.'

Celia's first illogical thought was for the poor, innocent ducks. She sat quite still for some seconds and then busied herself with the coffee pot, her hands shaking.

'How terribly sad,' she said faintly.

'Yes, the doctor agreed, accepting his refilled cup. 'It seems that he had quite a dramatic history. As a young man he had a prosperous small-holding, had the prettiest little garden for miles around, too. He used to win prizes at all the local shows for flowers and vegetables, oh, and honey. It seems he kept bees. But, alas, he had a very beautiful wife and that's where the tragedy lay.' He took a sip of coffee. 'Would you mind very much if I had a cigarette?' he asked. 'I allow myself an occasional one when I'm off-duty.'

'Of course not,' Celia said, having regained a little of her composure and, getting up to fetch a silver box, 'Don't smoke your own. Have one of these.'

His cigarette lit, the young man went on.

'Yes, his beautiful wife had a roving eye, apparently. Left him for a rich young farmer she'd met at a show. It quite turned the poor man's mind, he was never the same again: he got rid of his land, let his cottage fall into the most dreadful state and became a sort of hermit, a recluse.'

'How terribly sad,' Celia said again, her eyes clouded with distress for the man she had met only twice but so dramatically.

'Yes, it's a sad story but there's worse to come,' the young doctor said, putting down his cup. 'It appears the woman had a child rather suspiciously soon after leaving him and no one was too sure who it belonged to,' he stood up, preparing to take his leave. 'She didn't have long to enjoy her child or her new husband though. Tregaskis saw her in the street in Bodmin about a year later, followed her home and killed her.'

'Killed her?' Celia's voice was barely audible.

'Yes, strangled her, I think, I'm not sure, but anyway he pleaded diminished responsibility and only did twenty years or so in Broadmoor for it. I think it was Broadmoor, but it was a fairly garbled story I heard. The village was buzzing with it as you can imagine.' He reached for his bag, 'Look, I really must go!'

Celia helped him on with his coat and went with him to the door.

'Yes, very odd that you should mention Jack Tregaskis today,' he said stepping out into the February dusk. 'Don't over-do the gardening now, and get that prescription made up tomorrow!'

Celia took the sleeping pills the doctor had left with her and that night she slept without dreaming.

She woke in the morning and gazed about the small, stuffy bedroom crowded with heavy, ugly furniture, for a few seconds before glancing at the sleeping man beside her, his fair hair tousled on the pillow, his clear pale skin slightly flushed, strong arms flung outside the bedclothes.

She got out of the high brass bed and walked to the tiny window, drawing aside thin cotton curtains to look at the garden below. It was summer and bees from the gleaming white hives over by the hedge hummed in the roses that wreathed the window and sampled the sweet-smelling cottage flowers in the crowded borders. From the ford below the cottage she could hear the ripple of the stream and the gentle quacking of her muscovy ducks.

Her hands idly loosened the great mass of her hair from its plaits and started to brush it. The incredible hair, dark red, ruby-red, from which she had got her nickname, cascaded over her shoulders.

She glanced again at the man in the bed: his eyes were open

now, keen grey eyes watching her with adoration. He stretched his arms towards her but she ignored him. She was leaving him today and she hoped she never saw him again until the day she died.

XIV

Sixpence

It was a funny thing that, having lived next door to Bonython House for ten years, Evelyn Trelevan had never felt this way about it before.

When the Halworthys, Joan and Arthur and their three noisy, friendly children, had lived there she had been in and out nearly every day and the atmosphere had always been welcoming and normal; but now she had only to set foot inside the front door for a deep depression to descend upon her.

She became inexplicably weary and there was an ache in the pit of her stomach; her limbs felt leaden and her mind was clouded with a dejected yearning for something she did not understand. She just wanted to go home.

Perhaps she was going down with some mild sickness, she thought, but why should she only notice the enervating symptoms here?

Bonython House, and its semi-detached mirror-image, Carminow House where Evelyn lived, had been built at the beginning of the nineteenth century when the Cornish fishing village of Strode was starting to expand and become a fashionable little sea-side town. There was a whole row of semi-detached houses built at the same time, marching along the road above the sandy beach, four-square and well-proportioned, setting their good, plain faces to the sea.

Living with her solicitor husband in Carminow House it had always been Evelyn's dream to buy its neighbour and run the two as a guest house, so, when the Halworthys had decided to emigrate to Australia, she and Bill had been given first refusal, and it was now theirs.

Evelyn had been very fond of the Halworthys but their taste

in interior decoration was far from matching her own. Only last year they had recarpeted the stairs in what to her was the most unhappy orange.

'Right the way up to the top floor!' they had said, proudly, and Evelyn had hidden her amused horror and enthused with them over the dreadful carpet. Now it was hers, part of the fittings which went with the house, and she hated it, although seeing entirely the point Bill had made that, since there was so much to be done to make the two houses one, it would be madness to take up what was virtually a new carpet to buy another.

Anyway it couldn't be just the carpet that depressed her, Evelyn thought, gazing down at its brilliant pile in the sunshine that streamed through the skylight above, as she crossed the first floor landing. She turned and forced herself to smile at the two workmen coming up behind her, willing herself to feel better, as she started up the last flight of stairs which led to the top of the house.

To make the three attic rooms suitable for guests it had been decided to build out a flat roof at the back, thus giving more headroom. This was Bill's province really, Evelyn had not even been up to the top floor before, but he was at the office, and during the first stages of the alterations the workmen had found something that they wanted her to see.

'Nasty thing happened in this house a long time ago,' the older of the two men, Mr Backway, said as he puffed up the stairs. 'My Granny used to come in to fetch the washing once a week and I remember her telling me when I was a lad …'

Evie was so weary she could barely lift one numb, aching foot in front of the other to climb the stairs. Her too-small, broken shoes sounded hollow and lonely on the uncarpeted treads and she had difficulty in lifting up the skirt of the limp, black, cotton dress, made for a much larger girl, and at the same time holding the tin candle-stick in one small, chapped hand, while the other clutched the wooden bannister rail to help her climb to the mean little room under the slates which, for the next few hours, would be her refuge from grinding, back-breaking work.

She lifted her head and gazed through the bleared skylight at the few frosty stars snapping in the winter sky and her thin shoulders shook in a convulsive shudder under the shabby black material which covered them. She was cold right through to her immature bones and achingly hungry, but the weariness almost obliterated her other discomforts and the thought of being able to lie down at last, to sink into exhausted sleep, gave her the strength to drag herself up the last few steps: the thought of sleep and the silver sixpence which she had wrapped in a scrap of paper and hidden in her apron pocket urged her on.

'Madam! Mrs Trelevan!'

Evelyn opened her eyes to find Mr Backway bending over her as she lay on the stairs where she had fallen, his kindly red face creased with concern.

'My goodness, you gave us a turn, going down like that,' he said, 'Here, Jim,' turning to his young assistant hovering a step or two below him, 'Give me a hand to get her up, will you?'

She half knelt, half lay, the orange stair carpet beneath her cheek; one knee smarted badly and her ribs ached where she had fallen against a tread.

'What happened?' she gasped. 'Oh how silly of me, I must have tripped.'

The two men helped her gently to her feet and she swayed, clutching the bannister rail.

'If you don't mind,' she said faintly, 'I'll come up and look at what you've found a little later. Why don't we all go next door and have a cup of tea? I must admit I feel a bit shaken.'

The men could well believe it; she had taken a nasty fall, and, clucking solicitously, they shepherded her downstairs, out of the front door of Bonython House and in at her own.

'A nice strong cup'll soon put you right, madam,' Mr Backway said when they reached the kitchen. 'Put the kettle on for you, shall I?'

They sat round the table, when the tea was made, and drank the steaming liquid.

'Oh, that's so much better!' Evelyn said, quickly recovering her usual ebullience. 'Come on, we'll go and look at what you've found now,' and together they set off once more.

The silver sixpence in Evie's apron pocket was the most valuable coin she had ever found. On her errands to the shops for Cook she always carefully searched the pavements and gutters. On the all too rare occasions when she found a penny or a ha'penny she swooped on it, and when she went to bed at night would add it to the meagre collection she kept in an old boot-polish tin hidden between a rafter and the slates of the roof in her cold, bleak, little room.

Waking and sleeping she dreamed of running away, of going home to the little village where everyone knew her and cared about her; but she knew it was a long way away and that she could never manage the journey without money to buy food.

Her wages, only eight shillings a year, her so-called board and keep making up the rest, she had never set eyes on; Cook had taken possession of them, ostensibly for safe-keeping but in reality spending them on drink, so she had to rely on what she found in the street to realize her dream.

The people of Strode were careful with what little money they had and it was very seldom she found a penny in the gutter, but today when sweeping under the Master's dressing table she had found the sixpence and her heart had leapt with joy. With the little store of coppers it meant that she had over a shilling now, and surely that would be enough!

Evie had been working at Bonython House for nearly two years and every day had been a misery. Brought up as she had been in a crowded fisherman's cottage with a new brother or sister every year she had never been alone, but when her father had been drowned at sea her mother could not support her children on the little money she earned by taking in sewing and Evie, the eldest, had been sent to the poorhouse in the neighbouring town of St Kenelm Major.

Although her new life had been grim and cold and she was bitterly home-sick, at least she had had company at the poor-house, sleeping at night in a long room with twenty or so other girls and working with them during the day: but it was the practice of the establishment to send the strongest and most presentable girls into service and Evie had been packed off, her few belongings in a tiny bundle, to Strode, a long, rattling, wearisome coach-journey away.

Never before had she been inside such a well-to-do place as Bonython House, and never before had she been so lonely or worked so hard.

Cook, large, mean-minded and beady-eyed, was the only other servant kept, and had she not been party to the Mistress's weakness for gin, smuggling the full bottles in and the empty ones out, she would never have kept her position. She was lazy, greedy and malicious and as fond of her gin as was her mistress, doing as little as she could and leaving everything to the maid of all work.

Getting up at four o'clock in the morning the thin child had first to black-lead the range in the kitchen before lighting it to heat the water which had to be carried, laboriously and dangerously, up two flights of stairs to the bedrooms. From then on she cleaned, scoured, scrubbed, waited at table, fetched and carried, ran errands and washed up endlessly in the shallow cloam sink from under which darted the black beetles which infested the basement.

Cook, with an eye to her own well-being, saw to it that a succulent piece was carved off every joint for herself before it was carried to the dining-room, that an ample helping of the choicest vegetables and the richest puddings was kept back for her delectation, but Evie never had so much as a mouthful.

Once she had taken a piece of left-over chicken from the mistress's plate as she carried it down to the kitchen but she could not swallow it in time and Cook had made her spit it out, had caught her a swinging blow across the face and called her a thief. The woman seemed to have eyes in the back of her head, for all that she was very rarely sober, and should Evie so much as palm a crumb of pastry, a morsel of potato, to her mouth, Cook would see her and the same epithet, the same blows, were hurled at her.

Sometimes she was allowed to scrape the remains of semolina or bread and milk from the children's bowls, but should they have left any scraps of meat on their plates these

were scraped into the dog's dish by Cook, regarding the
hungry Evie with malicious satisfaction as she did so, and the
child's normal diet was stale bread with, on occasion, the
merest scrape of butter, and weak tea made from boiling the
used tea-leaves which were emptied from the silver teapot.

She was seldom warm, her gnawing hunger was never
satisfied and she was worked savagely from dawn till dark, but
it was the loneliness that seared her friendly little soul, the
lovelessness that broke her affectionate little heart.

The house, not large except by Evie's standards, was full of
people. The Master, out all day and oblivious of the scrawny
little servant when, her mousy hair hidden under a white cap
and her thin body enveloped in a large apron, she handed him
his food at dinner: the Mistress, pale and lack-lustre of eye,
professedly ailing, although in reality half stupid with drink,
terrified of Cook who kept her guilty secret since it suited her
to do so, and too far gone ever to notice the skivvy's small,
pinched face: the children, away at school a lot of the time and
too grand to acknowledge the lowly child of their own age who
cleaned their shoes and made their beds and fetched and
carried for them when they were at home; and Cook herself
who reigned in the dim basement like a fat, greasy spider in its
web, her gin bottle at her elbow, a plate of filched delicacies on
her lap, who never addressed the girl unless it was to accuse
her of her own vice of theft and to mutter an oath as she aimed
a blow at her head, demanding that she work harder. No one
ever actually spoke to Evie at all, no one smiled, no one even
looked at her, except, possibly, the woman who came in once a
week to fetch the washing but she was too frightened of Cook
to do more than glance curiously at her.

Her loneliness was absolute and she could only bear it by
dreaming of the day when she had collected enough money to
run away, to somehow find her way back to the crowded
cottage where poverty and lack of space seemed to matter not
at all, so steeped in love and companionship had it been.

Now, with the sixpence tucked into the corner of her apron
pocket, the longed-for day of escape had miraculously arrived.
She would go tomorrow! She would get up even earlier than
usual, would take some bread from the big crock in the pantry

and leave the house, getting clear of the town before Cook came grumbling and scratching down the stairs to discover her gone.

At the thought of the woman's rage Evie shuddered again and tripped over the trailing edge of her too long frock, falling forward across the stairs. She dropped the tin candle holder in an effort to save herself and the sharp clatter as it hit the uncarpeted wood, together with the thud of her falling, seemed to reverberate through the silent house; she held her breath, her heart racing, not noticing yet the smarting knee and bruised ribs in her terror that someone would come to investigate the noise.

It was past ten o'clock and Cook had creaked and swayed her way upstairs an hour ago, leaving Evie with seemingly endless chores to do in preparation for the morning; the Master was out playing whist at a friend's house but the Mistress had long since retired to her room where Evie imagined her lolling against the lace-trimmed pillows in the high brass bedstead; the children had been put to bed some hours ago. Silence fell again, no light flared in the blackness that the extinguished candle-end had left, no door opened. It seemed that the noise of her fall had disturbed no one and she picked herself up, shaken but thankful, feeling for the candle-stick and stealthily making her way up the last few stairs and into her tiny attic bedroom.

The room was little more than a cupboard. The dormer window showed a square of night sky and the rising moon gave a thin, grey glimmer which seemed to accentuate the frosty cold, washing the narrow iron bedstead with its thin mattress and its inadequate threadbare blanket in dim, grim light, the splintery floor boards and the underside of the slate roof gleaming bleakly pale; there was no comfort there but nevertheless it was the child's haven.

Pushing the door to, afraid to fasten it for fear of noise, she went down on her bruised knees by the small, hard bed and took the sixpence from her apron pocket. It gleamed and sparkled in the chilly light and fixing her eyes on it Evie prayed.

'Please God help me,' she whispered. 'Help me to find my

way home. Help me to find my mother and my brothers and sisters again. Forgive me for taking the sixpence; I know it isn't rightly mine, but no one won't miss it, or they'd have looked for it. I've never had no wages, Cook took 'em, so make *her* pay the sixpence back ...'

Suddenly the door was flung open and the dejected little room was bathed in yellow candle light.

'There, Madam!' Cook's voice was triumphant, 'There's the sixpence! She's not only a lazy slut but a thief as well, like I said!' She strode across to the child cowering by the bed, leaving the mistress leaning limply against the door in her pale peignoir. Setting her candle stick on the floor she grabbed Evie by the shoulder with one huge hand, pointing to the sixpence where it lay on the bed with the other.

'I put that sixpence under the Master's dressing table this morning just to test her, to show her up for what she is!'

Evie's thin body was shaken, not only by Cook's cruel hand, but by a succession of emotions; horrified guilt at being caught with the sixpence, abject terror of Cook's rage, and despair as the vision of her journey home seemed about to be wiped out. The sixpence glistened on the bed, as far away now as she cringed in Cook's grasp as though it had been one of the frosty stars; but something else glistened in the light from the candle burning directly below it, the shiny underside of the boot polish tin as one edge of it protruded from between the rafter and the slate in the roof, and it caught Cook's eye.

'What's that?' she roared, pointing to it, 'More of what doesn't belong to her, I'll be bound!'

Still holding the terrified child the woman turned to look at her mistress for approbation and was rewarded with the slackly nodding head of one who does not fully understand what is going on but knows what is expected of her.

'Disgraceful,' she murmured in a slurred voice, 'Yes, Cook, quite disgraceful.'

Suddenly, wiping out all the other emotions, Evie was filled with fury. Taking advantage of Cook's momentarily turned head she sank her teeth into the back of the fat hand that held her, biting hard and deep. Cook howled in agony and released her, and the child snatched the glinting coin from the bed and, pushing past her bewildered mistress, fled from the mean little room. Her small feet in their broken shoes hardly touched the stairs as she ran down to the first floor landing, but as she rounded the sharp turn to begin the lower flight she caught her ankle on the bannisters and fell: righting herself, holding her trailing black skirts high, she continued her head-long descent, but Cook, blood pouring from her bitten hand and red rage suffusing her vicious little eyes, had gained on her during those few stumbling seconds, and she aimed a blow at the child's head.

Evie was halfway down the last flight of stairs, within sight of the front door, its fanlight letting in the glow of the street lamps, when, with all the force of her beefy arm behind it, the huge woman's hand caught the back of her neck.

For a second which seemed like eternity her whole being was filled with pain, her brain seemed to explode in a red fog which spread all round her, blotting out vision and thought, as her little body, lifted off its feet by the lethal blow, crashed down onto the floor in the hall.

She lay, her neck broken and blood pouring from her mouth to spread in a black stain across the Turkish rug, soaking into the oak boards beneath, while Cook stood over her, still ranting and raving but with a note of uncertainty in her coarse voice now as she regarded the lifeless child. One small, work-roughened hand lay with its palm uppermost, that palm marked with a red circle from where she had clutched the precious sixpence. The small coin rolled across the hall and vanished in a crack under the skirting board.

Once more Evelyn entered the front door of Bonython House and once more depression engulfed her, for all the cheerful chatter of the two workmen.

Mr Backway told Jim to prepare the hall for them to start cutting a connecting door through the party wall the next day.

'That'll be our next job when we've done the roof,' he said. 'Mrs Trelevan won't want to be traipsing in and out of front doors when the autumn comes and the weather gets nippy. You take the carpet up, there's a good chap, and I'll be down again just so soon as I've shown madam what we found,' and he started up the stairs behind Evelyn.

'Now you watch your step this time, my lady,' he said, mock-sternly, 'We can't have you falling again.'

Evelyn took a firm hold of the bannister rail and kept her eyes steadily on the dreadful orange carpet as she ascended and, although nausea and near panic brought beads of sweat to her forehead, she gritted her teeth and carried on with determination, making a mental note to see her doctor in the morning. Eventually she arrived at the top of the house with Mr Backway panting along behind her.

Together they looked into the three rooms which the Halworthy children had used, where parts of the roof had already been removed. The sunlight filtered through chinks in the temporary tarpaulin covering, making dusty shafts of gold.

For all the cheerful posters on the walls and the sunshine Evelyn felt her skin creep as she stood looking round her. Her nostrils were filled with the smell of stale, greasy cooking, of foul breath, and she glanced over her shoulder, certain that there was someone behind her, someone malign and menacing, whose presence made it impossible to take in what the builder was saying to her.

'What is it that you found, Mr Backway?' she asked, desperate to be gone.

'Ah!' said the old man, 'that's in here.' He led the way out to the landing again and turned to a fourth door.

'Not much more than a cupboard, this isn't, where the watertank is. It's never had a ceiling put in.'

He opened the door and Evelyn looked into the small space almost entirely filled by the large, square, galvanized iron tank, and she was suddenly bitterly cold. Her feet hurt and her hands were numb and she could hardly see in the faint grey light.

She went towards the small bed, her hand seeking the tiny parcel deep in her apron pocket. Suddenly a yellow light flared, and, as Mr Backway followed her into the cramped space and pointed to a rusty tin wedged between a rafter and the slates, terror, despair and total misery swamped her mind.

She must have staggered and Mr Backway steadied her with a hand on her shoulder, but she turned her head sharply, almost as though she would bite him, the old man thought afterwards, and pushing him aside fled from the room and down the stairs.

She ran, tripping and stumbling, a salt taste on her lips and sheer terror in her heart. She must get out of the house! Must get out!

Turning swiftly on the first floor landing she caught her ankle on the bannisters and fell, righting herself at once, and Mr Backway coming down behind her as fast as he could, his face aghast at her sudden headlong flight, nearly caught her up: but it was not Mr Backway from whom she ran; the feet thundering down behind her, at first on bare boards and then on thinly carpeted stairs, were not those of the small, wiry man who smelt of tobacco and sawdust and old tweed coat but were those of a larger person, a bulky, dangerous person who smelt of stale sweat and grease, and whose breath reeked of gin, a person of whom she was mortally afraid.

She was halfway down the last flight now, in sight of the front door, in sight of freedom, when Mr Backway, desperately trying to save her with clutching hands as she hurtled forward, touched the back of her neck and she seemed no longer even to try to keep her balance.

An eternity of pain, totally unrelated to the old man's efforts to save her, suffused her mind and body and she fell down the last few steps and into the outstretched arms of Jim who had run, horrified, to the foot of the stairs.

She lay unconscious against Jim's chest, so pale that the two men thought her dead. Gently they laid her on the bare floor boards from which the orange carpet had been rolled back, stroking the wild hair from her cold forehead and anxiously looking for a sign of life. A faint pulse fluttered in her neck.

'Thank God,' breathed the older man, mopping his streaming face with a large handkerchief. 'It was a mercy you was there, Jim, she'm bound to have killed herself, else.'

They knelt beside her, watching her face. Jim took off his jacket and, folding it, placed it tenderly beneath her head where it lay on the stained boards.

'What's she got in her hand?' he whispered.

As he spoke the fingers of her clenched hand uncurled, showing that it contained nothing; but the palm was marked with a small, deeply indented red circle as though she had been holding a round object, a coin perhaps.

'Funny that,' Jim said. 'Look what I found when I ripped out the skirting board where the door's to be,' and from the breast pocket of his grubby sports shirt he produced a sixpence and gave it to his boss.

Mr Backway looked closely at it.

'That's an old one, Jim,' he said thoughtfully, 'Victorian, looks like,' and on impulse he placed it in Evelyn's limp hand where it lay on the red mark cut into her palm.

'Well I never,' he went on, as though to himself. 'Well I never,' and her fingers closed over it as her eyes opened.

She stirred, raising herself on one elbow and smiling uncertainly at the two men.

'Oh no!' she said, looking round her disbelievingly, 'I didn't fall again, did I? Whatever is the matter with me?'

The men assured her that indeed she had fallen and given them the fright of their lives.

She struggled to her feet with their help and looked curiously at the bare floor boards. She shuddered as she noticed a faint brownish stain which spread across the foot of the stairs where she had lain, and turned impulsively to the workmen.

'Could you take up those floorboards and replace them?' she asked. 'It was all so sad and so long ago. I don't want to remember it any more.'

She opened her clenched fingers and looked at the sixpence lying on her palm without surprise as though she had known it was there.

Mr Backway had taken a small, round tin from his pocket.

'Give me the tin,' she said gently, and when he had handed it to her she opened it and dropped the small silver coin onto the few coppers it held. She stirred the coins with her finger, counting them.

'I can go home now,' she said.

XV

Little Grey Home in the West

Number 10 Treveth Terrace was doomed.

Its owner, John Jago, had known it for years, but this morning's post had brought him an envelope bearing the County Council's stamp in which was a compulsory purchase order. The house was to be pulled down to make way for a ring-road. John heaved a sigh of relief and read the letter again. The purchase price was not generous, and no doubt the owners of the other houses in the terrace would be up in arms about it, but to John the price was unimportant. The fact that the house was to be demolished was all that mattered.

Number 10 was the last house in a short row, its blank end wall showing that originally the terrace was to have been longer. There seemed no reason why it should not have been extended to twice its present length over what was a roughly circular area of sour grass, dotted with heaps of half-burnt rubbish, old prams and sodden mattresses.

People said variously, half-remembering stories they had been told, that the speculator who built them had run out of money, that he had died horrendously, that the bedrock forming the foundations on which the other houses were built had ended abruptly and that building further would have been unwise.

John had done a great deal of research into the history of Treveth Terrace and found that all these stories, and a great many more, were true.

The terrace had been built during the last quarter of the nineteenth century by a far-sighted local builder who realized that when the railway had probed its way to the tiny, hitherto inaccessible town of Carveen it would abandon its previous role of fishing and farming community and become a watering place.

The builder had bought the land, known for hundreds of years as Treveth, for a song and the row of small stone-built houses was the first of many to radiate from the scatter of houses grouped round the church where the cliffs dipped down to the natural harbour.

The town of Carveen had prospered since then, although there were many who mourned its changed face. The small cliff castle, the *caer vean* from which it took its name, had for centuries been no more than undulating ridges in the turf of the headland, and now a vast hotel had been built on its site. Boarding houses had sprung up along the cliffs to east and west of the harbour, most of the original houses and cottages had long since given way to shops and offices and, now that the railway which had brought its first affluence had been abandoned, the cars which flooded in each summer choked its narrow streets.

Treveth Terrace was lost in modern development. Red brick villas rose in front and behind it looking out of place in this stone county, they themselves over-shadowed in their turn by concrete and plate-glass buildings.

The sour grass area beyond Number 10's blank wall remained unbuilt on. A chain grocery store backed on to it, as did a large garage and a block of flats, the high buildings keeping the sunlight from it. It was used as a dumping ground and occasional car park.

The town council had at last decided to demolish the terrace and, after years of experimenting with one-way streets and roundabouts, in a final attempt to alleviate the weight of traffic through the town, make a ring-road where it and its red brick opposite numbers stood.

Number 10 had stood empty for fifteen years. The other nine houses were all in good order. One had its sturdy stone bay removed and a shop window put in, the others did a thriving bed and breakfast trade in the summer. They were nice, honest little houses, the warm grey local stone giving them an air of permanence, and their brightly painted front doors put one in mind of dolls' houses.

All except Number 10. The paint on its front-door had bleached and blistered in many summer suns and winter gales untouched. Its windows, some of them having fallen prey to small boys' stones, were either boarded up or the glass filthy and opaque. Its tiny wall-enclosed garden boasted nothing but matted grass and nettles. If one looked carefully at the blank end wall a great crack could be seen, skilfully mended but sending the back wall slightly out of true. An elegant iron S, on the front wall, corresponding with one at the back, showed where a tie-bar had been inserted.

Dozens of people had wanted to buy or rent the house. The owners of Number 9 wanted to knock a way through the party wall to make the two houses into one, but John had turned down all offers.

The people in the red brick villas opposite, not numbered these, but with names like Peace Haven, Cricklewood and St Hilary, complained through their councillors to John, the absentee landlord, that its dilapidated appearance was an eyesore, but he dare not employ anyone to renovate it, even superficially, in case that malevolent something locked into its fabric should be disturbed.

The first owner of Number 10 was John Jago's grandfather, Richard.

Having worked hard all his life he was pleased and proud to buy the trim little house and in it to install his wife, Mary, and their son William who was to become John's father.

Richard saw to it that William received a good education in the small school in the town run by two indigent gentlewomen, and when in due course Mary presented him with three little girls, the two eldest were also sent to learn their lessons under the ladies' gentle guidance.

The fortunes of the Jago family seemed set fair, William by now a solicitors' clerk, two little girls at school and a babe in arms, when the first intimation of evil befell the house.

One morning Mary Jago was preparing some soup for her husband and herself to eat at dinner-time, the babe sleeping peacefully in her cradle, when the ground seemed to shudder and lurch under her feet. Grabbing at the kitchen mantelpiece to steady herself, she saw to her horror an ugly crack appear in the end wall, tearing the paper and exposing the stone as plaster fell into the room. At the same time the flagstones in the corner of the floor tilted crazily, unbalancing the table which crashed, sending crockery, knives and spoons hurtling across the room.

Richard, who had been in the front room, raced into the kitchen to find his wife still clutching the mantelpiece, her face contorted with fear and revulsion, and he was at once almost overcome, as was she, by the most appalling stench. The vile smell undoubtedly came from the dark space disclosed beneath the tilted slates of the floor.

Snatching up the baby, choking and sobbing in her cradle as the ghastly miasma attacked her tiny lungs, Richard dragged his wife across the room and attempted to open the back door. It had jammed as the wall of the house had eased open from the crack, and Mary's screams now mingling with those of the infant, he half carried the distraught woman to the inner door, down the short passage and out of the front door. They had only been in the room with the foul effluvium for a few minutes but even in the open air they found it difficult to breath, and the baby went into a convulsion.

Workmen with wet rags over their mouths and noses came to fill the shallow space under the flagstones and set them straight again. The yawning crack in the wall was carefully mended and a tie bar put through the house, between ceiling and floor, to hold the out-of-true wall firm.

The workmen who mended the floor reeled from the house, vomitting and choking, several times during the operation, but once the slates were cemented in place again no trace remained of the smell.

The family, who had been given shelter by kind neighbours during the repairs, moved back into the house, finding it difficult to remember the horror and revulsion they had felt. Subsidence was not uncommon in Cornwall, the ground being honeycombed with mine-workings, some of them hundreds of years old and uncharted, and the damage to the house was put down to this.

Within two days of returning to the house the baby died, but babies frequently died in those days of inadequate sanitation and no proper water supply.

Within a week Mary became gravely ill and followed her baby daughter to lie beside her in the old church-yard near the harbour.

Richard lasted another week and then he, too, succumbed to the strange disease that had carried off his wife and baby.

The Jagos' deaths were eventually accepted as being in some way due to the shock they had received. No one connected the deaths of two itinerant labourers who lived in another part of the parish with the tragedy that had befallen the family.

The three orphaned Jagos continued to live at Number 10.

Richard Jago's sister, Blanche, had been recently widowed and was only too glad to come and live with them. She was a kind woman and, with no children of her own, gave them all the love and devotion she was capable of, which was considerable.

William, old enough to realize how lucky they were to have Aunt Blanche, brought home his wages to her gladly, knowing that she would use them, and the money their father had left, wisely and for their general good. The two little girls, Rose, aged nine and Lizzie, aged seven, soon forgot their bereavement and flourished in the warmth and love lavished on them by the motherly woman.

A daguerreotype of Mary and Richard which hung over the mantelpiece in the front room was all that was left to remind them of the tragedy, and once again the family, having adjusted to circumstances, seemed set on an even keel.

The town of Carveen continued to grow, spreading out from the centre over green fields and windy cliffs, and the primitive water supply became totally inadequate to cope with the increase in the population.

Treveth Terrace had a communal pump in the little lane, known as an ope, behind the houses. Before going to work in the morning William would fill jugs and buckets and carry them back to Number 10, so that Aunt Blanche had nothing to carry for her washing and scrubbing during the day, but the well was being called upon to produce more and more water as new houses were built near it and it often ran dry, as did other wells serving other groups of dwellings.

The town council at last decided that matters must be improved and, not without opposition, a reservoir was built at the top of the town, collecting water from several streams. It was planned to pipe its water to every house in the town.

William had left home by now, having become a junior partner in the firm to which he had been clerk, and the two girls were working, Rose helping at the school she had so recently left, and Lizzie apprenticed to a milliner.

Aunt Blanche was alone in the house during the day and took great interest in the trench being dug in the lane behind Treveth Terrace which was to take the water pipes.

It was hard work for the labourers, digging deep into the rock on which the houses were built, and she and her neighbours took cups of tea and newly-baked cake to the sweating men who were glad to lay down their picks and long-handled Cornish shovels from time to time. It was hard work, that is, until the last yard of the trench, where it was planned to take the pipes into Number 10.

The brawny red haired labourer who was swinging his pick into the rock called to his mates that the ground had suddenly become softer and, as the point of the pick sunk deep, a foetid stench rose up, causing the man to stagger back against the wall of the house, retching and choking.

Aunt Blanche had gone out some seconds before to offer the men saffron cake and tea and ran to him. Before she reached him she was overpowered by the ghastly effluvia and had hardly staggered back to her kitchen before she collapsed, tearing at her throat with her hands.

The workman's mates carried him to the other end of the lane before, gagging on the appalling smell, they hastily replaced earth and stones in the part of the trench from which the stench came.

When Rose and Lizzie got home Aunt Blanche had recovered a little from her experience, but within a day or two she became acutely ill. The doctor could do nothing for her and in a week she was dead.

The red-headed workman and his gang were not seen in the lane again. Another group of men were employed to finish laying the pipes, the entry into Number 10 being made a yard short of where previously planned. No one thought this odd. There was so much work being done in the town that workmen were shifted from site to site as their particular skills were required.

Most of the other occupants of Treveth Terrace had moved there since the original Jago disaster, but there were one or two who remembered, and who discussed the coincidence of this second tragedy with their sons and daughters. The sons and daughters took scant notice, but nevertheless unconsciously stored the conversations in the back of their minds to be dredged up years later when John began his investigations.

Aunt Blanche's death hit the young Jagos very hard. They had all loved her deeply and she had cared for them with unfailing devotion. The three of them, dressed in black, stood round as the kindly woman was lowered into the ground beside her brother and sister-in-law, friends and neighbours behind them. If anyone looked at those other family gravestones and wondered they said nothing.

William was doing very well for himself now. Married to a local girl, he had bought a small house in the next town from which he practised law. He was the proud father of a baby son, John.

The girls continued to live at Number 10, Lizzie engaged to a young gardener who worked in a big country house some two miles inland from Carveen, Rose still devoting all her time to the children she taught in the rapidly expanding school of which she was now joint owner.

Once again the Jagos, having mourned the death of their dear aunt, settled down to live their various lives, prosperously and peacefully.

When Lizzie's young man, Paul Carne, became head gardener at the big house he asked Lizzie to marry him. She gladly accepted on condition that he come to live with her and Rose at Number 10, paying their share of the rent to brother William to whom the house belonged. This was agreed upon and Paul came to live in the family home. Lizzie devoted her time to looking after him and her hard-working sister, keeping the small house as neat and comfortable as had her mother and aunt before her.

About two years after their marriage Paul came home carrying what looked to Lizzie and Rose like a small tree, its roots wrapped in sacking. It was in fact a shrub, a pyracantha or firethorn, one surplus to requirements at the big house which Paul had been given. It would grow on an east wall, he said, and would cheer up the blank end of Number 10 with its masses of orange berries.

Planting the pyracantha was the last thing Paul ever did, coming in from doing so gasping and choking from the vile odour which emanated from the hole he had dug to take its roots.

The shrub died, and so did Paul and once again Rose and Lizzie were the sole occupants of the house.

From time to time over the years small repairs needed doing to the house. A new window frame where the wood had rotted, the brickwork of the chimney to be repointed, a gale dislodged slate to be replaced on the roof. The men whom the women employed to carry out these repairs all complained of difficulty in breathing and a feeling of faintness during and after doing the work. One of them actually fell from the roof, breaking his back.

It seemed that the fabric of the house had begun to soak up the evil which had hitherto remained underground, but the incidents were so separated by time that no one noticed that they followed a sinister pattern.

No one, that is, except William's small son John.

From a very early age John had sensed something strange about the house. He was a quiet child and on his frequent visits to his aunts, who adored him, he would listen avidly as they told him about the events which accounted for the crack in the end wall, and of dear Aunt Blanche, for whom the shock of modern drainage seemed to have been too much.

He would look at the faded picture of the grandparents he had never known and at the only slightly less faded one of his great aunt, and then across the room to the silver framed photograph, tinted, this one, of his Uncle Paul which stood on a small table in the bay window.

Unhampered by all the attendant detail with which those who had lived with these events had to contend, a vague pattern seemed to form in his mind. As he grew up it became clearer.

When his father, William, died and John became the owner of Number 10 he implored his aunts to move. The area was no longer a proper place for them to live, he said. They should move to the country, nearer him and his wife.

But the old ladies refused to move, although grateful to John for his concern. They had been born in the house and they intended to die in it, which they did, within six months of each other, of blessedly natural causes.

John had anxiously watched over them during their last years, but they were marred by only minor incidents when the old ladies became slightly unwell, as did the repair men, when things needed doing to the house.

When Aunt Lizzie finally died, having found life hard to bear without her sister who had preceded her, John scattered her ashes to mingle with those of Rose and his father on the family grave in the old crowded churchyard by the harbour.

He then returned to Number 10 Treveth Terrace and, with the photographs of his relatives under his arm, he turned the large key in the lock, vowing that no one else should ever live there.

At once he set about his investigations, consulting museums and libraries, asking questions of anyone whose family had lived in the district for any length of time, and gradually he compiled a dossier on Treveth.

From old books he discovered that the terrace was not the first group of houses to be built on the site. There had been a farm there in 1700, with attendant cottages and out-buildings. It had been dogged by disaster. Neither animals nor men could prosper there, but sickened and died. Crops withered in the ground and finally the place had been abandoned, the dwellings and cattle houses being allowed to disintegrate and return their stone to the ground from whence they came.

From an ancient map of 1630 he found that the ground had not always been level, but that an area roughly corresponding to the unbuilt upon grass plot had once been a deep round depression, due probably to the sea undermining the cliffs, and known as the Devil's Dish.

But between these two dates – ah, surely this explained it all! – had come that national disaster, the Plague.

John searched parish registers, those of Carveen and other nearby villages, and found that this part of the county had been hard hit by the pestilence. Where more obvious to bury the multitude of corpses than in the natural depression at a safe distance, as it was then, from the huddled cottages surrounding the harbour? Belatedly he translated the Cornish name into English – Treveth. House of the Grave.

John had kept his findings to himself. No good to tell people. They would either be upset or would laugh at him, and since Number 10 was the only house which extended over the edge of the grisly pit nothing would occur as long as it remained empty.

At first the demoliton order had been pure relief, but now he started to worry.

Would the building of the ring-road disturb the evil trapped beneath the surface? He consulted the engineers, ostensibly out of casual interest. No, the level of the road had to be raised. Hardcore would be added, nothing taken away.

He was anxious for the men who were to demolish the house, but found that the machine which operated the heavy ball used to smash the masonry was fitted with a cab to keep out dust and noise. That should be some protection.

One further thing. What was to happen to the resultant rubble? It was to be used to fill in a mine shaft down which cattle had been falling.

Once more John relaxed. It seemed that the small house was to be obliterated once and for all, and with it the fatal influence from which his family, and others, had suffered.

Meanwhile, far away in Berkshire, Philip Harris hurried home to his wife. He had good news for her.

Philip was a bank manager and was about to retire. His wife, Gwen, was about to achieve her heart's desire, a home in her native Cornwall.

Together they had chosen a site in a tiny unspoilt village on the north coast, far from any of the expanding holiday towns. Gwen had very definite ideas about this house of hers, her Little Grey Home in the West, as Philip laughingly called it. It had to look old. Yes, she knew that an entirely stone-built house would be too costly, but could it not, perhaps, be faced with old stone to blend in with the original cottage near it? *Old* stone, old *grey* stone, she stressed, not the new unweathered stuff being quarried now and used so badly by modern builders, like perpendicular crazy paving.

Philip had promised he would see what he could do, and had written to a friend and colleague, the manager of the bank's branch at Carveen. In his pocket was his colleague's answer.

As luck would have it one of his clients was a contractor, and again as luck would have it, he was at present demolishing a row of old stone houses. Most of the material had already been carried away and dumped, but one last house was still standing and the stone from this should be just what Philip Harris required.

On reaching the pleasant suburban house where he and Gwen lived Philip let himself in.

'Gwen? Where are you Gwen?' he called, 'Good news! The stone you wanted, we've got it!'

Gwen Harris swayed as she stood in the drawing room doorway ready to greet her husband. Her face was ashen and contorted.

'Gwennie!' Philip cried running to her, 'Gwennie dear, are you ill?' Gwen leant against his shoulder.

'No,' she said faintly, 'I'm not ill. I'm all right now. I just had the strangest sensation, as though I couldn't breathe, as though I was choking on a sort of evil fog.' She straightened up and stood away from Philip, smiling at him.

'I'm sorry, darling' she said, 'I didn't hear what you were saying. Was it about my Little Grey Home in the West?'

XVI

Grandmother's Footsteps

'Mummy! I want to come home for the weekend!' Jenny's voice was shrill and taut on the other end of the telephone.

Anne sat down on the bed beside her half-packed suitcase, spilling the evening dress she had been folding on the floor in a silken heap.

'But, darling, you can't! I'm just about to leave for London. Uncle Teddy's picking me up at any moment. Had you forgotten about my exhibition?'

'Yes, I had actually,' there was a pause. 'Must you go? Must you go for the weekend? Couldn't you just go up on Monday when it opens instead?'

Really! The utter selfishness of youth, Anne thought, exasperated.

'No, I couldn't, Jenny,' she said firmly. 'I asked you if you would like to come with me, I would have been thrilled to have you, but no: you wanted to stay in Exeter. Why the sudden desire to get away now?'

'I'm lonely,' still the rising note in Jenny's voice that presaged tears.

Anne fought back the urge to say 'I told you so!' Parents were never allowed to have known best.

Jenny could have gone to a university nearer home, Southampton had offered her a place, but she had insisted on going to Exeter. Also the idea of living in one of the halls of residence had been instantly dismissed in favour of sharing a flat. A flat! Anne remembered, appalled, the two dismal rooms with use of bath and kitchen which Jenny had found so exciting.

'Oh dear. But I thought it was going to be such fun,' she

said, in place of 'I told you so', but even that sounded sarcastic.

'It *is* fun,' the girl's voice was defiant but still with a tearful quiver. 'It's just that the others are away and I'm terribly *lonely* and I want to come *home!*'

Anne gripped the telephone receiver until her knuckles showed white. All Jenny's selfish little life she, her mother, had given up her own inclinations for the child's sake. When ever she had wanted an hour to herself to paint all the fantasies that she saw in her head Jenny had needed reading to, taking for walks, washing for, cooking for, and later her private school fees had been too much for her struggling architect husband to manage without help so Anne had designed run-of-the-mill Christmas cards, calendars and wrapping paper to bring in a little extra money. She had even stuck out a dreary and stultifying marriage until the child was old enough for her parents' separation to make little difference to her.

Now, when of her own accord the girl had moved away from home, now, when at last Anne had had time to paint and had been successful enough to warrant an exhibition in London, Jenny wanted to spoil it.

Born of long habit it was Anne's immediate reaction to cancel her weekend of excitement and preparation for the show, but she resisted it.

'Why not go and stay with Daddy in Shropshire?' she suggested.

'I can't. He's in Scotland. Had *you* forgotten?'

Anne felt a twinge of guilt. 'Touché,' she thought. On the eve of her own triumph she had indeed forgotten that Alan had achieved one, too, having been commissioned to design some vast municipal complex in Edinburgh. Because she preferred no longer to live with him didn't mean that she was not interested in his career. Mixed with the guilt was a pang of jealousy that Jenny had rung her father first, had wanted most to go to him.

'Well, my darling,' she said briskly. 'It looks as if you really will have to stick it out on your own for a little while.'

'Oh no, I shan't,' said Jenny venomously, 'I shall go and see

my grandmother in Cornwall.' Her tone was such that she
might just as well have said 'So there!'

Panic seized Anne. 'Jenny, no!' she cried. 'Please, darling,
don't do that! Look –' her former resolve instantly
undermined, ' –I'll ring Uncle Teddy and tell him not to come
for me tonight, that you and I will come up together
tomorrow.' It would mean rearrangements and irritation all
round but anything was better than that Jenny should go to
her grandmother. 'Besides,' she added quickly, 'You don't
know where she lives.'

'Yes I do,' retorted Jenny. 'Daddy told me.'

'*Daddy* told you?' Anne was amazed. She and Alan had
agreed that the girl was to be kept away from her
grandmother at all costs.

'Yes. He could hardly refuse, could he? After all I am
eighteen and she is my only grandparent.'

Anne was about to plead with her, to try to reason with her
when the door bell rang; Teddy had arrived to take her to
London.

'Darling child,' she cried into the telephone, 'please *please*
reconsider! I've got to go now but I do beg you not to go to
Cornwall! I'll ring you the moment I get back.'

Anne had met Alan Owen at Liverpool University where he
was studying architecture, she art and design. Alan's parents
were separated and he spent the holidays with his father, an
architect of some standing, in Shropshire.

He never spoke about his mother and, although she was
naturally invited to their wedding, she wrote a vague and
unconvincing excuse for not coming up from her home in
Cornwall, and sent no present.

They had spent their honeymoon touring the West
Country.

'I suppose you really ought to meet Mother now we are
within striking distance,' Alan said.

On their way through the narrow tree-tunnelled Cornish
lanes leading to the little south coast village of Porthzelah,
Anne realized that she had no idea what sort of person she was
about to meet.

'Oh, Mother's a bit of an odd-ball,' Alan said. 'She and I never hit it off very well; I'm too much like Father, I suppose. She grows herbs and things, in quite a big way I gather: she's mad about animals and flowers, doesn't care much for people.'

Anne visualized a retiring, countrified market gardener sort of woman, surrounded by dogs and geraniums in pots.

Nothing could have been more at variance with the actuality.

Alan turned the car off the narrow coast road into a steep, twisting drive. It climbed up between rocky outcrops festooned with azaleas of every colour and behind them lofty rhododendrons formed dramatic shapes against the sky. Eventually they came in sight of the house: it was a large, rambling, modern building on several levels, so much in tune with its surroundings that it seemed to grow out of the living rock.

Leaning against the balustrading of the balcony stood a tall, slim woman. The early evening sun was behind her and her silhouette was outlined in golden light. She made no sign of having seen them or having heard Alan's greeting, so they climbed the outside stair of granite blocks to join her on the balcony.

As they drew closer Anne saw an elegant woman in late middle age. She was dressed in an expensive cowl-necked angora jersey and trousers of some silky material which moulded itself to her long legs; a cascade of gold chains swung from her neck and several narrow gold bracelets encircled each wrist. Her hair was a soft, dense mass of black framing her face, a natural white streak slightly off-centre giving her a rakish look.

But there was nothing rakish about the small, dark face: all the features were too big for it, the arched nose, the wide, unsmiling mouth and the incredible eyes, huge and so pale as to be almost white, almost luminous, the lids shadowed with gold matching the nail varnish on the long, strong hands resting on the balustrade.

'Hullo, Mother!' Alan cried as they joined her on the balcony. 'This is Anne.'

The woman examined her new daughter-in-law in silence for some seconds, the great white eyes sweeping over the girl.

'I had expected you to be –' there was a pause during which she rearranged the cowl neck of her jersey, the bracelets on her wrists jangling, ' – much earlier,' she eventually finished.

She had a verbal trick of pausing in mid-sentence which totally unnerved most people to whom she spoke, giving them ample time to imagine she was going to say something alarming.

'What in the name of Hades –' she went on, her eyes still taking in every detail of Anne's appearance, ' – induced you to marry my son.' It was not a question but more a private observation of Alan on whom she now bent her white stare.

'You might ask Alan the same thing about me,' Anne said nervously with a little laugh, and then, 'What a wonderful place this is!' She turned to look down over the tumbled rocks and cascading flowers to the wide sea below. 'I never saw such a view! How lucky you are to live in such a lovely place, Mrs Owen.'

'Don't call me Mrs Owen,' the older woman commanded coldly. 'I gave *that* up years ago: I am always known by my – baptismal name, Myfanwy.'

'Oh, a Welsh name!' Anne said.

'It most certainly is *not*,' the white eyes regarded the girl sternly. 'The Welsh may use it now, but it was originally Cornish. The Welsh have *nothing* original.'

'Mother!' Alan said sharply.

'What's the matter?' his mother asked him. 'Just because your father was Welsh you needn't be so touchy. I have always said that the Welsh nation is the product of the union between a goat and a Cornish girl –'

'Mother!' Alan interrupted again warningly.

Myfanwy turned on him. 'Don't keep yelping "Mother" at me! Has Anne got Welsh blood or something that you should be so shocked?'

'I'm mostly English but I did have a Welsh grandmother,' Anne ventured.

'*Really*? How splendid!' Myfanwy looked at her with real interest for the first time. 'I'm delighted! If one can't be

Cornish to be Welsh is *quite* the next best thing! But why are you called Anne? Such a dull name I always think, Hebrew, too. I'm sure we can find you a more romantic Celtic name.'

'Mother, you really are preposterous,' Alan sighed exasperatedly.

'No I am not,' his mother retorted. 'Unless to be honest is preposterous. You should know me better than to expect pleasantries and inanities.'

'It's living by herself that makes her so outspoken,' her son explained, trying to excuse his mother to his new wife.

'Don't you feel very lonely sometimes?' Anne asked, glad, at least, that the conversation had moved away from herself.

'Certainly not,' Myfanwy said. 'I have ... friends all over the county. We ... get together at certain times, and besides, I'm never alone. Py! Bran! Come here!'

At her call a large grey cat emerged from the house and joined them on the balcony, twining his sinuous body round his mistress's legs, and with a black flutter of wings a jackdaw alighted on her shoulder.

She bent, careful not to upset the bird who buried his claws in the soft wool of her jersey, and gathered the cat in her arms.

'This is Py,' she said, 'No, *not* Pywacket,' the long mouth lengthened and the white eyes narrowed into a malicious smile as she looked at Anne, having guessed what she was thinking. 'He was brought to me from the next village, Pydar; he had a broken leg and when I had cured him he refused to stay at home, kept coming back, didn't you, my pretty?' The cat narrowed his yellow eyes exactly as his mistress did and gazed at her adoringly, his paws kneading her arm.

'And this,' Myfanwy put up a hand to the bird, 'is Bran. He came to me as an abandoned fledgling and I reared him by hand. He won't leave me either. People bring me sick and injured animals from miles around – children too, those who dare – and I cure them all.' The bird leant forward, turning his head so that his cold blue eyes looked straight into hers.

'Oh yes,' she said, dislodging the bird from her shoulder and putting down the cat, 'I see *quite* as much of people as I wish, and I'm never without a familiar –' she paused and shot another malicious smile at Anne, ' – face about the place,' she finished. 'Would you care to come round the garden with me? I like to reassure my plants that all is well before darkness falls.'

The garden was superb, and full of surprises. Sheltered nooks between rocks provided nursery beds for seedlings, all of which received a few soft words and a caressing touch from Myfanwy, and exotic shrubs and creepers luxuriated in this sub-tropical situation, the grey rock making a perfect background for them. Here and there between the dramatic flowers grew strange, dark plants with few or no flowers, but whose leaves were thick and lush, of dark or livid green, some with clasping tendrils, others crawling sinuously between the rocks.

Having made a tour of the garden they returned to the house through a heated conservatory, the cat at Myfanwy's heels, the bird fluttering back and forth. Here hibiscus, orange-blossom and orchids greeted them and at one end a large plant sprouted huge, dull, white bell flowers from which a strange and sickening odour exuded.

'What an extraordinary plant!' Anne exclaimed, putting a hand up to one of the white, trumpet-shaped blossoms.

'Don't touch that!' Myfanwy cried, 'It's Datura, and deadly poison! Come away from it!'

Anne recoiled. 'Why do you grow such a poisonous plant?' she asked.

'A great many plants are poisonous, my dear,' the woman said. 'Doronicum, Aconite, Atropia – even rhubarb leaves. They're all out there.' She waved an arm, bracelets jangling, towards the twilit garden. 'Any of them could wipe out an army if used … unwisely.'

'But why do you grow them if they are so dangerous?' Anne said.

'I use them in my –' Myfanwy bent to stroke the cat who put out a paw to play with the gold chains swinging from her neck, '– specifics.' She drew out the first letters of the word in a sibilant hiss and threw Anne her weird smile. 'And I sell them to others in my … profession. Used with knowledge they can do good or – harm. But that,' she pointed to the Datura, giving it a fond look, 'is a killer. Quite lethal. Its flowers open about now, at dusk, and the scent is very dangerous. It can make people blind, it can send them mad, and eventually it kills. Come along, we must shut the doors on it before it harms us,' she ushered them into the house and closed the conservatory. 'Once upon a time,' she went on, almost to herself, 'I would have been burnt at the stake for allowing it to grow.'

Leaving the dreadful plant to its evil devices Myfanwy turned her attention once more to the young people. 'Now,' she said, 'Come along, I must give you both a drink and something to eat. What will it be? Gin? Whisky? Or would you prefer one of my own ... brews?'

Followed by the cat and the bird she led the two young people into the dim, shadowy house; spacious, airy rooms, all with magnificent views led one from the other.

'I don't think I have ever been in such a beautiful house,' Anne said, when they were seated at a low table in a window beneath which the rocky garden seemed to plunge almost vertically to the sea below.

'I've always thought that the only reason Mother married Father was to get him to build her this house,' Alan laughed, handing his wife a gin and tonic and pouring whisky for himself.

His mother considered this for a moment, swirling a dark, purplish liquid in her glass.

'Yes,' she said at last, 'You're right. That and the fact that he was good breeding stock. One must not let talent die out and go to waste.'

'It's wonderful that Alan inherited his father's architectural skill,' Anne agreed.

'Oh, that,' Myfanwy said impatiently. 'No. I didn't mean that. I meant *my* talent, *my* genius.'

Anne was puzzled. 'But Alan's no good with animals,' she said, 'and he doesn't know one plant from another!'

'Of course he doesn't,' his mother regarded him without enthusiasm. 'These things always skip a generation.' She examined her long strong hands, holding them out in front of her and scrutinizing first the backs and then the palms. She raised her head and looked fixedly at Anne.

'It will be your child who inherits my gift. The gift of green fingers and healing hands,' she said and, her gaze shifting downwards to Anne's stomach, 'It will be a girl.'

Anne's hands flew automatically to her flat abdomen.

'But I'm not pregnant!' she protested.

'Oh yes you are,' Myfanwy said matter-of-factly.

As they drove away Anne held Alan's hand tightly.

'She's terrifying!' she whispered. 'She's weird! She's a –'

'Don't say it,' Alan said quickly, giving her hand a squeeze and putting it back in her lap in order to have both his free to negotiate the tortuous lane. 'I told you she was an odd-ball. She's good with animals and clever with plants and she likes to shock people with her outspokenness. No more than that. I couldn't live with myself if I allowed myself to think otherwise.' He manoeuvered the car round a hairpin bend, 'You're not pregnant, are you?' he said.

'Of course not,' Anne said crossly, 'At least, I don't think so.' She was silent for a minute as she calculated. 'Oh, Alan! I might be after all!'

They had not planned to have children until Alan's career was established and Anne had had a chance to see if her painting was any good, but nevertheless Jenny was born nine months after their wedding.

Myfanwy was delighted. She came to the christening, arriving too late for the church service but in time for the champagne celebration, protesting that her car had broken down.

She looked magnificently odd in flowing emerald green chiffon and a vast picture hat of the same shade, her glimmering eyeshadow and nail-varnish picking up the reflected colour as did her weird, white eyes.

'How clever of you to choose a Cornish name!' she cried.

'Is Jennifer Cornish?' Anne asked, surprised.

'Of course,' Myfanwy replied, 'It's a corruption of Guinevere. Another of the names that no doubt *you* would consider Welsh,' she added mockingly.

She bent her dark, small face, clouded in its mass of soft, black, white-streaked hair and shadowed by the huge hat, over the baby in her cot. Tiny hands went out to the jangling gold bracelets and swinging gold chains and the little face crinkled into a smile of pure delight.

'Yes, yes, my darling,' the woman murmured. 'Cornish gold, every one of them and very, very old. They shall all be yours one day, my pretty, and more, much more.'

As the baby grew Anne noticed with alarm how the small plain face became daily more like that of her grandmother, the infant nose taking on the arrogant arch, the little mouth becoming narrow-lipped and mocking. The baby blue eyes paled to translucent white and the fair, downy hair with which she was born was soon replaced by cloudy black, except for a white streak in front, slightly off centre. She and Alan resolved to avoid letting their daughter see more of her grandmother than they could help.

Jenny inherited her mother's artistic flair, her own bent being towards flower drawing. Anne convinced herself that her daughter's growing preoccupation with the plants themselves was only due to her having to examine them so minutely in order to draw them, but was alarmed when the girl expressed a desire to study botany.

She was an unattractive child, having, as yet, neither the confidence or the character to invest her small, plain, large-featured face with the arresting attraction that her grandmother possessed, and, being aware that she was plain, she was self-conscious, self-willed and spiteful.

The only love of which she appeared to be capable was for small, wild creatures that she found injured and which she nursed back to health with patient and tender care. Both Anne and Alan hoped that, as long as she did not fall under the influence of Myfanwy, she would grow out of her uncomfortable adolescence and mature into a normal happy young woman. They loved her with an anxious devotion, but like her they could not, and there is a subtle difference.

Anne's exhibition in London opened successfully; the critics were kind and quite a few paintings were sold on the first day. It was still drawing a satisfactory number of viewers when she left for home over a week later.

On arriving at her house she threw her luggage down and ran straight to the telephone. While she was dialling Jenny's number she noticed a vaguely unpleasant smell: houses got very stuffy when shut up for any length of time, she thought. The telephone rang for some time at the other end before it was answered, and then not by Jenny. Her flat-mate sounded worried; she had not returned from her weekend away and there had been no word from her since. Did Mrs Owen know where she had gone? Indeed Anne did know and it was with rising panic that she rang her mother-in-law's number. Her feelings were a mixture of relief and horror when Jenny answered – but *was* it Jenny? The petulant, shrill tone was no longer there, instead the voice was calm and confident.

'Jenny! Is that you, darling?'

There was a long pause and then

'Hello – Mother. Yes, this is Guinevere.'

'Darling! What are you doing still in Cornwall? Why aren't you back at college?'

'I'm not going back to college.' Jenny's tone brooked no argument.

'But, my dear, what about your course? Your degree?'

'I learnt more during Grandmother's last days than I could learn in a thousand years at college.'

'Last days? What do you mean?'

'Grandmother has been – taken. She has – paid her debt to nature. I was with her at the end.'

'Do you mean Myfanwy's *dead*?' Anne's mind was whirling, her vision was blurred and she felt dizzy.

'She will never be dead as long as *I* live,' the new calm Jenny, the new Guinevere, replied. 'She taught me all she knew. She has left everything to me.'

Anne pressed a hand to her eyes to clear the oppressive film from them, the heavy unpleasant smell seemed to be getting stronger.

'Mother?' Jenny's voice was steely.

'Yes, darling?'

'I want you to know that I shall never forgive you and my father for keeping me away from Grandmother for so long. *Never.*'

'Jenny, don't let us quarrel. Come home for a few days and we will discuss it,' Anne sank to her knees by the telephone table, her head swimming; the smell, the ghastly smell!

'I have *been* home, Mother,' Jenny's voice was heavy with meaning. 'While you were away. I visited my father's house, too.'

Anne heard a cat mew and the hoarse cry of a jackdaw, then the unmistakable jangle as thin gold bracelets slid down her daughter's arm before the telephone went dead. She pulled herself to her feet. She must open the windows to get rid of this sickening smell, and then, her blurred vision clearing for a moment, she saw it.

Standing in a corner, its great dull, white flowers opening to the dusk and exuding its foetid, lethal odour ever more powerfully, was a Datura.

XVII

Rose Lawn

Penelope gazed in terror at the full-blown rose. It stood in a slim, cut-glass vase, between the Rockingham Sheep and the gilt clock on the mantel shelf: she had not put it there, but now she knew who had – and only a moment since.

As she looked at it the fleshy pink petals seemed to quiver almost imperceptibly and then, with the slightest sound of release, they all fell, pattering onto the marble shelf and into the fireplace below. At the same instant the slanting evening sun slipped behind one of the cypress trees across the lawn and the room was plunged into shadow and a sudden chill pervaded it.

Penelope screamed. She knew that Mrs Pritchett was standing behind her.

At the end of a narrow lane in Exeter a sign projected from a tiny shop: 'GARIBALDI BULLOCK. ANTIQUES' it said.

Penelope stood amazed. There could not, surely, be two Garibaldi Bullocks, but here? In Exeter? Selling antiques?

A bell tinkled as she pushed open the door and a large, untidy man in an expensive, but crumpled, tweed suit emerged from behind a bric-à-brac laden dresser.

'Can I help you?' he murmured.

'Gari! It *is* you! Oh, how wonderful to see you!' Penelope cried.

The large man's face lit up as recognition dawned.

'Pen! I can't believe it! Come in! Come in!'

They embraced and then held each other at arms' length, exclaiming on how little the ten years since last they met seemed to have changed them, talking fast, laughing and interrupting each other with staccato questions.

Penelope had lost touch with Garibaldi when he had taken his family, precious paintings, furniture, dogs and cats to a remote farmhouse in the south of France, leaving England, so he said, for ever; but as this was but one in a long line of extravagant changes of life-style she was not surprised to hear that he had tired of the peasant existence and had gathered up people, things and animals and brought them all back again, only being delighted to have stumbled across him so unexpectedly.

Talking all the time Garibaldi made instant coffee in Sèvres cups – 'One day I *know* I shall find matching saucers,' he said – and stirred them with a wafer-thin silver spoon. Nursing her cup, Penelope wandered round the little shop. It was crammed with small, beautiful things, all desirable and not outrageously expensive. There were pieces of jewellery, glass, plates, silver boxes, footstools, a calf-bound book or two and pictures covered every inch of the wall.

'You clever old darling,' she said, 'to collect such a lot of heavenly things. I want to buy them all!'

'Oh, my dear! No, you mustn't buy a *thing*! It's all rubbish, utter rubbish!'

Garibaldi stooped hugely over her and removed from her hands everything she picked up and put it back nervously.

'Please! I insist! Put it down, put it down. This is just a junk shop. You know I've always wanted to have a junk shop.'

Penelope laughed. There had been a never-ending string of things Garibaldi had always wanted to do, and he had had the means to do most of them, but he was no salesman. It seemed that this article was rubbish, that that was not for sale, that the other was far too expensive or he couldn't bear to part with it.

'Darling Gari! How on earth do you expect to do business when you won't *sell* anything?' she said, allowing him to remove a small, bead-embroidered reticule from her hands.

'Oh, I don't!' Garibaldi sounded quite shocked. 'This isn't a business, it's my hobby. You know I've always had to have a hobby!'

Penelope did know, and remembered some of them: his

sudden urge to breed this or that exotic creature and his subsequent inability to part with their progeny so that at various times he had been over-run with Burmese cats, Afghan hounds, mink and Chinese geese; his passion to collect Austin 7 cars, until, when he had fifteen of them, even he couldn't, or wouldn't, afford to license them all, running them all on one number plate which he lashed on to whichever he happened to be driving. As he could only drive one car at a time it had seemed the height of folly to license them all, as he had told the Magistrate's Court in deeply wounded tones.

'Pamela said there was a limit to the stuff that could be crammed into the house,' he went on, 'and she forbade me to bring in another *thing*, and you know how I love to go to auctions and buy bits of nonsense, so a shop seemed the perfect answer.'

But Penelope suddenly wasn't listening. She had taken a small engraving in a wide black and gold frame down from the wall. It was of a slight woman in the high-waisted dress of the late eighteenth century, her hair an artless tumble of curls above and below the wide fillet that encircled her head. Her heart-shaped face was dominated by huge, black eyes and in slender fingers she held a full-blown rose. Underneath was printed her name: 'Mrs Pritchett'.

'Oh Gari! I really must have this! It's simply lovely! I've just moved into the most perfect little Georgian cottage and Mrs Pritchett shall move in with me to keep me company!'

Garibaldi's face was suddenly serious as he agitatedly tried to take the picture from her.

'No, no! You mustn't! Really you mustn't! I truly mean it this time,' and, as Penelope held it firmly to her chest, 'I'm not being neurotic, Pen, not now. I just have a feeling – a premonition – you know I do sometimes. Take the bead bag or the footstool or even the Chelsea figurine, anything, but this you must not have. It would be a *grave* mistake.'

But Penelope was not to be put off, and she eventually left the little shop carrying the engraving, carefully wrapped, under her arm.

Garibaldi had not known who Mrs Pritchett was but promised to try and find out for her, making a note of her

address and muttering dubiously that no good would come of
it, whoever she was.

On reaching home Penelope propped her purchase against the
wall on the bookcase and looked about her. Where should she
hang it? It looked very well where it was until she had decided,
and she regarded the delicate little figure affectionately: the
engraving was of a line drawing and only the face, the hands
and the rose they held were faintly tinted. Although there was
the ghost of a smile on the pretty mouth it did not reach the
great, dark eyes which regarded her steadily and coldly.

A chill breeze ruffled the long cream silk curtains at the
open French windows and Penelope shivered involuntarily:
although it was July she decided to light a fire.

She had only been in her new home for a week and could still
hardly believe how lucky she had been to find it.

A large estate had come up for sale, the mansion, long shut
up and empty, being sold as a hotel, the farmland parcelled off
and the small house on the outskirts of the park going
extremely cheaply because of its dilapidated state. It had been
called Cypress Cottage but Penelope learnt in the village that
it was locally known as Rose Lawns House, which she thought
much prettier.

Built in the late eighteenth century it almost qualified as a
cottage ornée, a tiny symmetrical doll's house set in half an
acre of what was once lawn, and roses which, although
woefully neglected and overgrown, still struggled to produce a
bloom here and there. Straggling lavender bushes lurked under
the yew hedge which bounded the garden and tall cypress
trees brooded over a small, white stucco summer house at the
far end.

The house seemed hardly to have been used, except as a
store by the tenant of the adjacent farm, since it was built and,
although the roof and windows had been maintained in a
weather-proof condition, the inside remained in its original
state with no plumbing or drainage, and of course no
electricity.

Penelope was extremely pleased with its condition. With no

unfortunate alterations to contend with she could carefully bring the little house up to date while losing none of its beautifully proportioned period quality.

The house was on three floors and the attic, whose dormer windows peered over the pediment, had been boarded off from the rest of the house for some reason, stout planks being nailed across the stairs. They were the only rooms to contain anything other than the remains of baled hay and balls of binder-twine: a chaise longue had stood dejectedly against a wall, its satin upholstery frayed and shredded; an oval mirror, the surface of the glass misted over with grime and the gilt frame gleaming dully through layers of dust, hung over a fireplace and below it on the mantelshelf stood a slim, cut-glass vase with a brittle twig, the remnant, no doubt, of the last bloom it had held, still in it.

The chaise longue had been recovered and it now stood in the drawing room between the French windows, elegant in gold and cream striped brocade; the mirror created a wash of gentle reflected light above the fireplace and below it, on the marble mantelshelf, between the pair of Rockingham Sheep and the gilt clock, stood the little cut-glass vase.

Gradually the small house, its modern lighting and plumbing skilfully and discreetly integrated, once more took on the graceful ambience it must originally have had. The work had taken a long time and had been expensive, but now it was nearly finished and Penelope was utterly delighted with it.

Or she had been, until her return from Garibaldi Bullock's antique shop.

A faint sense of unease seemed suddenly to pervade the peace and serenity of the small, beautiful rooms and a chill would be cast on the sunlit afternoons: shadows would assume human form when seen out of the corner of an eye, only to become shadows once more when examined closely; small sounds of movement would stop the heart for a moment until discovered to be the gentle susurration of a silk curtain swaying in the breeze from an open window; the reflection in the dim old mirror would seem to quiver and shift when there was no movement in the room for it to record, and the scent of lavender and roses from the borders that lined the ragged lawn would of a sudden take on a musty and long-dried character, resuming their normal freshness almost at once.

When working in the garden, tearing out the bind-weed and brambles that threatened to strangle the great old rose bushes, Penelope would sometimes think she heard a tiny, smothered peel of laughter coming from the cypress trees and at other times the suspicion of a smothered sob from the little summer house which stood between them would make her look up.

Being a sensible woman, and having lived on her own for too long to give in to flights of fancy, Penelope was able to explain away all these phenomena to her satisfaction. The half-heard step behind her on the stairs was merely the creak of old wood contracting in the lived-in warmth after years of damp neglect; the sounds that at first she took for laughter or weeping, both in and out of doors, could well be the chirps and murmurings of birds in the eaves and small animals in the undergrowth. The fact that sometimes things seemed not to be in exactly the same place as she had left them she put down to her own absent-mindedness and perhaps, she thought as she turned her head sharply to try and catch a shadow at its masquerading before it became a shadow again, she needed glasses.

All these things she could and did explain away to herself; even when she awoke with a start in the night, sure for an instant that someone stood beside her bed, she put it down to nightmare, turning over and going to sleep again almost without a qualm. But she could not explain away the roses.

Every few days a fresh bloom would appear in the cut-glass vase on the mantelshelf, a huge pink cabbage rose, of a variety she could not find in the garden. It would age gracefully as roses do, changing colour slightly from carmine to a paler, mauvish hue, and opening its layers of satin petals to reveal a golden heart; then it would be gone, the cut-glass vase empty, no sign of withered petals or the naked stem, only to be replaced immediately by unseen hands.

She never saw the coming or the going of the rose. It was obvious that someone put it there, but who? Apart from herself the only people to enter the house were the twice-weekly woman from the village, a dour, plain creature who did her housework efficiently and in silence, and the builder's men who were finishing the exterior painting. None of these were likely to be concerned with adorning her mantelshelf with cabbage roses. Could someone she did not know, someone who had been fond of the house before she had bought it, be coming on a sort of pilgrimage? And, if so, how did they get in without her seeing them? The thought was not pleasant.

One afternoon, as she regarded the rose with the usual perplexity she glanced into the oval mirror above the mantelshelf and noticed the engraving of Mrs Pritchett, still on the bookshelf opposite the fireplace.

'The pretty thing,' she thought. 'I must find a suitable place to put the dear lady,' turning and moving towards the picture. But she stopped in the middle of the room, staring in amazement.

The great, dark eyes glared at her balefully. Pretty she might be, but a dear lady she most certainly was not, not at this moment. The sheer hatred that poured out of the delicately tinted face made Penelope catch her breath, but there was something else about the picture that alarmed her even more. The slender hands clasped in the soft folds of the silken dress were empty; they held no rose.

Moving nearer the picture she put out a hand to pick it up, but withdrew it again sharply; the thing seemed to repel her, to repulse her, to defy her efforts to pick it up. Leaving it where it was she leaned forward to examine it more closely. The little hands, palest pink, clung together, every finger exquisitely drawn, each fold of the material behind them – which should have been hidden by the full-blown rose – correct and perfect.

She turned back to the great bloom on the mantelshelf and for a second its fresh, clean scent became dusty, dry and long-ago; the silk curtains at the open French window moved suddenly in a chill breeze with a sigh, as though of skirts drawn aside; the reflection of the quiet, still room in the oval mirror shuddered and shifted as though someone had moved across it, and the slightest sound of laughter, or of weeping, mingled with the murmurings of sparrows in the honeysuckle outside.

Penelope was at last aware that Mrs Pritchett had, indeed, moved in with her to keep her company: or, she thought with a start, had she not been here all the time? Perhaps it was she, Penelope, who was the newcomer.

Having acknowledged Mrs Pritchett's presence Penelope was determined to get rid of it. She remembered Garibaldi's urgent pleas that she should not buy the engraving. Funny old thing he might be, but she had to admit that more than once in the past his feelings – his premonitions – had been uncannily accurate, although she, in her matter-of-fact way, had maintained that they were no more than coincidental. This, too, might well be coincidental but she resolved, nevertheless, to return the picture to him the next time she went into Exeter, and in the meantime she would banish it so that at least she need not suffer the increasingly malevolent look in the great, dark eyes.

The next morning men from the Post Office came to install the telephone and, while the house rang with their cheerful whistling and the sound of hammering as they carefully tacked the fine wire along the top of the skirting board in the hall, Penelope strode purposefully into the drawing room carrying a large towel. Walking straight to the bookcase she seized the picture and swiftly bundled it up in the thick material, wrapping it round and round like an untidy parcel. Holding it at arm's length she carried it upstairs to the attic, put the whole thing into an empty trunk, slammed the lid and locked it.

When she was downstairs again she found she was breathing hard and fast and was close to tears. She tried to laugh at herself, it was unlike her to let fantasies reduce her to such a state of nerves, but at the same time she was uneasily aware that putting Mrs Pritchett's likeness under lock and key was not going to obliterate her oppressive presence. As if to endorse the feeling the curtain whispered and sighed in the breeze from the window, seeming somehow louder and more urgent than the workmen's voices from the hall, and the great

pink rose on the mantelshelf wafted a brittle, dry scent
towards her.

She rapidly crossed the room to the fireplace. She had had
enough of whatever nonsense was going on. She would get rid
of the wretched rose, would tear it to shreds, would fling it
out; but no. She could not. She was suddenly overwhelmingly
aware that if she destroyed the rose, if indeed the bloom were
harmed in any way, that she herself would be in dire peril, and
she backed away from it. Tomorrow she would take the
accursed engraving back to Garibaldi. Once it was out of the
house surely, surely things would become normal again and
she would be safe.

All the rest of that day strange noises came from the attic,
mingled with the cheerful banter of the telephone engineers.
The men seemed not to notice anything but Penelope was
aware, as though with some sense other than hearing, of
footsteps running back and forth on the floor at the top of the
house, of tempestuous sobbing, of shrill screams and urgent
bangings as though of fists on a locked door.

When the engineers finished the installation she kept them
in the house a little longer, making tea for them, asking about
their families, where they lived, anything to put off the
moment when she would be alone – or not alone – in the
house. But finally the bright yellow van drove down the path
and away, leaving Penelope standing on the sun-drenched
lawn. Almost with dread she walked towards the house,
entering the drawing room through the French windows.

The house was quiet now, as though whatever had been
imprisoned against its will had escaped and was at liberty
again. On impulse, noticing fleetingly that the cut-glass vase
on the mantelshelf was empty, she ran to the stairs. She must
go up to the attic to make sure that the engraving was safely
locked inside the trunk.

There was very little in the attic but what boxes and
oddments there were were still piled tidily just as she had left
them, the trunk containing the likeness of Mrs Pritchett
fastened and locked. But there was something different about
the room.

The end wall was lined with thin, tongued and grooved

boarding and this had unaccountably come away in one place, sagging forward and revealing the stained and patchy distemper behind it on which there seemed to be faint, dull brown writing; huge wild letters straggled across the wall at a crazy angle. Pulling the boarding a little further away Penelope saw that they read:

'THIS IS ROSE LAWN'S HOUSE', amid splashes and splutters of the same dull brown colour.

She smiled, relieved that it seemed to be nothing sinister; some child, she imagined, had whiled away a rainy afternoon in the attic with a paint-box and had made sure that everyone knew what the house was called.

But there seemed to be an unnatural hush as she went downstairs again. No birds murmured in the honeysuckle, no old wood creaked and contracted as the day cooled towards evening, and yet she felt, more than ever before, the oppressive, malignant presence.

She decided she could no longer stay another minute in the house. Without even stopping to collect night things she would get into her car and drive away, anywhere, as fast as she could. She ran across the hall and into the drawing room to pick up the ignition key that lay on the Davenport in the corner, but the great rose in the cut-glass vase on the mantelshelf seemed to draw her to it. It had not been there only minutes ago and it seemed to transfix her as its petals quivered almost imperceptibly.

Garibaldi Bullock ushered the two large American ladies out of his shop with a sigh of relief and closed the door. He watched the strong, handsome, well made-up faces withdraw, reluctantly, from their last lingering appraisal of his crowded window and then turn, avid for culture, towards the Cathedral; the tightly-trousered bottoms took up nearly the entire width of the narrow lane as they walked away.

It had been only with the greatest difficulty that he had dissuaded them from buying anything. Really, he thought, the strain of running a shop where nothing was for sale was becoming too much for him. Perhaps it was time for a change: he had always wanted to live on a Scottish island and breed rare sheep. He brightened up at once; it was an idea! It was ages since he had bred anything.

He pottered round his shop carefully rearranging things that the Americans had displaced. Picking up a fragile silver filigree necklace that one of the women had wanted very badly he shuddered at the thought of anything so delicate condemned to adorn that vast bosom. The thought of *any* of his treasures being taken to – what outlandish place did they say they came from? – Milwaukee? – was too appalling. It had been bad enough selling the eighteenth century engraving to Penelope – ah! Penelope! He had heard from Monty Masters concerning Mrs Pritchett and he must write to Pen at once.

Tenderly putting the silver necklace down he hung the 'Closed' sign on the shop door and locked it, going into the small back room he sat mountainously at a little escritoire and drew writing paper towards him.

'Dearest Pen,' he wrote:

> I have made enquiries about our Mistress Pritchett as I promised. Monty Masters came up with the whole story, and it turns out to be not at all a savoury one. She was, as we have seen, as pretty as a picture and, as we might have guessed, no better than she should be ...

Mrs Pritchett had been born Rose Lawn, Monty Masters had disclosed, and had been brought up in a London slum, the eldest of an ever increasing number of children, one of which her mother was delivered of yearly, in pain, weariness and squalor. Some of the babies died but a great many did not, and by the time she was twelve Rose had seven brothers and sisters and, as usual, another one was on its way.

Her father was a drunken lout and her mother was a beaten, defeated drab; the family's living conditions were appalling.

From some remote ancestor Rose had inherited a fastidious streak and she resolved to leave the slum by any means she could. Going into service was her only way of escape so at twelve she exchanged the misery of the filthy, overcrowded life she had been born to for the drudgery of a kitchen maid.

She had worked hard and moved from position to position, each time climbing one rung of the ladder of servitude, until, having been careful to learn whatever she could from her employers, she obtained a place as parlour maid to a well-to-do family in Belgravia.

By now she was seventeen and quite beautiful, and she inevitably caught the eye of many a young gentleman who visited the house where she worked. Hugh Pritchett, the son and heir of Sir Robert Pritchett, was one of these and she made herself available to him in such a way that she was able to tell him, untruthfully, that she was pregnant. Hugh Pritchett was not only an honourable young man but was besotted with her and he married her at once.

When Sir Robert discovered that his son had married a servant girl he promptly disinherited him and, although Hugh had a modest income of his own from his late mother, this did not suit Rose at all. Gathering as many valuables as she could carry, and all the money she could lay hands on, she left the pleasant little house in which they had lived and moved to Brighton where before long she became the toast of a certain society and moved swiftly from one lucrative liaison to another.

On hearing of the disrepute into which she was bringing the name of Pritchett her reluctant father-in-law offered her a considerable sum of money to renounce it. Rose refused until he had doubled the sum and then happily accepted his condition, reverting to her maiden name of Rose Lawn.

She was in her prime, beautiful, elegant and intelligent, dressing always in pink and always carrying a rose, the flower whose name she bore. It was thus that the Marquis of Stratton saw her for the first time and lost his heart to her.

The Marquis was a man in early middle-age, tall, well built, handsome and fabulously rich. He was a keen botanist and had been on a protracted tour of the Americas where he had collected rare trees and plants for the vast gardens of his country seat in Devonshire, and it was here that he eventually installed his rare and lovely Rose, in a small house he had built for her on the edge of his estate, and at a discreet distance from the mansion.

The Marquis had a wife, older than himself and suffering from a lingering disease. Rose settled happily into her delightful little house, secure in the knowledge that the lady would die very soon and that she would be the next Marchioness of Stratton.

But the lady did not die. Years went by and Rose became restive in her position as mistress. She demanded more and more of the Marquis's time, more and more money, more and more amusements, and gave him less and less affection, showing him the less beautiful side of her nature.

She became a shrew: she scolded and raved at him or maintained a cold and sullen silence. In desperation she suggested that he should hasten his wife's end so that she could step into her shoes.

It was not at all in the Marquis's best interests to help his wife to her demise. She was the sole heiress of an extremely wealthy father and he must at all costs keep her alive until the old man died, leaving her his fortune which would of course, at once become the Marquis's. But the idea appealed to him in quite another way.

Whereas there was every reason to keep his wife alive there was none why he should put up with Rose with her moods and tantrums any longer. Ladies there were a plenty who would be glad to fill her place far more gracefully; in fact he had met just such a one, a young widow, pretty and plump and willing, only last month in Bath.

The Marquis put it about that Rose was going abroad for her health, dismissed all her servants and, leading her up to the attic of her little house on the pretext of a surprise he had hidden for her there, he locked her in and left her to starve.

The house was quite isolated and no one heard her screams. Just before she died she managed to open a vein in her arm with a splinter of wood and in blood, wrote a curse on the wall of her prison. She could do nothing to help herself, but she would see to it that at least no one else should be happily installed in the little house that had been built for her and her alone.

The Marquis was a cold-blooded man. Having ordered that the attic should be boarded up, after the secret removal of the pathetic corpse, he did, indeed, install other mistresses in the house, but first the plump widow and then her replacements died in peculiar circumstances. Even his spinster sister and her companion, who were to have been only temporary residents, met with untimely ends, and eventually it became obvious that the little house had an evil aura and it was not safe for anyone to live there.

and so you see, dearest Pen [Garibaldi finished] our Mistress Pritchett's story is a sad and sorry one, and not a little sinister. Of course a lot of it must be conjecture, but Monty assures me the basic facts are true. Why I should have felt it had anything to do with you I don't know, but I always trust my premonitions and think it would only be sensible for you to bring the engraving back to me where she can do no harm.

He would be delighted to have the little picture back, he thought, it was a pretty thing and even more fascinating now he knew its story. He signed his name with a flourish and put the letter in an envelope. Now, what had he done with Penelope's address? He searched through the jumble of papers on the desk – ah, yes, he had written it down on the edge of an auction catalogue. Charlton Borham, that was the name of the village. Borham? Wasn't that the family name of the Marquises of Stratton? Yes, he was sure it was. What a strange coincidence! Now, what was the name of the house again? Here it was, Rose Lawn's House. Rose Lawn's House! *With an apostrophe!*

Immediately everything fell into place. Penelope's new little Georgian cottage, his feeling of doom and disaster when she picked up the engraving of Mrs Pritchett.

Garibaldi erupted to his feet, knocking over the gilt chair he had been sitting on, nearly toppling the escritoire and, running his hands through his already dishevelled hair in his distress, he raced from the little shop towards the Cathedral Close where his car was parked.

He arrived at Rose Lawn's House just as the sun went behind the cypress trees, drawing black fingers of shadow across the ragged lawn, and the scent of roses was heavy on the suddenly chilling air. As he ran towards the open French windows he heard Penelope scream.

She lay on the drawing room floor in front of the fireplace with her head at an awkward angle on the elegant brass fender, blood dripping from a huge gash across her forehead. She was quite dead.

She appeared to have fallen heavily against the marble mantelshelf on which stood a huge full-blown rose in a slim, cut-glass vase. The rose shifted slightly, as though it had only that moment been put there.

XVIII

Miss Meekle

Miss Meekle stood quite still and stared at the white envelope lying on the old, filthy doormat. She stood for a full minute regarding the clean white square, so incongruous in its dejected grey surroundings, as though any movement might precipitate some attack on its part.

She had lived alone and withdrawn for so long that her communication with the outside world was of the slightest, and of her own choosing. This gleaming white shape was an intrusion and could mean nothing but a threat to the gaunt old woman.

It was Thursday and she was dressed to go out. Over the layers of ancient, shapeless garments that she wore day and night she had put a man's tattered raincoat. On her head was a felt hat, stained and faded in patches, with only a thin stripe where the ribbon had been to show what colour it might once have had. Her feets were encased in Wellington boots, split and far too big for her.

The envelope lay between her and the door and she could not ignore it. She picked it up, turning it over and over in dirty, shaking fingers, and carried it back into the cluttered kitchen where she held it close to the window. The light was bad on this bleak November morning, and made infinitely worse since the window had not been cleaned, inside or out, for years. Confident black handwriting told her without a doubt that it was addressed to –

> Miss Alice Meekle,
> Chantry House,
> Chantry Green,
> Westcombe

– in fact to her.

Her fingers were shaking so badly that she could scarcely open the envelope, but she eventually managed it and extracted a single sheet of paper covered with the same confident black writing.

'Dear Aunt Alice,' she read. 'Aunt Alice' – who could be writing to her under this alien title? She was Miss Meekle, she was also, she knew, Mad Meekle, Batty Meekle to the local children, who half feared and half laughed at her, and she had been Alice, once, long ago, but Aunt Alice? No! She read on.

You will be sorry, I am sure, to hear that your brother John died last month after a short illness. Just before he died he mentioned your name and asked me, his elder daughter, to look you up.

My sister Rosemary and I will be staying in Westcombe for the next few days and will call in sometime on Thursday.

The letter went on, hoping she were well, hoping the news had not been too great a shock, looking forward to making her acquaintance, and ended 'Yours sincerely, your niece, Ruth Meekle'.

Miss Meekle swayed slightly and clutched the torn and greasy curtain beside the window, feeling the rotten material give under her fingers. She had not thought of her brother for years. When her mother had turned him out of the house, for reasons she had not properly understood at the time and had not cared to consider since, she had been forbidden ever to mention his name, and since every indication that he had existed had been removed, she gradually ceased even to remember him. Now, through his death, she was forced to remember him – through his death and through his daughters, her nieces.

'I don't want them to come!' Miss Meekle whispered harshly to herself.

Twenty years ago, even ten, it might have been possible to accept them, to speak to them, but not now! Not now! Her privacy had become much more precious since those others had come to her. She looked at the letter again. Thursday – her nieces were coming to-day!

Thursday was the only day of the week that meant anything to Miss Meekle. On that day every week, year in year out, she would put on the filthy raincoat and the ancient hat and let herself out of the heavy back door, unlocking it and then locking it behind her again with the huge iron key that she wore on a thick piece of string round her neck. Picking her way between the piles of rubbish and clumps of rank weeds she would cross the yard and collect the large rusty old bicycle from the shed, whose door needed to be lifted open and shut on its screaming hinges. The bicycle out of its shed, she did not attempt to ride it but pushed it, clanking and creaking, down the dank overgrown drive and out of the nearly obscured gateway into the road, the large basket hanging lop-sided from the handlebars and holding an empty paraffin can.

About half a mile down the road was a knot of cottages, the church and a small post-office-shop. From the cottages in years gone by had come cooks, gardeners and housemaids to work for Miss Meekle's parents at the big house. Now they had mostly been bought up by retired business people and transformed into smart, quaint residences, all coach lamps and scarlet geraniums, but the shop, although changing with the times and stocking frozen scampi, nylon tights and the more exotic jams and tinned fruits, was still owned by the same family that had known Miss Meekle in happier times.

It was to the shop that the old lady made her Thursday journeys, pausing every now and then along the way to peer into the hedge at a wild flower or a bird's nest, and ignoring the little boys who whizzed backwards and forwards on their bright painted bikes taunting her with cries of 'Batty Meekle'. Rain or shine she made the journey, and as regularly young Mrs Blake, who was sixty and the daughter-in-law of old Mrs Blake (relegated now to the back room) would have put her meagre weekly order ready in a small cardboard box on the corner of the counter, a can of paraffin on the floor beneath it.

Miss Meekle would go first to the post office counter, having left her empty paraffin can beside the full one, to present her old age pension book. Having received her pension money from young Mrs Blake in her capacity of postmistress she then crossed the shop to hand some of the money back to her in her capacity of shopkeeper, and then together they would carry the small cardboard box and the full can outside to stow them in the bicycle basket.

Young Mrs Blake was fond of Miss Meekle. Her mother-in-law had told her how things used to be up at the big house, and she herself had watched the old lady's growing strangeness and withdrawal. If newcomers made disparaging remarks about her ridiculous looks and pungent smell she would roundly tell them to mind their own business as, she pointed out, Miss Meekle minded hers. On the regular Thursday visits she would talk kindly to her, not expecting more than the few words Miss Meekle would utter, diffidently and abruptly in answer, and the wintry out-of-practice smile of thanks.

Having pushed the bicycle, more difficult to control now with its heavy basket, back up the road, Miss Meekle would prop it against one of the granite gateposts, festooned with ivy, which marked the entry to her drive, and pick up the two bottles of milk which stood in the grass. Concealed in the ivy behind them was an old cocoa tin. Each Thursday she peered inside the tin to see if there seemed to be enough money in it for next week's two pints of milk. She didn't know how much milk cost, in fact she didn't understand the new decimalized money at all, but she knew that the milkman's maxim was 'No money, no milk', and added to it whenever it seemed necessary.

Wheeling the bicycle up the tree-tunnelled, bramble-lined drive and across the yard the old lady would lean it by the back door and go in search of firewood. The overgrown garden in front of the house was criss-crossed with paths and tracks she had made through the long grass and weed-choked bushes on her journeys to collect sticks. The gloomy ilex and fir trees were constantly shedding rotten branches and she had no difficulty in finding enough wood for the small fires she permitted herself in the rusty kitchen range.

As she got older she found she could carry less and so made several journeys back and forth across the garden, her faded filthy clothes, the dead lichened wood and her gnarled grey hands and face all being much the same colour, had there been anyone to notice.

Having collected her money, her food, her milk, and her firewood Miss Meekle would thankfully let herself in, fumbling under layers of garments for the huge key with which to unlock the door and lock herself in again, knowing she was safe for another week. Thursdays were a nightmare but she knew she must venture out into the world once a week if she were to keep body and soul together, 'Though heaven knows' she said to herself from time to time 'why I bother'.

The big house was at once her haven and her prison. Once inside it closed round her, protectively yet menacingly. It ached with darkness and silence, it reeked with dust and damp and dirt. The rooms, some of them unvisited for thirty years, still with their furniture and ornaments, carpets and curtains in place, seemed to weigh her down with their very presence, and even the kitchen, where she lived and slept now, had very little in it that she wanted and too much that she did not.

Until one Thursday about a year ago.

It was pouring with rain and bitterly cold when Miss Meekle, her tattered coat soaked through and the brown paper young Mrs Blake had tucked over the box of groceries sodden, had let herself into the kitchen. She was amazed to find it warm and to smell the unmistakable smell of ironing. In a flash sixty-five years fell away and she was a little girl again, sitting on the rug in front of the glowing black-leaded range watching Bertha, her nurse, iron her white lawn lace-trimmed nightgown. Just as quickly the warmth and the comforting smell had gone and the kitchen was as dark, untidy, dirty and cold as it always was, and she was old and rain-soaked and weary, leaning against the door, thankful at least to be indoors.

But the memory of that smell, that warmth remained, and in fact returned. Miss Meekle could never tell when it would happen, could never make it happen, but happen it did from time to time.

She would be sitting in the decrepit chair, close to her small

stick fire in the range, in the dim light of the paraffin lamp
when suddenly the light would intensify, the heat from the fire
become an all-pervasive warmth and the smell, the hot dry
smell of ironing, would waft across the room to her.

As time went on the warm, well-lit interludes in the kitchen
became more frequent, stronger and more diverse. Sometimes
she could smell bread baking, sometimes meat roasting, and
gradually she began to hear voices and movements, and
eventually very nearly to see people. The sensations were so
faint, and at the same time so intense, that the old lady
became quite exhausted from the effort to cling to the sounds
and the scents, to completely see the vague forms, and also
from the emotional surge that she felt each time. She would sit
quite still, her dirty fingers gripping the equally dirty arms of
the chair, holding her breath and trying so hard, so hard to
realize, to comprehend, to possess or be possessed by those
others who were there.

Over the months she began to distinguish separate entities.
Her beloved nurse, Bertha, she knew not only by the crackle of
her starched apron and the squeak of her shoes, so well
remembered, but by the sense of comfort and love that seemed
to emanate from the large buxom shape she could so nearly
see, and the smell of ironing that had been her first
presentiment that she was no longer entirely alone. Other
forms, besides Bertha, seemed to be there, one larger and two
slighter women, sometimes all at once, sometimes one or two
of them, the cook she thought, and the two maids – what were
they called? Mildred and Jane – all of whom had left soon
after her father had died, due to her mother's ill-nature and
harsh treatment of them. At times there was a strong sense of
man, of outdoors, earth, green things and fragrance. She felt
rather than saw the gardener leaning through the door so as
not to track mud on Cook's clean floor, handing in baskets of
vegetables and flowers. She racked her brain for his name –
Cheeseman! – he that had had a soft spot for little Miss Alice,
smuggling in the very first strawberries especially for her.

Only once was she frightened by what she experienced,
when the warm muddled kitchen smells were suddenly cut
across by the chill, sharp scent of eau-de-Cologne and she

knew her mother had appeared in the doorway to the hall. The sense of comfort and half-heard laughter ceased at once. All attention focussed on the doorway. Alice froze, not daring to look. She was not allowed in the kitchen, and waited for her mother's rebuke, but it was not forthcoming. Perhaps she, so small a child, could not be seen deep in the big armchair, but the shock broke the reverie at once and she was old and cold and alone again in the desolate kitchen, terrified that those others would have been frightened away for ever by that alien presence.

But they were not. They still came and went, talked and worked, and each time Miss Meekle could grasp them more clearly, realize them more nearly with her senses and her lonely groping mind.

And then the letter had come.

Still looking at the stiff white paper with its aggressive black writing Miss Meekle took off the shapeless hat and threw it on the table. It landed among piles of china, good china – Spode and Crown Derby but chipped now and filthy with the remains of food. Half-empty butter papers lay on calf-bound books, some open and broken-backed, and there were other things, rags, boots, on the table which had arrived on it when and for what reason the old lady had long forgotten and which she absently pushed aside to make small spaces for her scrappy meals.

The letter joined the chaos on the table and she ran both hands through her thin grey hair, clenching her fists in its roots as though she would tear it out. She looked wildly round the atrocious room and saw in her mind's eye the other downstairs rooms, the curtains rotted away from their blackened brass rings and draped crazily across the filthy windows, the furniture spilling stuffing and woodworm dust on to the damp, moth-ruined carpets.

'I don't want them!' she said, this time on a scream of panic, 'They can't come!' But she knew that they would and that they would come today.

Sometimes during the summer visitors to the district would chance upon the entrance of the drive to the big house, now not much more than a gap in the hedge, and venture up it.

They thought the house abandoned and would walk all round, exclaiming at how it must have been quite grand once, as they pushed back the roses which had once covered the walls and had now collapsed. Occasionally, as they peered through the dirt-obscured windows it appeared that they might try to force an entrance to explore inside, and quite deliberately Miss Meekle had gone close to the glass so that they could just distinguish the long pale face surrounded by wild hair looming out at them. That soon sent them off, and in such disorder that it even brought Miss Meekle's wintry smile to play momentarily across her grey lips.

But this would not do today. She must not be seen. It must appear to Ruth and Rosemary that the house was indeed deserted, that she had gone away, or died. She must go upstairs and watch unseen for her unwelcome visitors.

Miss Meekle stood, well hidden by the threadbare, once-velvet curtain and the grimy glass at the landing window and watched the two middle-aged women in the yard. They had picked their way through the heaps of ashes, broken crockery and rotting garments towards the house, distaste written on their square, florid faces, and were now standing, stocky legs apart, looking round them in amazement.

One was slightly larger, more florid of face and stocky of leg, than the other, but both were the image of Miss Meekle's mother. Her fingers plucked at the remaining pile of the velvet curtain as she strained to hear what they said.

The smaller of the two pulled at her sister's arm and said 'This can't be the place, Ruth, it's derelict, Aunt Alice can't live here. No one could – do let's go.'

The larger woman turned on her angrily, shaking a piece of paper: 'This is the address Father gave me, and we checked with the man at the shop. I admit it looks ghastly but I'm sure it's the right place.'

Although every nerve in Miss Meekle's body was tightened with horror at the nearness of the women, a part of her mind registered 'Man? At the shop? What man?' and then she remembered young Mrs Blake had told her she was going to London for a week, and her son-in-law was looking after the shop for her. She turned her full attention on her nieces again.

What unattractive women they were, she thought, one arrogant and domineering, the other surly and resentful of her sister's dominance. Their expensive shoes, suede jackets and tweed skirts marked them down as well-to-do, probably even spoilt, but their ill-nature hung round them like an aura.

'Just like Mother,' thought Miss Meekle, 'I expect they thought they would come down here and browbeat me, see what they could get out of me', the wintry smile crept out for a second.

Whatever they had been like she would have feared and resented them, would have hidden from them and set her face against them, but it seemed a pity that these two relatives, of whose existence she had only known for a matter of hours, should so closely resemble the person she had so much disliked and feared.

The two women in the yard bickered on as to whether this was the right place. They attempted to get near the kitchen window to peer in, but the brambles and collapsed rambler roses, dank and dripping, clutched at their tweed skirts and, their well-shod feet slithering on the piles of rubbish, they abandoned their efforts. Turning round from time to time to glower back at the house they left the yard, and, with a long shuddering sigh, Miss Meekle slid to her knees, her face buried in the musty material of the curtain.

For some minutes the old lady remained on her knees, thankful that the women had gone, but gradually her mind began to function again and she knew that they would come back, perhaps even later today. They would find out more about their aunt, that she did indeed live in the seemingly derelict house, that she was a recluse, odd, even mad, and that as far as anyone knew the silver, the china and the jewellery were still locked in with her. As indeed they were.

She sighed once more and with stiff, painful movements eased herself into a sitting position with her back to the mildewed curtain, her thin legs, encased in several layers of torn and dirty stockings and still wearing the split Wellington boots, stuck out in front of her. She pulled the skirts of the tattered raincoat round her. It was cold, terribly cold, but she felt too shaken to attempt the long flight of stairs just yet.

The carpet under her hands was gritty and damp, felted and grey with age and disuse. She stroked it idly, trying to make out its once bright pattern, and remembering with a shock that it must be over thirty years since she had been upstairs.

She looked across the landing to her mother's bedroom door, closed, as were all the other doors on either side of her. She had closed that door after the undertaker's men had carried her mother's coffin through it, and had never opened it again. A grimace of distaste disturbed the wrinkles on the old grey face as she pictured the fat, obsequious undertaker directing the kindly village men as they negotiated the bend of the stairs with the heavy coffin 'Up a bit Fred, steady now Charlie, mind the bannisters', tiptoeing about on his small fat feet and smiling what he presumably hoped was a sympathetic smile at the sorrowing daughter.

Miss Meekle hadn't been sorrowing. She had heartily disliked her mother all her life, that dislike deepening into hatred over the years when, first with Bertha's help, and latterly on her own, she had looked after the large square woman. When she had shut that door, its paint now yellowed and peeling, its panels outlined with dust, she had felt nothing but relief, and if sorrow had come later it was sorrow that there was none.

She pictured the room behind the shut door, the sheets and blankets thrown back on the high half-tester bed from which the stout corpse had been lifted; the silver photograph frames on the dressing-table, those that had held pictures of her brother empty; the velvet jewel boxes still guarding the rings, bracelets and necklaces inside them; the cupboards still protecting furs and dresses.

She knew from the state of the downstairs rooms what it must be like behind that door. Silver blackened; furs, bed hangings, carpets, rotten and moth-eaten; a pile of soot, dead leaves and jackdaw droppings in the fireplace.

Shuddering, she gathered her arthritic legs underneath her and, pushing with her hands, stood up, supporting herself against the wall whose once-elegant wallpaper hung in damp rags disclosing the stained plaster behind it, and started towards the head of the stairs.

On the half-landing she came face to face with a pastel portrait of herself when she was ten. Her gentle, beloved father had commissioned it just before he died. Through the dusty glass surrounded by its oval frame, a thin, solemn little face looked back at her, long fair hair falling in ringlets on each side of it.

She remembered how her mother had hated her fine straight hair, comparing it unfavourably with her own coarse black curls. 'What a plain child you are!' she would exclaim, and Bertha's kindly mouth would tighten with annoyance. She didn't think her Alice, her little lamb, plain, and each night she would wind thin slithery strands of hair round curling rags and knot them firmly, close to the child's head, undoing them in the morning to release slender shining spirals which bounced on her shoulders until, too soon for her mother's liking, they became straight again. Rats' tails, her mother called them.

Suddenly Miss Meekle found it imperative to seek the comfort of Bertha, and she stumbled down the stairs, clinging to the greasy bannister rail, her old feet in the ill-fitting boots tripping on the worn and rotting carpet. She made her way across the shadowy hall and into the kitchen.

There was no warmth, no comfort there either, but there would be. She would light her tiny fire, turn the wick of the paraffin lamp up against the November afternoon gloom and wait for those others.

But then she remembered.

The letter, and its consequences, had made it impossible for her to go to the shop or to gather firewood. She shook the paraffin can. There was a little left in it, but dare she light the fire? No. Her nieces might come back, having made sure they had found the right house, and she could not risk their seeing a glimmer of light. She realized that she had had nothing to eat that day, and that there was nothing to eat. 'Nothing at all? Nothing at all?' She whimpered to herself, scrabbling among the piles of clothes, books and breadcrumbs on the table in the half-darkness until her fingers found a bread-wrapper, still with the two end crusts of a loaf inside, crusts

she would have given to the birds this morning had she gone
out. She found a greasy, crumpled paper with some butter still
clinging to it, and scraped the butter over the stale bread
crusts and ate them ravenously. If only she could light the fire
she could make a cup of tea, but she dared not show a light. She
held up one of the two clouded milk bottles which stood amid
the clutter and tipping it against the grey light from the
window saw that there was still a drain of last Thursday's
milk in it. She drank it, thin and sour, straight from the bottle.
That would have to do.

Rubbing her hands to get a little warmth into the dirty old
fingers she went across to the ragged armchair near the range
and began to wrap herself in the torn rugs and blankets in
which she slept every night. Settling herself as comfortably as
she could she prepared to wait, either for her nieces or those
others.

The evening's desolate grey light deepened into darkness.
Miss Meekle slept fitfully. No one came to visit her. The house
hung round her, heavy and damp, only the occasional twitter
from the birds that nested in the creepers outside breaking the
thick silence.

When morning came the old lady unwound herself from her
tattered cocoon of blankets, her joints stiff and aching. Would
the nieces return today?

She looked wearily round the dismal kitchen. No milk, no
food, no warmth. She shuffled into the small scullery which
contained a stone sink and the only tap in the house, and
drank some water out of a dirty, cracked Crown Derby tea
cup. The cup lay among a jumble of other crockery and
tarnished silver in a few inches of scummed water, speckled
with tea leaves. The waste-pipe had become blocked long ago,
but then Miss Meekle had given up washing herself, or
anything else, long ago, so it mattered little.

The day stretched endless before her. Listlessly the old
woman went back to her chair, and at once the atmosphere
warmed, the mildewed, stuffy smell vanished and the
sensation of being no longer alone swept over her.

Those others came and went several times through the day,
filling Miss Meekle with such joy that she forgot how hungry

she was, forgot the cold, forgot the ever-present threat of her nieces' return. She could nearly see them now, and their presence was so earnestly desired, so much more important to her than anything else, that she no longer strained to see them better.

The room got colder, but she didn't feel it, warmed as she was by that other warmth. The rain outside the filthy windows obliterated most of the dreary November light, but she didn't notice it, lit by that other light. From time to time voices called outside in the yard and hands banged on the door, but she didn't hear, listening only for those other sounds.

As she got weaker, from cold and from hunger, she could see them more and more clearly; Cook, the two slim girls and dear, stout Bertha, and could even make out some of their chatter, their good-natured banter.

Miss Meekle was no longer aware of day and night. She had no idea how much time had passed when those others became aware of her.

The old rickety chair creaked as she shifted a cramped arm, and Bertha started.

'Did you hear something?'

'Probably a mouse in the cupboard,' said Jane.

'Better not be a mouse in my kitchen,' Cook retorted.

Miss Meekle moved again, desperate for them to be aware of her. Bertha looked fixedly at the chair by the range.

'I thought for a moment my Alice was curled up in that chair,' she said.

'Poor child, it's more than her life's worth to come in here,' Millicent replied.

Too weak to speak, too weak to move again, Miss Meekle cried in her mind 'I *am* here! I *am* here' and as she did so there came a beating on the back door. After the knocking came heavy thuds and the sound of splintering wood. Those others noticed nothing, Miss Meekle noticed nothing. All that was left of her yearned out to Bertha, to be picked up, to be comforted, to be loved. She started to scream, a high wailing scream, and was instantly surrounded by people, all talking at once.

'It *is* Miss Alice!' – Jane.

'My God! *Poor* Aunt Alice!' – Rosemary.

'Oh, Miss Meekle! Miss Meekle!' – Young Mrs Blake.

'Whatever is the matter with the child?' – Cook.

'Hypothermia.' – Ruth.

'Stand back now, ladies' – the village policeman.

And then Bertha, large, loving Bertha, came fully and clearly into Miss Meekle's vision, as tangible, as real as anything in her life had ever been.

She held up her arms, tears streaming down her face, and Bertha bent down to pick her up.

She felt the crisp lawn of her nightdress slither over her warm skin as the firm hands went round her waist and swung her from the chair to rest against the soft bosom.

She felt the curling rags pull at her hair as she buried her head in the warm fold between Bertha's shoulder and chin.

'There, there, my Alice, my little lamb,' Bertha comforted, rocking her gently, 'You're worn out, aren't you? Let Bertha rock you to sleep.'

A thin sigh, barely audible, escaped from the old, emaciated body in the wretched armchair.

'She's gone, poor old lady,' young Mrs Blake whispered through her tears.

She had. The little girl slept peacefully in the arms of her beloved nurse.